CW01080384

SAIL OR RETURN

To Nuala, with all my love,
this will come as no surprise.

❊ Chapter One ❊

Thea came out of the kitchen, wearing bra and pants, laddered tights and green wellingtons.

Pax did not ask her why she was cooking Sunday lunch in her underwear. It was her usual outfit when they were expecting guests. It was the best way she could think of for not getting splashes and spots on the dress she planned to wear. The Browns did not go in for aprons. He suspected she was the only woman in the Square whose knickers you could inspect to know what you were having for lunch.

But why the wellingtons?

"I dropped a jar of mint sauce on the floor. There's broken glass everywhere. I don't have time to clean it up."

There's a reason for everything.

Pax rummaged in the top drawer of the stripped pine sideboard. It was full of broken pencils, half-used candles, bits of Lego, useless keys and other rubbish no-one dared throw away.

"Where's the corkscrew?" he asked.

Thea picked up the bottle of wine from the top of the sideboard. He knew she was trying to curl her lip. It came out as a leer. He was much better at lip curling. "You're not giving them that are you?"

"It's perfectly good plonk. Nothing the matter with it. They won't know the difference when it's in the decanter. Your brother couldn't tell if it was Ribena and meths."

"You know perfectly well that Nick knows a lot about wine."

"Then why does he carry round a plastic card in his wallet that tells him where the wines come from and what the good years are? He left his little crib card in his other jacket at

1

Christmas. He told me he'd rather have a red Bordeaux than a claret any day."

"What's wrong with that?"

"They're the same thing."

He brandished a rusty corkscrew that had been lurking in the back of the drawer. With the point he ripped the plastic off the top of the bottle.

"Oh look. It didn't need a corkscrew after all. It doesn't have a cork."

"I'm surprised they bother with a bottle. An old Harpic jar would do for that stuff. I wish you'd open another one."

"We haven't drunk this one yet. Waste not want not."

"Please, Pax, open another bottle of wine."

"I tell you what. We'll use your brother's trick. He always serves his wine in a decanter. At the beginning of the meal he pours himself a drop, tastes it, wrinkles his nose, passes it to whoever his wife or girlfriend happens to be at the time. She agrees it's off. He rushes to the sideboard and drags out a bottle of Mouton Rothschild and flashes it around so we can all see the label. He takes it off to the kitchen to open it. Woman of his dreams stops him half way and tells him to empty the decanter down the sink while he's about it. Exit Nick with full bottle and full decanter. Enter Nick again with full decanter. He apologises that it hasn't had time to breathe but it'll do. So we all drink the jollop that was in the decanter in the first place."

"That's not true. It's another of your inventions."

"It's not my invention. It's his. And he puts his ideas into practice. He's done it twice on us in the past year."

"Coincidence."

"No such thing as coincidence. There's a reason for everything. The last time he had a party I looked in the broom cupboard for tonic and found the unopened bottle. The trouble with Nick is he always gets found out."

He knelt down to look for the decanter in the bottom of the sideboard. He unloaded onto the carpet a clump of half-finished macramé, a distorted wicker bread-basket and a children's bicycle stabiliser.

"While you're there, could you get out the place mats please.

I think that's why I came out of the kitchen. It might not have been, of course. I probably wanted something else. Then I'll only remember when it's too late. And now I'll worry about what it was I really wanted and burn the vegetables. But it was probably the mats all the time. So don't worry. Are they there?"

"London Street Cries or the straw ones my mother brought back from Tangier?"

"Thomas took three of the straw ones to school last term for the crib. They never came back. Give me the others. They'll need a wipe."

"They'll need more than that. Look, we had spaghetti last time."

He followed her through the louvred pine door into the kitchen with an empty Malvern Water bottle to fill from the tap. His shoes crunched on the floor and the scent of mint and vinegar rose from his feet.

"It smells lovely in here. Like an embalming room. We should scatter herbs on the floor every day."

"We do. And carrots and mince and biscuit crumbs. And then your mother comes in before I've had a chance to clear it up."

He put his arms round her from the back while she rinsed the place mats. He kissed the back of her neck and caressed her stretch marks. She carried on rinsing. He wondered whether pinching her bottom would get a reaction.

"I wonder what she's like," she said.

"Who?"

"Who do you think? Nick's latest girlfriend."

"Blonde. Sexy. Thick. The usual riff-raff he leaps in and out of bed with."

"She's a model."

"Like I said."

She tore a length off the toilet roll that served as kitchen paper and wiped the place mats. She took a handful of forks out of the sink and wiped those too. She wriggled out of his arms, turned round and thrust the mats and the cutlery into his hands. Bits of toilet paper were clinging to the teeth of the

3

forks. "Can you draw the curtains in the dining room so I can lay the table?"

"If you wore matching underwear I wouldn't have to do that."

He went back through the louvred door and dumped the mats and cutlery on the table with a clatter. He took the plastic cap off the wine bottle and held it upside down over the upright decanter. The wine bubbled and gurgled and made a red froth like an ice-cream soda. Thea shouted through the door. "You're always so unpleasant when we're having people in. If you don't want them to come, don't invite them. I'll do fish fingers instead of wasting my weekend cooking Sunday lunch. You asked them to come, not me. I don't know why you bother."

Pax put the wine down on the sideboard. While he composed a reply to Thea's outburst he stuck his middle finger down the neck of the decanter. He wiped away the pink scum that the wine froth had left behind when it subsided. He was careful not to get his finger stuck.

"We invite people for parties and dinner and drinks for the same reason everyone else does: so we're invited back to their place where we hope we'll have a nicer time than we do in our own. We're all going round in circles trying to find a good time."

"Then let's stop. Right now. I'm going to phone my brother and tell him not to come."

Pax licked the acid scum off his finger and put it back in the neck of the decanter for a final wipe.

"You wouldn't do that. You want to see what his latest floosie's like. She might turn out to be your sister-in-law. Anyway, if we didn't invite anyone here we wouldn't get invited back. Then we'd feel lonely and inadequate. That's why we put up with other people making a mess and drinking our drink and wasting our time when we could be reading the paper. The only consolation is that we do the same to them when we go back to their houses."

He wondered whether he should use the toilet paper instead of his finger. Bad idea. Bits of cork floating in the wine were

4

socially acceptable. Bits of bog roll were not.

Thea burst through the door brandishing a saucepan. "You make me angry. You're petty minded and cynical."

She clumped back into the kitchen, her wellies leaving a little trail of mint sauce on the carpet. The swing door slammed behind her. Pax could see her shadow through the slats and hear her banging saucepans in the sink. He took a swig out of the decanter and tried to suppress the rictus in his facial muscles. It was bloody awful but he couldn't back down now and open something else.

It was obvious to him why Thea was on edge. She was always nervous when she met her brother's new mistresses. By convention, Nick always referred to them as his fiancées. If Nick's previous relationships were a guide they would indeed get married as a necessary prelude to getting divorced.

"Better send your bridesmaid's dress to the cleaners," he shouted.

She came out of the kitchen again, this time waving a wooden spoon. "You're on edge because my brother's bringing his new fiancée. Please don't take your anxieties out on me. I've quite enough to worry about cooking lunch."

She disappeared back into the kitchen like a bird in a cuckoo clock.

Pax took another swig. Why should the idea of an attractive mistress put him on edge? What a silly idea.

Pax went upstairs to get dressed. He would have liked a bath but he could not be bothered to clear out the jugs and sieves and plastic tubes and curly-wurly straws and soap that had melted through the night and stuck on the bottom. He did not shave at weekends, not only to save money but as a gesture. What exactly it was a gesture of he couldn't quite put his finger on but it was something to do with not going to the office. He splashed water on his face and sprayed deodorant under his arms. He stood up on tiptoe to reach his toothbrush in the holder that he had fixed near the ceiling. This was a precaution against it being used as a bath toy or an Action Man accessory or to clean the hamster cage. He found the toothpaste behind

5

the toilet bowl and squeezed out the last little blob from the crack in the middle of the tube.

From the bathroom it was but one step to the bedroom. It was as good as having a bathroom en suite, he once told Thea when she was feeling claustrophobic. The whole bloody house is en suite was her reply. Sometimes he felt she was not suited to open plan living.

He took out of the wardrobe his best blue guernsey sweater and blue denim jeans and put away the second best guernsey sweater he had just taken off. His natural inclination was to throw them on the chair or the bed or the floor or the dressing table but these spaces were already taken by Thea's clothes so he was forced to put them away.

If they lived on a boat they would have to keep it tidy. Until they were in harbour and could festoon the rails and rigging with towels and underwear like bunting. Marinas always looked so festive.

He put thoughts of boats out of his mind. They were not for the weekends. He would only feel miserable for the rest of the day. Boats were for dreaming about in the office and going to see at lunchtime down at Saint Katherine's Dock. Boats like the *Swan* with its honey-coloured hull and teak decks and tall mast, big enough for a family of four and a hamster to throw all this up and sail away to a new life together. Small enough to hide in tiny creeks and bays and creep over coral reefs to deserted islands.

He combed his hair in the wardrobe mirror. He should have shaved. The stubble highlighted his jowls and made his face look fatter. He kneaded the flesh on his jaw until it hurt, willing the fat to melt away and reveal the determined chin he knew was there. Hard tack and sea salt was the answer. It had been a mistake to buy a mirror that made you look suntanned. Every time he looked in it he worried if he had jaundice and looked carefully at the whites of his eyes. There were no short cuts to the lean and weatherbeaten look.

He ran through his repertoire of facial expressions from careless bonhomie to studied superciliousness. It was hard living in an age when you had to pretend to be natural. There

6

was a lot to be said for elegant falseness. He decided on an expression of disarming frankness with a touch of humour around the corners of the mouth.

He threw the comb down on the dressing table among the lipstick-stained Kleenex and used cotton buds and screwed-up sticking plaster. Amidst the litter stood a photograph in a Perspex frame of him and Thea on their wedding day. The photographer had posed them in front of a statue of an obese cherub, a hideous Cupid who was not so much a symbol of their undying love as a warning not to overfeed the first-born of their blissful union.

Pax was grinning out of the photograph with what appeared to be spontaneous happiness. Thea's smile was more deliberate to match the carefully arranged train of her wedding dress but it did not look strained. Did they choose their expressions then as carefully as they chose them now? He couldn't remember.

Poor fools. Poor innocent fools.

The Browns had moved into the Square five years before when Thomas was two and Thea was pregnant with Sarah. It was their first mortgage.

The house was ten years old. There were four terraces of six making the Square around a patch of grass and a car park. Half of them had blue PVC cladding over the front door and half had black. The doors were painted different colours. Otherwise the houses were identical.

The ground floor consisted of a garage and a bedroom. The middle floor was an open plan living room with a small kitchen in one corner. The top floor had three small bedrooms and a bathroom. Most of the owners had bought them not because they liked them but because they thought a building society would like them. After they had painted the front door a different colour they started to look for houses that building societies probably would not like.

Estate agents pointed out that the houses in the Square were bigger than those in the next-door council estate. And that their road was private. The only time residents of the Private

7

Square went into the Council Square was to find out why the cleaning lady had not turned up.

The picture window in the living room looked out onto the picture windows on the other side of the Square. Thea worried about it. The people opposite or passers-by could look straight in. She would not put up net curtains. Only the windows in the council estate had net curtains. She did not like to draw the ordinary curtains during the day, except when she was laying the table in her underwear, in case the neighbours thought she was peculiar or someone had died.

Sometimes she could not shake off the feeling she was being watched. From time to time Pax tried to reason her gently out of her delusion.

"Who the hell would be interested in us?" he used to say.

Pax could tell from the cries of outrage and pain coming from the kitchen that Thea was getting the children to wash their hands and faces. Then a reminder about some of the rules of social intercourse:

- Do not ask Uncle Nick or his fiancée for money.
- If they give you any money say thank you. Even if it's not very much.
- Do not take your trousers down and shake your willie. Uncle Nick saw it last time.
- If you think anyone has done a whoopsie do not cheer or hold your noses or pretend to faint.
- When someone goes upstairs to the loo do not sing out "I know where you're going."
- Do not make personal remarks of any kind to anyone even if they're true. Especially about Uncle Nick's hair.

(But why did your real hair fall out, Uncle Nick? There's plenty growing out of your nose.)

Uncle Nick had had a hair transplant. It had been planted in rows across the top of his head like lines of cabbages in a field. The intervals were so regular they made diagonal lines as well.

8

The way the patterns changed as he moved his head was like op-art. Just when they had got used to his hairpiece. It was much harder to tear your eyes away from the patterns than the little cap of neatly permed hair that he had before.

"All these things make people unhappy and we don't want to make people unhappy, do we? We want everyone to be happy and think what nice people we are, don't we? And then we'll all be happy, won't we? We have to make other people as happy as we are. Of course Mummy and Daddy are happy, Sarah. That's why we want everyone else to be happy. If you do that again, Thomas, I'll smack you."

It was the end of a hot summer's day. A warm breeze from the land brought the scent of wild thyme and honeysuckle down to the sheltered inlet. A boat with a honey-coloured hull and tall mast was anchored a few yards from the white sand beach where a man and a woman were lighting a driftwood fire to cook the fish that still flapped on a line at the water's edge. Two children were gathering the first course in the shrimp pools at the edge of the beach. Their happy laughter mingled with the gentle lapping of the waves.

The man and the woman smiled at each other. Their smiles, their words, their gestures welled up spontaneously from the deep pool of inner happiness they shared.

A black bird with a long neck dived into the water for a fish and came up dripping. It sat on the bowsprit of their boat to eat, silhouetted against the sunset. Seagulls were calling as they flew happily home to roost, looking in the distance like those birds everyone can draw, V-shaped ticks in the porcelain blue sky. As the sun set the moon rose, laying a silver path across the silver sea towards them.

The moonlight was chill. They put on natural-dyed fishermen's smocks over their cut-offs. He went happily down to the water's edge for the fish and the bottle of wine buried in the wet sand to cool. It needed the corkscrew that dangled with the marlin spike from his belt.

He took a mouthful of wine and without swallowing it kissed the woman so it trickled into her mouth, tart and sweet.

After supper the children washed their hands and faces and cleaned their teeth and went happily off to bed of their own accord, as they did every night, saying how tired they were. The man and the woman lay on the soft sand looking up at the full moon and holding hands. They decided to stay in the inlet for a couple of days before sailing on up the atoll.

They talked about the old days and smiled that he had carried on working at the bank for so long. They laughed happily at the things they thought were important then – money and houses and schools. Now they had little but it was more than enough to live on. They caught fresh fish every day and bartered them for vegetables with passing natives. In the villages where they bought their other provisions like coffee and wine and toothpaste they traded in batik.

She kissed him and ran her gentle fingers over his bony, weatherbeaten face. They made love happily in the moonlight. After a year at sea her body was like a young girl's. His body was more or less like it was before, only muscular instead of podgy and without the wrinkly bits that had started to develop under his nipples.

"Are you happy?" he whispered.

"Yes. I'm so happy. Are you happy?"

"I'm happy. And the children are happy."

"We're all so happy."

"That's what it's all about, isn't it? Happiness."

"Yes. Being happy."

"Do I make you happy?"

"You make me so happy. Do I make you happy?"

"You make me so happy too."

"It's a funny word, isn't it?"

"What?"

"Happy."

While Thea was upstairs putting on her dress, Pax made the last-minute preparations. He swept the broken glass and puddles of mint sauce into the corner by the fridge. He threw away the incriminating wine bottle he had just emptied into the decanter. On top of it he threw away the plastic bags the frozen

10

vegetables had come in. Then he thought again and fished the bags out of the garbage. He rinsed off the tea leaves and other glop under the tap. If Thea did not have the instructions on the back of the packet she would panic and forget how to cook them.

In the living room he took the flokati off the large wicker laundry basket that stood against one wall underneath the framed Toulouse Lautrec poster of Aristide Bruant, the man in the cloak and floppy hat. He opened the basket and filled it with old newspapers, broken toys, jigsaw puzzle pieces, dirty washing, clean washing waiting to be ironed, ironed washing waiting to be taken upstairs and all the other ornaments of domestic life that lay on the floor and tables and chairs and any other available flat surface. He closed the lid and covered it again with the flokati. Now the room looked strangely barren.

He went downstairs for the Hoover they kept in the garage. With it he ruffled up the plain brown fitted carpet into furrow marks and pushed the hard bits like peg people and peanuts under the sideboard with the dried apple-cores and orange peel and sweet papers and tops of felt-tip pens, for the cleaning lady to ignore the next time she came.

He arranged the cushions on the Habitat sofas so they covered up the stains and adjusted the lace antimacassar so it hid the crack in the glass on the bamboo coffee table. He pushed the sofas so they faced each other across the table. It is a symptom of contemporary social relationships, he informed Aristide Bruant, that seating is placed for confrontation. In the old days you sat round the walls and looked at the fire.

If Nick's new girlfriend was like his last wife the sofas could end up back to back.

He could not think of anything else he could do which would add to the unnatural symmetry and tidiness of the room that Thea insisted on when they had guests. He wished they could cultivate the lived-in look instead of a waiting room ambience but their attempts at studied informality always ended up making the place a worse mess than it did before.

Still in her underwear, Thea ran through the living room on

her way downstairs, explaining that her wellingtons had made her tights smell of old socks and she wanted another pair out of the drier in the garage.

"I've cleaned up now. It looks nice," he lied. It was in everyone's interests to calm her down.

"I suppose you've tossed all my clean washing into that damned basket. It's got to go."

"But we got it from *The Observer*. And we need it for Auxiliary Seating."

She did not hear. She was in the garage, banging the door of the drier. She ran back upstairs two at a time and through the living room again.

"You may like living in an empty goldfish bowl but I'm getting tired of it. I want a house with a lounge on the ground floor that I can clean and lock up the day before and doesn't look as though the bailiffs have just been in. And that's got proper curtains."

"What have we got to hide?" he called upstairs but she had already slammed the bedroom door.

Bugger all was the answer.

"Is my dress all right?"

She was wearing a calf-length batik shift with a pattern of purple crescent moons on a crackly brown and yellow background. It was stitched together out of a rectangle of material that was supposed to drape itself sensuously around the female form. The batik had made it so stiff that it stood out where it should have folded in. Her shoulders were like an American footballer's. She had made it at evening classes. It looked terrible.

"It looks absolutely lovely, darling. Aren't you clever? But isn't it a bit formal for today? We don't want to overwhelm the poor girl. Aren't your jeans clean?"

"You don't like it, do you?"

She stood flatfooted in her stockinged feet, silently pleading for encouragement and confidence like a lost puppy, knowing in her heart of hearts that she looked awful, wanting to be told that she was beautiful.

12

Why do we do this to ourselves? Why do we act and dress and live like this? Surely there's some other way.

He put his arms round her and hugged her. The batik felt sticky. He tried to kiss her but she wriggled away so her lipstick would not smudge.

"I'll wear it," she said defiantly, "who cares? At least I did it myself."

"That's my girl," he forced himself to say.

She went downstairs to call Thomas and Sarah in to have their faces washed again.

"Cor Mum. You're like someone out of *Doctor Who*."

"It's like Thomas's army tent."

"Are you going as a witch?"

So much for confidence boosting. His well-meant insincerity had all been wasted.

Nick parked his bright yellow Jag in their tiny drive, its boot sticking out over the pavement. Passers-by would have to step out into the road to get past. He sounded the horn three times to save ringing the doorbell. Pax hurried downstairs to open the door before he could do anything else to attract the attention of the whole Square.

I mustn't look at his hair. I mustn't look at his hair.

He was confronted with a large bunch of white lilies. "What lovely transplants! I mean plants!"

"Flowers, Pax, cut flowers," said Nick. "Pax, I'd like you to meet Annabel."

She was the most beautiful girl he had ever seen.

Slim, blonde, wide blue eyes, straight nose, full mouth, teasing pout, clear skin, golden tan. A smile full of innocence and knowingness and sensuality. And mischief. There had to be something wrong. Her voice? Squeaky? Gruff? Missing consonants and distorted vowels like Brummie or Belgravia? But her voice was beautiful and exciting too. A hint of breathlessness and an intriguing lilt.

"Sorry about the lilies. They're really for funerals. Nick insisted. I don't care for death, do you?"

"No. I'm against it. I'm definitely against death. Do come in," he stuttered.

They shook hands. Her fingers were long and strong and soft. They were like a bird's wing, gentle feathers and firm quills. He held her hand for as long as he dared.

"We got the flowers at the cemetery. It's the only place that's open on a Sunday," said Nick, cheerfully.

"Did you nick them from a grave?" asked Pax, closing the door. The fleshy leaves, sickly yellow pistils and cloying scent brought dead bodies to mind. Annabel laughed a thrilling laugh.

"Oh silly! There's a flower seller outside the cemetery gates. We nearly got you a wreath but Nick said you only had one foot in the grave . . ."

"Joke, Pax, joke," said Nick, squeezing Annabel's arm.

Nick made the narrow hall seem smaller. He was not tall or well-built but his restlessness made any room he was in seem inadequate, like a squash ball in a squash court. He was dressed in a blue double-breasted blazer, open-necked shirt with a Liberty print cravat, cream trousers and white shoes. He was ten years older than Pax but looked the same age. His innocent, cherubic face was beginning to sag into the expression of a youthful satyr. He tried to arrest the process with expensive exercise equipment, a hair transplant, a sunlamp and blue tinted contact lenses. On the few occasions when he was in repose he reminded Pax of a waxwork.

Annabel's appearance was just as contrived but opposite in its effect. Her contact lenses were plain but they moistened her large eyes and enlarged the pupils. Her long lashes were barely touched with mascara. Her make-up was meticulous but minimal, bringing out the natural pink of her cheeks and the light, even tan on the rest of her skin. Her lipstick was a delicate line to mark the boundary of her full mouth. Her hair fell in waves to her shoulders, its tinted streaks only the slightest shade lighter than its natural blonde. Her bra-less breasts filled her plain white silk shirt and her narrow waist did not seem unnaturally pinched by her wide red belt. Her stone-washed designer jeans hugged her slender hips and long legs but there were creases here and there to show that there was a real body inside them.

The only flaw in her image was being associated with Nick.

The stairs from the hall led directly up into the living room. The first that newcomers saw of anyone else was feet, then knees, then the rest of the body. Conversely, those in the living room saw the top of the newcomer's head, then an upturned face, then the rest of the person rising from the depths. It spared everyone the shock of a sudden introduction, let them size up the others before they were confronted on the same level.

What would Annabel make of Thea's flatties and the tacked-up hem of her home-made dress?

"What a pretty dress, Thea, so original. Where did you get it?" she asked after the introductions had been made.

"Nowhere special," said Thea, keeping her eyes off Annabel's silk shirt and expensive jeans.

"She made it herself," said Pax with more malice than pride. "She's been going to evening classes, haven't you dear?"

"How creative," purred Annabel, "how brave."

"She started at the beginning of the alphabet, didn't you dear? She missed out Astronomy because she's frightened of the dark and started on Basketwork. That was last year. This year we moved on to Batik. It's your first attempt, isn't it dear?"

"When do you get to D for Dressmaking?" guffawed Nick. "Joke, Thea, joke."

"I've got Bridge and Candlemaking to do first. If you'll excuse me, I have to take the peas out of the oven."

Thea fled to the kitchen, leaving Pax with the bitter taste of victory. But it was her own fault. She should have known better than to wear that dress in public. And what was she doing with peas in the oven?

"I think it's time for a drink," said Pax, "anything you like as long as it's red wine, sweet sherry or gin and tonic."

"Bacardi please," said Annabel in a velvety voice.

Bacardi was something that people brought back from their holidays or which filled the screen between Coming Releases and the main film. For the first time in his life he felt inadequate for the lack of a bottle of Bacardi.

"Never mind, honeybee, drinkiepoos is drinkiepoos. Gin will do us," oozed Nick.

In the kitchen Thea was banging saucepans in the sink and standing on a carpet of half-cooked peas. Pax pushed past her to get to the fridge. He hammered and twisted the rubber ice tray until a few recalcitrant lumps fell into the pool of mint sauce and peelings he had swept into the corner.

"Nice, isn't she?" he whispered.

"Bitch," was her only reply. Did she mean Annabel or him?

He went back to the living room with the drinks. Thomas was standing at the top of the stairs with chocolate round his mouth, grass stains on his best white shirt and a cricket bat in his hand.

"Uncle Nick, you promised to come out and play cricket when you'd had a snifter and patted Mummy's fanny. Are you ready yet?"

"Snifter on the way, Thomas. I would have said arse but it would have been rude," apologised Nick as he relieved Pax of his drinkiepoos. He followed Thomas down the stairs, ice cubes tinkling in his glass, baggsing first bat.

Pax was alone with Annabel. He looked at his shoes and the wall behind her head, trying desperately to think of something suave or witty to say. He had not felt like this since adolescence. Those feelings had gone the way of acne and square dances and the last bus home. He blushed while his stomach muscles tightened from the larynx to the groin. He wanted to run away to the kitchen and even more to stay where he was in spite of the bursting, embarrassing emptiness.

"Is this mint in the gin and tonic? How clever," she purred.

"Speciality of the maison. You should try it in Bacardi."

"Nick's a character."

"He has a gift of bringing trouble into our well ordered family life."

He looked at her and swigged his drink. She was smiling and looking at him. He had to keep the conversation going.

"I'm even worse than he is with the children. Thea says she

16

spends all week bringing the children up and I spend the weekend bringing them down again."

He had never been a leg man or a breast man as much as a face man. He had fallen in love with Thea for her face. Annabel had the loveliest face he had ever seen outside a Bacardi advertisement. He had to keep talking.

"All we owe our children is board and lodging and clean clothes. We don't bring them into the world for their own good and happiness do we? We conceive them out of self-gratification. They don't owe us anything either. Least of all our happiness."

"That depends on what you mean by happiness," she said.

My God, perhaps she's an intellectual as well.

"I've never had children. And I never knew my parents," she continued.

A surge of compassion welled up inside him for this poor orphan girl, alone in the world but for Nick.

"But who do you blame things on? I blame my mother for everything. She carries the can because I never knew my father. It was her genes and her upbringing that made me what I am. Why shouldn't she take the blame? When I couldn't ride my bike or failed my 'A' levels or got fired from my first job I blamed my mother. It's all her fault."

"You have to break out of that. I hate the thought of being conditioned from birth. You can do exactly what you like, when you like. It's up to you."

"I'd rather blame my mother. It's easier."

"I'd rather do just what I like. I make a choice and I do it."

How on earth had they got round to free will and determinism? He should have been beguiling this gorgeous girl with sparkle and wit. She knew there was no-one else in the room but she was still looking round for someone to rescue her from this boring man who talked about his children and his mother.

"You choose to take your clothes off all day for a living. Wasn't that conditioned?"

"What the hell do you mean by that?"

Oh God. If Nick had made that remark she would have laughed. Whenever he tried to be daring it always misfired.

"I thought you were a model. Don't you have to keep dressing up in different outfits?"

"I don't do that sort of work. I specialise."

"What in?"

"Ears."

She smiled sweetly. Was she making fun of him or looking for a conversation stopper?

"You just model ears?"

"I sometimes do neck work as well. And I might get something in a crowd scene on a big budget commercial if there's nothing else going. But the speciality is ears."

"What a waste of the rest of you."

Thank God. She smiled and fluttered her eyelashes.

"Can I see?"

She turned her head sideways and lifted the hair from the side of her head. Her ear was pale and small. He was not a connoisseur but it did look like an ear of above average quality.

"It's the most beautiful ear I've ever seen." He could not remember ever saying that to a woman before. And she smiled again. "Is there a lot of demand?"

"Of course. Jewellery. Hi-fi. Perfume. I did a hearing aid last week. A girl's got to eat."

She was smiling at him with mischief in her eyes but he was not deceived. She was mocking his small talk and small house and small life and small self. He had always been a failure at chatting up. He took a large swig of gin and tonic to buttress his self-esteem.

"You're right. We have to eat. And then we have to do the washing-up and sweep the floor."

"You can get out of that. Nick has found some Vietnamese boat people to live in and do the cooking and the housework for us. He says they can live in the utility room next to the kitchen."

"A whole boatload in the utility room? That's a heavy price to pay for freedom."

"Silly. Just two girls. They'll learn English and have a home and a job. Nick says it will give them back their dignity. The alternative is social security and a council flat in Brixton."

"Plenty of people find that dignified enough. How much do you pay them?"

"I don't know. Nick arranged all that. He did a deal."

"I bet he did. His contribution to the household is a yellow Jag and a pair of oriental slaves. And a wardrobe of Liberty print cravats."

"They made a choice. They will be happy."

"I thought we only had cheap domestics from the Philippines and the Seychelles these days. Vietnamese must be really avant-garde. They probably cook better too."

"Now who's been conditioned? Why don't you think of what it's like for them instead of what *The Guardian* would say? Of their own free will they escape from Vietnam in a tiny boat and spend months drifting around until they run out of food and water. Typhoons. Storms. Pirates. They could have been raped and tortured and murdered. The utility room must be heaven."

"Until you put the washing machine on Fast Spin. Scares the hell out of me when I go in the garage."

Thea came out of the kitchen carrying a dish of roast lamb and put it on the table. Blood and juices slopped onto the table cloth.

"Shall I carve, Thea? We were just talking about torture and rape."

He found the carving knife in the top drawer of the sideboard under a collection of last year's Christmas cards and an old string vest now used as a duster. He stood by the window to carve where he could see Nick and the children playing cricket in the Square. Nick was batting. He had probably been hogging the bat since they started playing. Pax heard the chock of the bat against the ball. Thomas knew they weren't allowed to play with a hard ball because of the windows and small children. Nick had doubtless persuaded them to break the rules.

Annabel offered to help Thea in the kitchen but was politely declined. She came to stand next to Pax at the window. Her silk sleeve rubbed against his sweater.

"Overgrown schoolboy," she sighed. It didn't sound like an endearment. She was frowning.

19

"At least he looks the part. White trousers. Blue blazer."

"Terrible aren't they? I thought we were going to a fancy dress."

"Nick is conventional in a very unconventional way. A free spirit. One of the boat people. Cast off on the water and sail for freedom. That's what we'd all like to do, isn't it? Bugger the pirates. Unless they bugger you first."

Thea came out of the kitchen with a dish of roast potatoes and a dish of swept-up peas.

"I've nearly finished carving, dear. We were just talking about being buggered by pirates."

Thea went back into the kitchen with a scowl to locate the gravy. Outside in the Square, Thomas bowled a jerky overarm down the leg side. It was slow and pitched up and irresistible to any schoolboy. With a graceful swing Nick brought the bat down and across in a perfect hook to leg. Pax watched the ball soar towards them, inevitable and unstoppable, growing larger in his vision. At the last moment, a split second before the ball hit the window, he ducked so that the broken glass showered harmlessly over his back and the meat and vegetables on the table.

"At least we got a free Chinese meal out of it," said Pax that evening as he dabbed the carpet under the table with a pad of wet toilet paper.

"The one day in the week when I take the trouble to cook a decent meal and look what happens. We were having real meat and vegetables and still we end up with rice and monosodium glutamate."

"It was a meal out. Saved washing up."

"The whole point of eating out is to avoid cooking. All we did was avoid eating it. And we still had to wash everything up because of all the broken glass."

"Stop complaining. Now we've got cardboard over the window you won't think everyone is looking at you."

Pax brought the toilet paper into the light to inspect it for tiny, glistening shards. He had covered the whole of the living room carpet in this way after going over it with the vacuum

20

cleaner while Thea put the children to bed. He pushed two cardboard boxes in front of him. One was for the used toilet paper, apple cores and other rubbish like the mouldy bits of chewed carrot he found on the ledges under the dining table. The other was for treasures he found along the way, such as the spare ignition keys for the car, long lost pieces of jewellery, foreign coins, all of which were destined for the sideboard drawer.

If it's true that the outside world is just a creation of my own mind, then I have a very sick mind, he thought to himself.

Thea came upstairs from the garage loaded with unironed washing.

"Are you sure this is really necessary," he complained, "I'm shampooing every square millimetre of this dammed carpet by hand. It's never been as clean since the last people moved out. This is Sunday night, for God's sake."

"Leave it if you like," she said, "and you can take the children to the hospital to have the little bits of glass taken out of their feet."

She was wearing the green wellingtons again for protection against the hostile carpet. She had taken off the batik dress and thrown it to the back of the wardrobe where it would stay until one of the children wanted it for a school play. She was wearing an old pair of jeans too tight to do up around the waist and a pregnancy smock to cover the gap.

"If I had broken a window in Nick's flat he would have made a gang of Vietnamese coolies go over the carpet in their bare feet. You wouldn't find him or Annabel with their bottoms in the air like something out of the *Mikado*. Why do we live like this, Thea? Why do we live like this? Why can't we have a few Asiatics living in the loft to do the dirty work? We could give them the dignity of labour and eat Chinese food every day in our own home."

He appropriately burped sweet and sour.

"We don't have a loft. The house has a flat roof. We don't have room for ourselves. And if labour is so dignified, why don't you do it with better grace."

She dragged the ironing board out of the broom cupboard in

21

the kitchen and set it up on an area of damp carpet that had been treated and pronounced safe. She took the steam iron out of its place in the bottom of the stereo cabinet and filled it with sterile water from the drinks cupboard in the sideboard. Then she rummaged in the Auxiliary Seating hamper for tomorrow's school uniform and a clean shirt for Pax.

Now was not the time to have a sensible conversation with Thea. When she was washing the kitchen floor or tidying up the Lego or doing the ironing she had nothing good to say about anything or anyone. They carried on with their respective chores until Pax had dabbed the carpet for the last time and Thea was surrounded by neat little piles of ironed washing.

"Whisky?"

"No thanks. I'll have a sip of yours."

"The hell you will," he thought. He poured her a small one and himself a large.

"I thought you got on well with Annabel at the restaurant," he said, watering his whisky from the Malvern Water bottle. Even though he had filled it himself from the kitchen tap it tasted better. The power of self-delusion.

"She makes a big effort to come down to our level. It's easy to be humble in a Christian Dior silk shirt."

"I think she's got depths."

"What's that old line? Deep down she's a very superficial person. Poor Nick. He's so irresponsible and carefree and the price he pays is living with a succession of women like Annabel."

Pax tried to imagine what the disadvantages were of living with Annabel in Nick's little love nest in Orpington waited on by oriental girls.

"You're right. Orpington is a heavy price to pay."

"And I don't know what he's doing for money since the electronic roulette business went bankrupt. I'm glad we don't live hand to mouth."

Hand to mouth with a woman like Annabel. Hand to hand. Mouth to mouth. Back to back and belly to belly. He swigged the whisky.

22

"He's got a new business idea. He wanted to know if I would go in with him. It sounded quite interesting."

"Nick's my brother, and I won't have a word said against him, but I wouldn't trust him an inch. What's this new business?" she asked.

"Import-export. Something to do with stamps and coins and that sort of thing. He's found a source somewhere on the Continent and he thinks he can make a profit selling them over here."

"What does he need you for?"

"I would be his financial advisor. Do the books. Open the bank accounts, that sort of thing."

"He can't have bank accounts. He's an undischarged bank-rupt."

"That's where I come in. I'm the expert. He needs that sort of advice."

"He needs a patsy to open his accounts, and as you work for a bank you're the obvious candidate. You'll be suckered, Pax Brown."

"I'm nobody's fool. I can look after myself. And what's this about not saying a word against him."

"He swindled me out of my pocket money too often. I stick up for him but I wouldn't touch his schemes with a barge pole."

She drained her glass, stood up and piled the ironed washing at the foot of the stairs. She slammed the lid on the Auxiliary Seating hamper and replaced the flokati. Pax carried the hissing iron gingerly into the kitchen.

"He offered fifteen per cent. That would come in useful."

"Fifteen per cent of what? His debts?"

"You're always pouring cold water on everything. A real wet blanket. If we're ever going to break away from all this you're going to need a bit of imagination as well. Annabel supports him. She's all for it."

Nick had brought up the idea over the lychees while Thea was taking Sarah to the loo to be sick. Annabel had smiled and had said how lovely it would be if the two men did something together. She had squeezed his thigh under the table.

He was glad he had still had his napkin on his lap.

While Thea carried the washing upstairs Pax took the milk bottles downstairs to the front step and turned out the lights. On his way back up he took another swig straight out of the whisky bottle. They had not made love for days.

"Coming, darling," he called upstairs.

The routine never varied. Pax tucked the children in and turned off their lights while Thea was in the bathroom. They left the landing light on in case a child woke with a screaming nightmare. He undressed while he waited for Thea to come out of the bathroom carrying the glass of water that stood all night on her bedside table. She never drank it but she couldn't get to sleep without knowing it was there. Pax was similarly conditioned. He had to have a clean handkerchief on his side.

While he was in the bathroom Thea mucked out the bed. This consisted in gathering up the clothes, toys, newspapers and damp towels from the morning and other bits and pieces that had accumulated on the bed during the day and dumping them on the floor. She gave the duvet a couple of good shakes and got into bed among the swirling feathers and dust that her bedmaking created and lay on her back looking at the ceiling. Before she could go to sleep she had to count the cracks in the ceiling to make sure there were no new ones. She sometimes wished there was a medical term for the fear of the ceiling falling down on you in the middle of the night while you were asleep.

Pax came back from the bathroom, naked, and rummaged for his pyjamas on the floor. He put them on trousers first. If he put them on top first he would invariably have a nightmare about going to work dressed only in a string vest too short to pull down over his bottom. He got into bed and adjusted the alarm clock. By common consent it was ten minutes fast although they both knew that he added another five minutes for safety.

Thea turned out the light and they both lay on their backs looking up at the shadows and the yellow patches on the ceiling from the street lamp outside. They listened for unusual sounds over the noise of the traffic building to a crescendo at pub closing time.

He felt her hand on the inside of his thigh, diffidently stroking his pyjama poplin and he carefully moved so that her fingers would find the opening in the front.

"You know, Thea, I feel as though we've spent the last ten years of our life carefully building a house of brick and stone. It has a concrete floor and solid roof. The inside is reinforced with steel. All the windows have got solid bars and the doors are solid oak with massive locks that you can only open from the outside. It's a nice house. Mock Tudor with leaded lights and two bathrooms and fitted carpets. No complaints on that score. But we've locked ourselves in and thrown the key out through the bars and now we're looking at the world outside and wondering how we can get out. Do you ever feel like that?"

He would have to ask her again another time. Her hand had stopped stroking him and he could not hear her breathing. Her face was turned towards him, looking waxen in the yellow light. Her eyes were closed. Was this what corpses looked like?

Perhaps we're all dead after all. Pass the lilies. Two feet in the grave.

He closed his eyes and tried to think of something to distract him from the nightly fear of dying. In the Catholic primary school he went to they said you had to think of death last thing at night. A cheap trick to make you say your prayers. His mother always told him to think of something cheerful like what he wanted for Christmas. A cheap trick to make him go to sleep quickly. Apart from a brief period of adolescent despair he chose Christmas presents over the terror of the abyss.

Hoping the whisky burning in his stomach was not going to keep him awake he turned his back on Thea, closed his eyes, and thought of little yachts scudding in a sunlit sea.

❋ Chapter Two ❋

Thea stood at the kitchen window, cooling the eggs under running water. She saw John Thornton from Number Nine, striding pontifically and swinging his umbrella like incense, on his way to the accountancy firm where he was a partner. She wiped her hands on a tea-towel and went to the foot of the stairs. "Thornton," she shouted.

She was answered by mumblings about lack of clean socks and deduced that Pax had his head deep in the airing cupboard. Then she called down to the ground floor. "Breakfast. Come and wash your hands."

The children came to the table, slapping and pinching each other.

"Yuwert me," yelled Thomas.

"Pissoff," yelled Sarah.

Thea carried the teapot from the draining board and watched Mister Trees beginning his brisk little walk, almost a trot, to the station. He worked somewhere in Whitehall. Thea went to the foot of the stairs and shouted. "Mister Trees."

The children slurped their runny eggs. They tried to smear yolk on the ends of their noses with their tongues. On the other side of the square the Campbells got into their car.

"The Campbells," shouted Thea.

Pax jumped off the second stair into the living room. He avoided the bottom stair because the carpet was beginning to wear on the tread. He came into the dining area and pulled out a chair. The back came off in his hand. The children screamed and guffawed.

"You were going to mend that over the weekend," said Thea, without reproach. The list of things to be done about the house was too long for recrimination over a single item. This

26

was saved up for periodic litanies of complaint.

"Good morning everybody. Daddy's here to make you smile," said Pax, helping himself to the last egg from the saucepan in the middle of the table. He tickled Thea under the chin and then Thomas and then Sarah. He looked down accusingly at the egg yolk on his finger. "Mummy, you're such a messy eater," he said. The children screamed and guffawed and carried on screaming and guffawing long after the moment of humour had passed. Thea wiped the egg from under Sarah's chin.

"Pissoff," said the little girl. Her parents exchanged glances and forced themselves not to react. The books said you should never reinforce, just explain how certain behaviour is undesirable.

"You know I didn't have time for the chair over the weekend, love. I'll do it tonight, I promise. It just needs some glue and a wedge."

"It just needs a new set of dining room chairs, *love*. There's so much glue and wedge and screws and bits of Meccano on those chairs that the wood they were made from isn't necessary any more," said Thea, buttering toast and licking misplaced butter off her fingers.

"Do you know how much furniture costs? The window your brother broke is going to cost a week's salary."

"I'll ring up the glass man this morning. And I'll get him to do the upstairs bathroom and the playroom door and put safety glass in the front door before Thomas rides his bicycle through it."

"You're not serious? I'll have to take out a second mortgage." Pax waved his eggy spoon in the direction of the boarded-up window and a yellow teardrop dripped to the carpet. Thea jumped up from the table to throw a teacloth over the toaster which had caught fire.

"And we need a new toaster. This one's costing us a fortune in teacloths." She opened the kitchen window to let the smoke out and saw Mrs Peters from Number Ten mince delicately past on her high heels to the chemist's in the village which she managed. "Mrs Peters!" she called. "Quick, Pax, you're on next."

She followed Pax downstairs.

"Sarah's started to say 'pissoff' now," she whispered while Pax buttoned up his nylon shortie raincoat.

"She gets it from you. You shouldn't use such rude language around the house."

Pax stood on tiptoe and bit her on the ear. He pushed her towards the coat cupboard, muttering about a quickie before he went to work.

"Stop it, Pax, it's serious. What if your mother heard her? She gets it from that playgroup. I don't mind myself what language she uses," she lied, "but I do mind if other mothers won't have her to play because she swears like a navvy." She opened the door.

"We chose Saint George's Playgroup because it had the children of workers and blacks and one parent families so she wouldn't grow up in a social ghetto. And also because it costs a pound a term. If you don't like the language she picks up from the children of workers and blacks then send her to Cilla Debrett's Infant Academy and pay a hundred pounds a term. I bet you anything you like she would come home saying 'Piss orf' at the end of the first day. All you'd get for your money would be 'off' rhyming with 'dwarf'. Goodbye."

"Goodbye. I'm going to the estate agent this morning to put this place on the market and see if there's anything on the Manor Estate."

"Over my dead body," he wanted to say, but there was no time to argue. He pecked her on the cheek and half-ran, half-walked into the Square and out onto the road in the direction of the station. The despairing bonhomie with which he coped with Monday morning was already wearing off.

On the other side of the Square in Number Eighteen Sandra Smith stood at the bottom of the stairs wiping her apron.

"Brown!" she called up to her husband. So it continued until the first wave of commuters had left for the day.

The beautiful Vietnamese girl came out of the cabin and walked barefoot across the warm teak deck to where he stood at the tiller. She was wearing one of his shirts, open to the waist

28

and billowing loosely around her thighs. She pressed herself against his body, pleading for his love. He had mastered her wildness and her fear.

He eyed the sails, the glowering sky. He slipped the strap over the tiller to hold it on course. He took her in his arms, felt her softness and tears on his lean, tanned face. She clung to him. Her full lips sought his eyes, his cheeks, his temples. Her fingers caressed his scalp, his back, his chest. He winced as she touched the wound in his side. She kissed away the pain.

Gently he lowered her to the deck. It was clean now. The last rain of the dying monsoon had washed away the blood. With the following wind they would soon be clear of the Straits and danger.

She begged him to do with her whatever he willed. He felt a twinge of compassion for her. A short time ago she had been an innocent virgin fleeing with her family to freedom. He would be gentle with her. He began to kiss her ear. She had the most beautiful ears he had ever seen. He took her hand and guided it.

"Excuse me, Mr Brown, you have a lunch at the Auditors' Association at half-past twelve."

Pax looked up over the rampart of files he had built around himself. Doreen, his secretary, held his diary open in front of him. Today she had chosen to clothe her pear-shaped body in black and white zigzags. With her long face, sad brown eyes and mane of straggling hair she looked like a hideously mutant zebra.

"Thank you, Doreen, I'll be back at three. What a pretty dress."

With a whinny of pleasure she emptied his out-tray and went back to her own office, leaving him to lapse back into his daydream. But it was no good. However hard he tried he could not bring back the image of the half-tamed oriental virgin with exquisite ears. In her place was the vision of Doreen in a zebra-striped shift.

Mastering Doreen's wildness could put you off fantasy for ever.

Pax avoided business lunches whenever he could. The stress of talking about his job took all the pleasure out of eating and gave him indigestion. The only advantage of a business lunch was that nobody minded if you stayed out of the office for two hours or more.

He preferred a sandwich on his own followed by a good read or a long walk along the river. He was an expert on warm deserted places to hide with a book, like the waiting room at Fenchurch Street Station or the mahogany-panelled lavatories on the third floor of the Grand Hotel. But he was only supposed to take an hour off for lunch.

The answer was to fill his diary with dummy appointments. This worked so well that in addition to two or three spurious lunches a week he allotted himself a fictional afternoon meeting so he could go to the cinema. He didn't mind what the film was. The main pleasure was to come out blinking in the daylight on a weekday afternoon.

The bogus appointments had to look genuine and be made some time in advance to forestall genuine ones. In the beginning this sometimes led to confusion on the day. He would arrive at someone's office and announce his arrival for a fictitious meeting. Once he was watching *The Magnificent Seven* when he should have been at the Bank of England.

The solution was to put a tiny pencilled cross next to the dummy appointment. His lunch at the Auditors' Association had such a mark. He could go down to the marina by the Tower of London and look at the *Swan*.

The *Swan* was moored at the end of a pontoon between a large white catamaran and a motor cruiser. She was a wooden sailing boat, about thirty feet long, very low in the water and broad of beam. The bow was full and curved, sweeping up from the water to meet the bowsprit, the shape of a honey-coloured toffee-apple.

Pax knew her well. She had been in the marina all winter. She wasn't as flashy as many of the other boats, not designed to impress. She had a functional, serviceable look about her, as if the sweeping lines and curves fulfilled a purpose other than to look beautiful. Her broad beam and bluff bows weren't built for speed but she would hold her own in a rough sea. She reminded him of an old-fashioned fishing boat or the *caiques* he had seen on Corfu on his honeymoon.

A massive oak tiller hooked over the rudder which rose in a curve high above the stern, like a canal barge. It was carved with a swan, painted white. The open cockpit was mahogany and big enough to take half a dozen passengers in comfort. Around the cabin doors were carvings of grapes and leaves and little swans. The cabin was low and sleek, varnished to a deep, rich brown, with shiny brass portholes in the sides.

Where the cabin ended and the foredeck began was the mast. It tapered tall and gleaming to the grey sky, supporting itself without stays or rigging. The slender boom stretched back towards the cockpit, supported by a crutch above the tiller. A jaunty bowsprit pointed the way ahead. The foredeck was grey teak, pencil-lined with black caulking, wide and practical for fishing or sunbathing or toying with oriental girls.

Pax kicked a pebble off the quayside, hoping his petty vandalism would not be noticed. It plopped loudly in the oily water. Ripples spread languidly towards the *Swan*.

It was the same shape as the twee Dutch clog that hung in the hall at home. Who would want a boat like that?

"This is nice," said Thea as she arranged her knees around the wine barrel, "it's the first time we've been out together for months."

They had been to the parents' evening at Thomas's school. After they had seen his teacher they had had another hour before the babysitter had to go home. They decided to treat themselves to supper in a new wine bar in the village. They sat downstairs in the white-painted cellar and ordered a traditional wine bar meal – chilli con carne for him and moussaka for her, heated up in the microwave in little brown pots, washed down with a carafe of the house white.

Pax put the cutlery and Christmassy red paper napkins down on the barrel top. It was warm and damp in the cellar and they drank the first glass of wine greedily.

"Quite a good report for young Thomas," said Pax with forced optimism. He liked to push through the post mortems on parents' evenings as quickly as possible. Thea liked to linger over them and draw the worst conclusions from everything they had heard.

"His handwriting is terrible," said Thea. "Did you see the other children's books? His 'o's are appalling. He can't draw a circle."

"That's just psychological. It will pass with puberty. In any case, people with neat handwriting become auditors and teachers and people who write the menu up on wine bar blackboards."

As he said this the girl came with their food. He gave her an embarrassed smile. He waited until she had gone before he continued.

"Have you ever seen an auditor's figures? All tiny and well formed and in neat little columns with ticks by them. Talk about anal repression."

"But you're an auditor," she said, breaking through the scab on top of her moussaka as if she were lancing a boil.

"Do you think I want my son to grow up like me?"

He scooped up a forkful of red beans from his brown pot, masochistically, knowing they would give him terrible wind. He waited for Thea to tell him what a wonderful role model he was but all she did was wipe away pus-like *béchamel* from her chin.

"How would you like to see him grow up?" she asked at last.

"I'd like him to do just what he wants to do. Just what would make him happy. No hang-ups about what he should be doing instead."

He made a show of topping up Thea's full glass so he could politely fill up his empty one. She said nothing so he carried on speaking.

"I'd like him to do something useful for others and be happy and successful and make lots of money. The simple things one wants for one's children. What about you?"

She appeared to be thinking while she devoted herself to the task of cutting up with her fork the last big bit of rubbery aubergine in the bottom of her brown pot. She succeeded only in making perforations and gave up. She drained her glass and

32

spoke. "I was sitting on his chair in that old Victorian class-room and wondering what it was like to be Thomas. You remember how we agonised about what school to send him to?"

"We still do."

Every so often they stayed awake at night wondering whether they should scrounge the money for private educa-tion. This was followed by a few days of reading programmes and visits to museums and friends round for tea until the impetus wore off and they lapsed back into simply surviving their children instead of bringing them up.

"Before we had Thomas we were against the class system and the public schools and the public day schools and the grammar schools and secondary modern schools we grew up with. We supported comprehensives – "

"Only the sort of comprehensives that Labour politicians send their children to. Not the others."

"Let me finish. We decided that when our children went to school they had to be exposed to children from all kinds of different backgrounds. The teaching and the facilities didn't really matter – "

"Now we feel guilty because the school has only got one computer."

"Please let me finish, Pax. Where was I? Well, I sat on his little chair with my knees under my chin and I looked at the picture of the yacht he'd painted that was stuck up on the wall and thought that if I were little Thomas I would just want people to leave me alone. And I felt so sorry for him."

"Are you sure you weren't feeling sorry for us?"

She wiped away a tear with the Christmassy napkin and left in its place a smear of tomato sauce. She drained her glass and he refilled it, squeezing out the last drops from the bottle. He reached out for her hand across the brown pots.

"What's the point of it all?" she asked.

"I can't answer that, Thea. I can't even imagine what the answer would look like."

She stared in despair at her perforated aubergine and took her hand away from his.

"Then if you can't imagine what the answer would look like, the question is meaningless. There *is* no point."

Pax grappled in silence with this philosophical statement. He gave up trying to understand it because an even more terrible thought was gnawing into his mind. Thea's behaviour, unless it was just pre-menstrual tension, implied that she was having the same kind of self-doubts as he was. Was this possible? Could they indulge in two identity crises at the same time?

He was about to suggest they carried on talking over another half carafe of the house white when she picked up her handbag and plonked it on the barrel as a sign that he should ask for the bill. It was getting late. If they were home after eleven the babysitter got time and a half.

"We can talk on the way home," she said.

But they didn't.

Pax looked down at the *Swan* from the quayside. He noticed for the first time that half way down each side was a flat, oval board on the outside of the hull, sticking up like a stubby cygnet's wing. He had no idea what they were for but they looked workmanlike and useful. Perhaps they were some kind of stabiliser.

Although boats played a large part in his imaginative life there was a large gap in his seafaring experience between a pedalo on the park pool and a cross-channel ferry. Sailing was something other people did. Somehow the opportunity had passed him by.

Whenever he wanted to make himself depressed about the increasing speed with which life was passing he made a mental list of things he had always meant to get round to. Sailing came top, above riding a horse, going on a Big Dipper, sniffing cocaine, running a marathon, going to bed with two girls and countless other experiences he would probably never taste before he was old or dead.

As a result, his ignorance about the practical aspects of boating was almost total.

Boats livened up a tedious seascape. They decorated little

34

harbours. They lay like dead things on the sand, waiting for the wind to breathe life into them. They made tiny kinks in the horizon on the borders of infinity. Boats were air and water. Fish and bird. Licking ice-cream on a deckchair or plodding along the promenade behind a push-chair he did not connect them with his own mundane existence.

Other people spent money on boats. They struggled to get them on the roof of the car. They drove along like grotesque mechanical beetles, causing accidents. They hit overhead electric cables with the metal mast and frizzled. They capsized. They drowned. Boats were unreliable, unstable, dangerous.

But he wished he could walk down the ramp to the pontoon, board the *Swan* and float off through the lock to the river and the open sea instead of going back to the office to tick off numbers on a computer print-out.

Many other things were preferable to going back to the bank. Sitting in a warm cinema, reading a book in a coffee bar, feeding the pigeons in Trafalgar Square were all attractive alternatives to pretending to be an auditor for the rest of that lovely spring afternoon. Indeed he had opted for them on many occasions in the past. But what he would most like to do was sail away on his own.

How do you start the engine on a boat? Is it like a car with a clutch and an accelerator? How do you put the brakes on? Can you reverse? Can you do a three point turn? Which side of the river do you drive down? Sail gave way to steam, he remembered from somewhere. Or was it the other way round?

Stepping onto the *Swan* was as improbable and impractical as hang-gliding from the walls of the Bank of England.

✳ Chapter Three ✳

"Why do you think Thomas and Sarah draw yachts all the time?" asked Pax, picking up the current gas bill from the kitchen floor. On the payment counterfoil a yacht and a flock of distant seagulls had been drawn with red felt-tip.

"Why shouldn't they?" asked Thea. She was sitting at the dining table browsing through an Open University brochure.

"No reason. There were lots of pictures of boats stuck round the classroom walls. And in picture books. You know, little sailboats on a blue sea with a yellow sun. I wonder what kind of impression they make on kids' minds. Most of them will never go near a boat."

He screwed up the gas bill and threw it into the rubbish. It was only the blue one.

'If you're illustrating the alphabet you don't have a lot of choice when you get down to the letter Y. It's either Yachts or Yaks. They stand even less chance of going near a yak. I suspect the zebra gets a lot more publicity than it's entitled to."

"Whatever the reason, the image stays in the mind. You never know when it's going to pop up again. You could go on for years without ever thinking about boats and suddenly, hey presto, there's a yacht. Takes you right back. If we wanted true happiness we would surround ourselves with apples and balls and cats and dogs and elephants and so on. We've been conditioned."

He sat down at the table opposite her. She furrowed her brow and tried to persist with the brochure but he sat staring at her, twiddling his thumbs. She gave in.

"I don't think I've been conditioned by elephants or frogs or giraffes."

36

"What about yachts? Doesn't the idea of a yacht make you feel warm and furry all over?"

"I can't say it does, no. In fact quite the opposite. The idea of yachts makes me feel quite cold all over." She returned to the brochure.

"Are you sure? It crossed my mind just now as I was doing the washing-up that we could try out sailing. As a family. You know, lots of fun together, out in the open air. Nice blue sea, yellow sun. I'm sure there's an evening class in it."

"Yes dear. The perfect hobby for a family with two young children. Sarah can't even swim yet."

"It would give her an incentive to learn. She'd learn much faster if she had some kind of incentive."

"Go on Sarah, there's a good girl. Beachy Head's only two miles away. Now you just let go of the life-raft like Daddy. You'll soon get the hang of it. Let Mummy hold your chin. Wave to the rescue helicopter, sweetie."

"But it's perfectly safe if you take the right precautions. It's something we could all do together," persevered Pax, racking his brains for a more convincing argument.

Thea slapped the brochure down on the table.

"Can you imagine us in a boat for the day? Or the afternoon? Or even an hour? We'd have to wear lifejackets for a start. I have enough trouble getting Sarah into her ordinary clothes without having to make her keep a lifejacket on all day. It's like wearing a straight-jacket all the time."

"They'd get used to it," said Pax, lamely. It was true, he hadn't thought about the lifejacket problem. Did you have to sleep in a lifejacket too?

"Sure, they'd get used to it. And they'd get used to being in a little box miles from anywhere with no chance of getting out to run around. You can't bear to be in the same room with them for more than half an hour without sending them out into the Square to play. How would you like to spend the afternoon cooped up in a boat with them?"

"Perhaps it's something you and I could do together at first until the children are a bit older," he said hopefully.

"And what are they going to do while we sail off into the

sunset? Play quietly on the beach by themselves until we come back?"

"It was just an idea."

"A bloody silly one if you ask me."

"I thought that sailing would be a good way to get away from things."

"Get away from what things? Sailing is one of those activities that get you further into the things you were trying to get away from in the first place. I for one do not wish to spend what little spare time I have piled on top of each other in the wet with nowhere to go and nothing to do except dangle our fingers in the water. We can do that at home."

Pax stood up from the table. He went into the kitchen to put the kettle on for a cup of coffee, leaving the table to Thea. She opened the brochure again.

"Can I just ask why you're so bitter about it? It was only a suggestion."

"I spent enough weeks with my brother and my parents in caravans to know what I'm talking about. At least in a caravan you could get out and walk around. If you're looking for something for us to do in the holidays think about a big hotel in the sun with a swimming pool."

Pax spooned coffee into the mugs and stirred in boiling water. He would have to be more subtle in future. It was not going to be easy to bring Thea round to the idea of giving up everything and sailing off to a new life on the nice blue sea.

She had a point about the lifejackets though.

❊ Chapter Four ❊

"I went into the estate agents in the village this afternoon. There's a house for sale in Romona Terrace. One of the three-storey ones."

Pax was sitting at the dining table waiting for the rest of his dinner. He looked down at the two blackened lamb chops on his white plate like empty quotation marks. He had to say something quickly to nip this conversation in the bud before it spread like convolvulus through the rest of the evening.

The terrace had been built at the turn of the century by an impresario who had invested the profits of his hit operetta, *Romona*, in speculative housing. The houses were named after the characters. They had elaborate stained glass in the front doors and tiled porches and fancy gables. Before Sarah was born Pax and Thea used to walk Thomas past them in his push-chair and laugh at the names and the net curtains and the ornaments on the front window ledges. Now they were being gentrified with stripped-pine doors and kitchens in the dining room.

"Which one is for sale?"

"Number Three. Mavis."

Thea came out of the kitchen. She plonked the peas on the table and flopped mashed potato out of the saucepan onto their plates with the masher. Very deliberately Pax scooped up a blob of potato from the table cloth with his little finger.

"The gravy got burnt. Sorry."

Pax licked the potato off his finger. "I refuse to live in a house called Mavis."

"But they're the nicest houses around here. That we can afford. You know they are. They've got all that stained glass and plaster mouldings. They're ever so easy to restore. You use a toothpick and an electric toothbrush."

Pax forced himself to take a deep breath and a mouthful of peas. He chewed them and took a sip of water.

"I have no objection to titivating the cornices like some unhinged dental hygienist but I put my foot down about living in a house called Mavis. And that's flat. It is a lovely name for a person. Or a flower. Or a goldfish. But not a house."

"We can change the name."

"What to? Ethel? Frank?"

"Please, Pax. Don't be unreasonable. We can blank out the name. It's only in the pane above the door."

"I thought we were looking at that Georgian cottage in Brixton."

"You said it needed underpinning, a new roof and wire mesh on the windows for the summer evenings. You said you weren't going to live in Inner City Bandit Country."

"Ah. But it was you who were worried about the schools. Don't blame it all on me."

The time before it had been a little farm worker's house at the end of a two mile dirt track, no sanitation and an acre of garden to reclaim from the wilderness. Before that a tumble-down water mill, a deconsecrated church, a fire-gutted alms-house and other eccentric follies had presented themselves as the house of their dreams.

"I thought you didn't want anything as modern as that. Romona Terrace isn't even a hundred years old. It's got to be old to be any good, hasn't it?" asked Pax, resolutely chewing on the nugget of resilient flesh he had picked out of the eye of his chop.

"But this has lots of character. Some of the rooms have got the original wallpaper. You can have your own study upstairs on the third floor. There's an attic room with a dormer window."

Why did she always bring up a study for him? He had nothing to study. The only time he begged for privacy was when he was concentrating on the pools coupon. For some reason she imagined he pined for a book-lined room and a place at the Open University.

"We'd have to change the car. You couldn't park a Morris Ital in the drive of Romona Terrace. We'd have to buy a Renault."

"It's easy to make the back two rooms into a proper kitchen where we can all sit down to breakfast. The children could have the dining room as a playroom until they get a bit older. We'd still have one room we could lock so the children don't mess it up. And a downstairs lavatory. Upstairs we could have a proper guest room for your mother. There's a proper garden with a lawn."

This was getting serious. Mavis sounded like a practical proposition. Up to now he had joined in happily in building highly desirable castles in conveniently situated air. They had discussed improvement grants, the location of schools and bus stops, extensions, demolitions, new bathrooms and old panelling for many hours over the kitchen table or in bed at night. He had not been indulgent or patronising. He had been genuinely enthusiastic. But there had never been any serious possibility that their plans would come to anything.

"What about the Jacobean workers' cottages and the Georgian town houses? What about the little hotel in the Cotswolds? You doing the cooking, me doing the gardening?" (The last was perhaps the most extraordinary of their fantasies.)

"Let some other idiots devote their lives and money to old wrecks. Who cares where we live as long as it's got a bit of character and the space? It's how we live that counts. It's us that matters, not the architecture."

This was disturbing. Pax got up from the table and fetched the wine box from the fridge. Thea had obviously Been Thinking. Been Thinking meant Taking Stock, New Resolutions, Reordering of Lives. It might be something as short-lived as hiding the television or going to Ancient Greek classes three or four times. Or it could be as drastic as doubling their mortgage to buy a house in Romona Terrace.

"I've been thinking," she said, chewing the lumps in her mashed potato, "if we're going to make a move we have to do

41

it soon. The children are getting older and will need more space. We all need physical space to grow and develop and be ourselves. And privacy when we need it. But then a place where we can all come together as a family. This isn't a family house. It's an aquarium."

"Vivarium. No water."

"Whatever."

Pax put his knife and fork together and pushed his plate away like a man who has had a satisfying meal. "You do realise that Mavis won't make any difference to our lives. If anything we shall be even more boring. Look at the Wilsons. They bought a Victorian vicarage and tried to make it as much like this place as possible. Central heating, fitted kitchen, through lounge, picture window. All they talk about is Irish Jays."

"I'm not going to talk to you if you're going to be flippant. You know what I mean. It's time we took stock."

"I know exactly what you mean. We need the *Lebensraum* of Mavis to develop our potential for personal fulfilment and satisfying family relationships. But why do we have to move house to do it? Let's spend our time and energy on personal relationships now and then move when we can afford it. How are we going to pay for it? We'll have to get a bigger mortgage."

"I'm going back to college. And I'm going back to work. That will be my contribution. Sarah's going to nursery school now."

"What are you going to do?"

"I'm going to go back to work as a secretary and study to be a Probation Officer."

Pax filled a Mister Men tumbler from the wine box and drained half of it. Thea stabbed moodily at her peas. This was the first time she had brought up the Probation Officer idea. He was stumped for anything to say. Sometimes when Thea announced her ideas it was like being struck by a thunderbolt from a clear blue sky.

'Thea, can I ask a question?"

"If it's not flippant or sarcastic."

"Are you establishing us in a spacious family home of

character as a prelude to liberating yourself into the self-fulfilment of socially useful work?"

"If you really want to know, yes."

"Just as long as I know."

He held his empty Mister Men tumbler under the tap of the wine box. An inch of wine came out. He tipped the box up on its corner and got another inch. He took the greasy knife from his plate and sawed open the box. He yanked out the aluminium bag and squeezed the last half-inch into his glass. He sucked the tap like a nipple.

"Could I make just one point?" he said.

"If you like."

"In my personal opinion restoring an Edwardian house and taking on a bigger mortgage and going out to work all day is not liberation. For me, liberation is just the opposite."

"You are entitled to your opinion. I think it's now my turn to decide what I want to do and go out and do it for myself."

She picked up the plates and took them out to the kitchen leaving him to flick errant peas thoughtfully onto the floor.

'Does that mean I've had my turn already?" he asked the eviscerated wine box.

Pax's job at the bank was to make sure that all the internal systems and controls were working and all the rules and regulations and procedures were being followed. He did this by random inspection of the records of the various departments of the branch on the orders of the Auditing Office in the bank's Head Office in the United States.

There were only sixty people in the branch. There was not enough work to justify a full-time auditor so he also inspected the Frankfurt and Bahrain branches from time to time. These trips meant a welcome change from the everyday routine and a few duty-free bottles.

Auditing requires meticulous attention to detail, a methodical mind and an inherent mistrust of computer systems and human nature. Pax had a horror of detail, a congenitally untidy mind, a timid respect for machinery and an abiding faith in the essential goodness of human nature. Above all, he couldn't give a fig if someone ripped off the bank for millions. Good luck to them.

He sometimes wondered if he was the right man for the job.

In his idle moments, which were frequent, he brooded with bitterness how he had drifted into this occupation and more frequently worried how he was going to drift out of it again. The bank attached a lot of importance to avoiding expensive mistakes and fraud and embezzlement so the job was well paid, including a car and a five per cent mortgage. Job security was high as long as he avoided gross negligence. There was little material incentive to overcome his natural inertia and look for something else.

"It's one thing to know you're a square peg in a round hole," he muttered to himself as he climbed the stairs to his office, "but another thing to find out where they've hidden the square holes."

His office was on the second floor and he stood at the top of the stairs taking deep breaths to recover from the climb before he went in. It was the only exercise he got. Too clumsy for games and too easily bored for jogging, he assuaged his guilt by avoiding the lift and by annual forays into his book of Canadian Air Force exercises, which lasted about a week.

The internal auditor had the privilege of his own office. His work was often confidential and he was expected to keep a little distance from the rest of the staff. The main advantage was that he could read books and magazines at his desk instead of skulking off to the lavatory. Since he embarked on his professional career at the age of eighteen as an articled clerk in a firm of accountants all his serious reading had been done with his trousers round his ankles.

This had two main consequences. The first was that he could never go to the lavatory unless he had a book in his hand. The second was that whenever he went into a bookshop or a library he had an irresistible urge to empty his bowels. He was only just beginning to overcome this Pavlovian association of literature and shit by being able to do his reading at his desk.

He took his last deep breath and opened the door into his office. His secretary, Doreen, was putting files and papers into his in-tray and emptying the out-tray. She flicked her long, straggly hair coquettishly over one shoulder. She was wearing a dress modelled in shape and colour on the original Montgolfier balloon. She waved a thick procedure manual accusingly at him.

"Have you read this already, Mr Brown? I only gave it to you yesterday."

"Speed reading, Doreen. It's what makes me so productive. How do you think I get through so much work? It's the secret of my successful business career."

"Is that what it is?" she said sceptically, flicking her hair over her other shoulder.

As she floated majestically out of his office with the unread manual under her arm he asked her to make an appointment for him to see the Branch Manager, Gilbert Pinkish.

"What about?" she asked, her little eyes screwing up with curiosity.

"Confidential, Doreen. Highly confidential," he said, as if the fate of the banking industry depended on it.

When she had gone he settled down to his daily routine. While he waited for the tea lady to come round he would read the cartoon page of the *International Herald Tribune*, make a stab at the *Daily Telegraph* crossword and flip through the headlines of the *Financial Times*. He resisted the urge to dump the files in his in-tray straight into the out-tray. Doreen was beginning to suspect the real reason for his productivity. He would have to be more careful. He spread a couple of files industriously on his desk and settled down to Peanuts and the Wizard of Id.

He was on the third clue of the crossword when Gilbert Pinkish phoned, asking him to come up. His office was at the top of the building with a panoramic view of the high stone wall that surrounds the Bank of England. When Pax walked in he was standing at the window, staring at the wall and jiggling the coins in his trouser pockets with a clinking sound like chains.

When foreign banks establish themselves in London, one of the conditions is that they employ a senior man who has

45

worked in a British bank and therefore knows the ropes. Old chap. Since Gilbert had left school he had worked in one of the large English banks, which, in order to induce him to retire early, had encouraged him to become the token Brit in the management of the new London branch of that little American bank.

Gilbert was surprised and flattered when they offered him the Manager's title and not really upset when he found out that all the banking decisions would be taken by the American Assistant Manager. Gilbert went to the cocktail parties and receptions and made sure the lifts and central heating were working and approved salary rises and mortgages for the British staff.

He turned round from the window and looked at Pax histrionically over his half spectacles. His grey hair was carefully brushed back into a suspicion of a ducktail over his collar. He wore a dark three-piece suit of an old-fashioned cut that was still available in the subterranean tailors around Fenchurch Street station, a striped shirt, dark blue tie, a matching silk handkerchief flopping over the top pocket, a discreet gold chain across his ample waistcoat. The studied distinction of his appearance enhanced the persistent aura of insignificance which clung to him.

He waved Pax towards the visitor's chair in front of his desk. It was low and uncomfortable and specially chosen by Gilbert to put him at an advantage when he sat behind his massive mahogany desk on his leather swivel chair with the extra cushion.

"Morning Pax. How's the canary?"

"Tickety-boo, thank you sir."

"Wife and children?"

"Likewise. Everyone's chirpy and bright-eyed."

Gilbert was a canary fancier. It was his passion in life. His speciality was Norwich Fancies which he exhibited at every major show in the country. He tried to keep his hobby separate from his business life but was often betrayed by tiny seed husks clinging to the sleeve of his suit or a blob of white shit on the back.

When Pax joined the bank they had a canary which had been part of Thea's dowry. It died soon after but Pax never had the courage to admit this to Gilbert. Since neither of them were very interested in banking, it was all they had in common.

"I say, Pax, how well do you know young Randolph? Can you get him to stop calling himself Randy? I heard one of the secretaries tittering about it in the lift the other day. I mean, what if you or I went round Head Office telling everyone we were horny, eh?"

Randolph S. Rifenbach the Fourth was a new arrival from Head Office. He was the Comptroller, as the chief accountant was archaically called. His responsibilities overlapped with Pax's but he took them more seriously.

Had Gilbert started talking about him as a hint to Pax? Was Doreen not the only one who suspected his lack of dedication?

"I'll try to take him on one side."

"As the actress said to the bishop. You know, the first time I went to Head Office I was walking through the banking hall with the Chairman when he suddenly pointed at someone and said in a loud voice, 'Why, Randy!' I said to myself, Well, here's a man who can spot an erection at fifty yards."

Pax laughed politely. Although he preferred the company of canaries Gilbert tried hard to be one of the boys and he believed that men's talk was always ribald. He made a point of making a few risqué remarks at the beginning of the conversation before getting down to business.

"Now, what can we do for you?"

Pax listened to himself mouth the words increasing his mortgage to buy a larger house. His heart sank as the prepared speech continued. He remembered films where the hero is made to sign his own death warrant. Is this really me, saying all these things?

He finished and Gilbert looked down at the blotting paper on his desk where he had been doodling. He looked up over the half-moon spectacles and pronounced sentence.

"I think it's stretching your limit, Pax old chap, but you say you have a few thousand in savings. If you put those in too to

47

increase your equity stake I daresay we could come up with the rest."

Pax forced a smile. "Thank you, Gilbert."

Gilbert leaned back in his chair and put his thumbs in his waistcoat pockets. Gilbert attached a great deal of importance to his managerial responsibility to give personal help and guidance to those in his charge even when unasked for. Pax steeled himself for a heart-to-heart.

"I know you ambitious young chaps think it's very important to get on in your careers, and so it is. Banks like ours depend on the total dedication of all their staff. You also want to have the right kind of house and car and so on. Good luck to you. You only live once. But you have to be very careful not to get so totally involved in your career and the material things that you wish your life away."

"I'll try not to Gilbert. But you know how it is when you've got a responsible and well-paid job. I want to do the best I can. I believe in putting everything into the task at hand."

If the old bugger was giving him a warning about pulling his finger out, this was a very subtle way of doing it.

"I know just what it's like. But you ought to find something outside the bank and the usual domestic duties to take your mind off things, broaden the mind, free the spirit. Take canaries for example. I've found the Fancy a wonderful hobby over the years. You've got a canary. Why not develop your interest? I could help you along, you know, if you felt that way inclined."

"That's very generous, Gilbert. When we've moved into the new place I'll think about it seriously. There'll be more room then."

"We can always do you a home improvement loan for an aviary," added Gilbert plaintively.

As he left the office, Pax glanced back at Gilbert. He was standing at the window, staring at the blank wall of the Bank of England, clinking the coins in his pocket.

There but for the grace of God . . .

Pax plodded down the stairs, past his office, and although it was only half past eleven left the building and headed in the direction of Saint Katherine's Dock. He needed to do something to shake off the heavy black pall settling over his head and shoulders.

"Hurry up. We have to give the keys back to the estate agent by seven o'clock," said Pax impatiently.

They were standing in the front room of Number Three, alias Mavis, desirable family residence in fash Romona Terrace. Fash meant Fashionable, not Fascist. Pax had verified this with the agent, to Thea's annoyance.

"It's like the *Marie Celeste*," he said. "Look, there's a tea cup in the corner of the fireplace."

The owners had been a couple in their seventies who had both caught flu and died within a week of each other in hospital. Their children had emigrated to Australia many years before and there were no other relatives. Only the executor and the estate agent had been in the house since the ambulance had driven away.

"We could move in, lock, stock and barrel," said Pax. "Just sell our own house, contents and all, and move in here. We could take over their lives."

The ceiling was thickly encrusted with brown paint. The wallpaper had faded to a pattern of pale yellow flowers from the floral riot of bright red and orange that was still visible behind the picture frames. The pictures and ornaments were souvenirs of holidays hung up at random on the walls.

Pax picked up a pair of crutches that was leaning against a walking frame by the fireplace and fitted them to his elbows. He stooped and hobbled towards Thea. "See. They fit perfectly. I could get a few weeks off work with these. A lifetime even."

The blue patterned carpet was old but the bright green loose covers on the three-piece suite were new. They were made of dralon and sparkled in the light from the wooden chandelier. The shades were hung with cobwebs. There were more souvenirs, ornaments and ash-trays on half a dozen coffee tables, all covered with a thick layer of dust.

"Look at that lovely marble fireplace. I've always wanted a

fireplace like that," said Thea, looking desperately round the room for something to like.

On the mantelpiece stood black and white photographs of two schoolchildren in school uniform. In one they held a white cat. There was one colour photograph. Four adults and several children stood in their shirtsleeves round a plastic Christmas tree in the garden of a modern bungalow. Thea picked up a black and white portrait of a couple with two young children dressed in their best party clothes, smiling self-consciously.

"I suppose they didn't come back," she said.

"No point is there? The solicitors will just send them the money through the post."

"I mean for the funeral."

"You can't blame them. I hate funerals. Although I've never been to a double one. Are you allowed to put them in the same coffin?"

"You're being awful. Deliberately. You're trying to start a row so we don't buy this place."

Pax put his hand on his wallet pocket and screwed his face into a hurt you-are-misjudging-me expression. "That's nonsense. Absolute nonsense. I think it's a wonderful fash house. And like I said, we could slip in without touching a thing. I wouldn't touch a single ornament. Look at our walls at home. Plain white with one picture of a geezer in a floppy hat. What has Aristide Bruant to do with us? We have nothing to show for our lives. Nothing to look back on. No identity. But this room is packed with incident and anecdote. We'd have an identity at last."

Thea turned and walked out of the room to the front door without saying anything. Wistfully, Pax leaned the crutches back against the walking frame and followed her.

❋ Chapter Five ❋

Nick telephoned Pax at the bank to ask if he was free for lunch. He had some business in the City that would be over by noon. They could talk about the new import-export company he was setting up and what banking arrangements would be necessary. Pax said it was a bit short notice but he would look in the diary.

There was a lunch engagement in the diary but there was a tiny pencilled cross next to it. A dummy. He kept Nick holding on for a couple of minutes before telling him he had managed to put someone off but would have to be back early for an important meeting.

At half past twelve Nick was waiting for him downstairs in the lobby. He was wearing a calf-length dark-blue cashmere overcoat with a velvet collar, a dark mohair suit and a regimental tie sufficiently different from the genuine article that he would not be openly accosted by a pukka ex-Guards officer on the steps of Lloyd's or the Stock Exchange. "Bankrupt spiv," thought Pax to himself but he wished he wasn't wearing a brown nylon shortie raincoat and a Marks and Spencer polyester tie.

They shook hands formally and went outside. It was a lovely spring day. The City was stirring like a municipal cemetery on the day of judgement as the sun shone down on its cold stone and spent lives. Flowers in narrow window boxes on the office buildings looked as if they were springing from cracks in the dead marble. The measly parks and churchyards began to fill with the white bodies of sunbathers. Office workers who kept on their funeral clothes cast off the weight of files and ledgers and walked with their heads in the air. The tourists who strayed into the City from the Tower of London and Saint

Paul's Cathedral in a vain search for something interesting to photograph looked less outlandish than usual. They meandered among the risen dead in their beach clothes, craning their necks, hiding their navels with cameras, harbingers of a better life to come.

"I thought we could go to Saint Katherine's Dock," said Nick, steering Pax by the elbow down Lombard Street away from the mausoleum-like walls of the Bank of England. "It's the old dock by the Tower of London, old boy. They've been tarting it up. It's not bad, but gentrifying dockland is a bit like polishing a turd, don't you know."

Pax just grunted. There were so many things to resent in Nick's short statement that he didn't know where to start. The hearty City Gent parody. Treating him like a country cousin when he'd worked here for fifteen years. The denigration of *his* Saint Katherine's Dock, where he escaped at lunchtime.

Nick let go of Pax's arm and put his hand back in the top of his pocket, the fingers inside and the thumb outside, the approved posture for walking in a velvet-collared coat. Pax wished there was a posture to dignify a nylon shortie raincoat and opted for the Prince Philip, hands behind the back.

As they walked eastwards the addresses became less respectable. The Bank of England squats in the middle of the City like an old mother hen gathering her chicks as close as she can around her. She clucks loudly if her charges stray too far away towards the fringes among the commodity traders and insurance brokers and shipping companies that rub shoulders with the barrow boys of Whitechapel or spill over the river into the transpontine wastelands of Southwark.

At last they came into the open and caught a glimpse of the Thames behind the newly-cleaned stone of the Tower of London. They picked their way through the milling crowd of tourists to the cobbled promenade between the Tower and the river. Even the oily water sparkled in the sunshine and the stink of mud had an aftertaste of fresh seaweed. They carried on past the Traitors' Gate and the old cannons, gobstoppered with red cannon balls. Pax suddenly felt as though he were on holiday and was tempted to ogle a Beefeater or buy an ice-cream.

They went under Tower Bridge, past the forecourt of the Tower Hotel and at last came in sight of Saint Katherine's Dock. Nick took a hand out of its pocket and waved it proprietorially as if he were somehow personally responsible for the development of the old tea and spice and ivory port into a smart marina.

The old warehouses had been restored as offices and shops and the three connecting pools of the dock were crowded with boats of every description – ocean-going yachts, motor cruisers, dinghies, old Thames sailing barges, houseboats, catamarans, a three-masted sailing ship and even a lightship.

"Wonderful," said Pax, "I always think it's just like Monte Carlo or Piraeus."

"I suppose so," said Nick, "if you screw your eyes up enough."

They had lunch in the Yacht Club overlooking the main pool. Nick wanted to sit facing the bar where he could see who came in. Pax wanted to face the window where he could look out on the boats. So they were both happy.

Pax asked for a Pernod to go with his holiday mood. Nick stuck to gin and tonic.

"Sorry about your window the other day, old chap. I haven't hit a cricket ball like that since I was at prep school."

Pax knew that Nick and Thea were at a South London primary school until they were eleven and not a fee-paying private school, but he let it pass. The fine day, the boats, the Pernod were making him feel well disposed even towards his brother-in-law.

"We had the glazier round yesterday. He did all the other broken windows in the house at the same time. Thea's put the house on the market so she had the lot done," said Pax, using the part of the brain reserved for routine conversations. The active part of his mind was concentrating on the sparkling water and the pretty boats outside.

"That's jolly sporting, old chap. Where are you moving to?" mouthed Nick, his thoughts obviously elsewhere as he scanned the other patrons of the yacht club.

"Thea's found an Edwardian semi with stained glass

windows and plaster mouldings. It'll cost a fortune to reno-vate. We'd have to sell the ducks off the dining room wall," he heard himself say as he watched a red light flashing on the bridge that crossed the lock. A voice from a loudspeaker warned people to stay behind the barriers. You had to go through the lock to get into the river.

"Good old Thea. When are you moving?" Nick pretended to adjust his shirt cuff so he could look at his watch.

"The later the better. I've got nothing against gentrified Edwardian so long as it's not mine. Even after we've done it up it would cost a fortune to furnish it. The only thing we've got that would go with Three Romona Terrace is the SDP poster in the bedroom window."

The bridge over the lock was rising slowly and the inside gates were opening to admit a little white yacht steered by a man in a blue fisherman's jersey.

"The offer's still open to come in with me, old chap, if that would help. I could use a bit of the old financial wizardry. Never hurts to have a banker on the team."

For a moment Pax was distracted from the boats. He had never thought of himself as a banker, much less a financial wizard. Was Nick's project really so grandiose? The little white yacht was nosing gently into the lock and he let his voice switch back to automatic pilot.

"What exactly is the business?" he asked.

"I have a few contacts in the antiquarian coin business on the Continent. Right now there's a big market in this country for gold coins, mainly the Arabs but also local investors. A rare gold coin has value in excess of its gold content. So we buy them abroad and sell them here. Five or ten per cent profit. Not bad pickings for a riskless trading operation with no over-heads."

"Is it legal?" asked Pax, while the hull of the white yacht dropped out of sight as the level of water in the lock went down. The red pennant at the top of the mast made small circles against the china-blue sky. He sighed and directed more of his mind to his brother-in-law who was impatiently sloshing the remains of his gin and tonic round the bottom of the glass.

"What an unworthy question!" he said, in a voice long practised at dealing with creditors. But Pax worked for a bank and was used to dealing with debtors.

"But I'd like a worthy answer."

"Of course it's legal. We've got valid import licences, the whole caboodle. Listen, Pax old chap, you know my situation. Through absolutely no fault of my own I am legally, though not morally bankrupt. I have every intention of discharging my obligations to the last penny. This means two things. Firstly it is totally in my own interest to stay within the very letter of the law and sound business practice. Secondly, I am inhibited by what any sensible person would regard as unfair and discriminatory bankruptcy regulations from carrying on a proper business so I can recoup my losses and pay back what I owe. Is that a worthy enough answer?"

Nick looked at Pax with wide, innocent eyes and a world-weary smile. Still Pax was distracted by the hair transplant and looked away. A sail that had been hoisted on the mast with the red pennant filled with wind and disappeared from view downstream.

"So what do you want from me?"

"I need a couple of people I can trust to be directors of the new company. I thought Annabel could be one and you could be the other. Then we'll need a bank account, a small overdraft perhaps, safe deposit facilities and a reference or two. That would be your contribution while I look after the buying and selling side. It's all pretty straightforward and above board and it might mean an extra few thou for you to spend on the house of my sister's dreams. I can't be fairer than that, can I?"

The extra money would come in handy. There would be no harm in introducing an account to the bank. The business sounded legitimate. These thoughts ran through Pax's head as he watched the lock gates close and the bridge come down.

"I'll think about it," he said as a waitress put down plates of beef curry in front of them.

"I'm sure you will," said Nick, with a warm and trustful smile, "but I need an answer by Friday, there's a good chap."

There was one other thought which would have run through

Pax's head if he had allowed it. Annabel was the other director. There would be board meetings. Regular reviews of the business situation. Drinks, lunches, dinners. The most beautiful and exciting woman he had ever met. Feelings he had not known since adolescence.

He drove the image of Annabel out of his mind as he drained the gall of the Pernod's last dregs, bringing back the aniseed balls of a half-remembered youth.

"Tell me more about these coins."

He got up from his desk and went over to the cupboard. He took out the navy blue canvas holdall and closed the door on the tooled leather executive case and the velvet-collared cashmere coat. He would not be needing them for a few days. He gave a warm smile to his secretary as he passed her desk.

"Board meeting, Doreen. See you Monday."

He strode briskly towards Saint Katherine's, away from the Bank of England. The spring sun glittered on the office windows and made sharp shadows in the narrow City streets. A fresh breeze cut through the vehicle fumes and somewhere above the noise of the traffic a seabird sang in the china-blue sky.

He skipped down the steep ramp onto the pontoon. He knew that envious eyes watched him from the offices and flats and the Yacht Club dining room. He strode along to the end where his little white yacht was moored between two monstrous motor cruisers. He fiddled expertly with the lock on the cabin and went below with the canvas holdall.

He changed out of the dark blue mohair suit, maroon tie and Gucci shoes into a blue guernsey, white jeans and rope-soled shoes. He kept his white shirt on. He went back into the cockpit, turned a switch and watched for the cloud of blue smoke from the exhaust at the back. Quick but unhurried, he walked to the front of the boat and confidently cast off. He came back and untied the stern in the same expert way. He took the tiller and the boat began to nose away from the pontoon towards the lock.

A man on the quayside, hunched up in a shortie nylon

raincoat, took a hand out of his pocket and gave him a shy wave.

As the level of water in the lock went down the offices and warehouses and the workers in their ties and suits dropped out of sight. The red pennant at the top of the mast scored small circles on the porcelain-blue sky.

Once he was in midstream he hoisted the mainsail and the foresail with a few swift and expert movements. There was a following wind but it was light and he left on the engine until they were well clear of the City. He breathed deeply and felt the cares of financial wizardry slough off into the water that rippled along the hull.

The cabin doors swung open. Framed in the doorway was a beautiful blonde girl dressed in a bright-pink jump-suit. She smiled a warm, exciting, mischievous smile. In each hand she held a tall glass of milky Pernod, tinkling with ice.

"Here you are my darling."

"Thanks, Annabel."

"I can't wait to start our board meeting."

He pointed the nose of the little white yacht towards a secluded inlet he knew just the other side of the Thames barrier at Woolwich.

Pax was swallowing the last mouthful of rice when Nick stood up and shook hands with a massive man in an unseasonal gaberdine suit and white polo-necked sweater. He was totally hairless, with not even an eyebrow or a nostril hair to mar his smooth, buttery skin. He had the wide-eyed, newborn look of a slightly jaundiced baby.

"This is Carlo, an old friend of mine. My brother-in-law and partner, Pax Brown."

They shook hands. Carlo's hands were big and muscular.

"Carlo is a consultant," said Nick, as if that explained everything.

"My pleasure entirely," said Carlo in a North American accent and a voice that was surprisingly deep.

"Unfortunately Pax has an urgent meeting back at his office.

He's a senior executive in a bank in the City. Don't let us keep you, Pax."

Nick put out his hand authoritatively. Pax took it without demur and picked up his shortie nylon raincoat from where he had hidden it in a bundle under his chair.

Pax promised to telephone Nick on Friday, thanked him effusively for lunch, made him promise solemnly to convey his love to Annabel and undertook to take back to Thea a declaration of brotherly devotion. They told each other to be good, drive carefully, not work too hard and look after themselves. Carlo nodded while they expressed these heartfelt sentiments as if he was a notary, witnessing them.

Pax sidled away hastily through the tables, looking at his watch and trying to look important and waved as he went through the door. The other two remained standing side by side while they watched him leave, as if they needed to make sure that he had gone before they carried on with their conversation.

As soon as he was out of sight of the Yacht Club Pax slowed down to a stroll. He was not sorry to leave. Carlo made him feel uneasy. If he were buying an old gold coin from Carlo he would bite it very hard indeed.

At the same time he indulged in feeling wounded that Nick had brushed him away so hastily. Nick's real rendezvous was with Carlo. Why then had he asked Pax? To show Carlo he knew financial wizards from the City? To show off the patsy he had found?

It was not yet two o'clock. He had another half an hour at least before he had to go back to the office. He strolled round the quays, keeping his mind off the couple in the Yacht Club by ogling the boats and diverting his injured pride into a familiar envy of those who owned them.

"Why shouldn't I feel envious? That's why they bought the things in the first place. Bloody fibreglass confections. Just trying to impress other people with how much money they have to throw away. I'd do the same if I had a lot of money. Buy a boat for the price of a house in Romona Terrace. Maintain it and moor it and insure it for the money an average bank auditor gets paid. Potter round the water for ten days a year in a blazer and a yachting cap. If they didn't make people like me envious there'd be no point in owning boats."

He grumbled to himself as he walked round the marina, feeding the embers of his resentment, picking on boats that bore the names of seas and storms and faraway places when most of their time was spent in bobbing up and down in the marina. There were names evoking the wild and free spirits of seabirds and fishes while their owners led the lives of pigeons and goldfish. There were the names of exotic places in the Mediterranean and the Indian Ocean and the South Seas which would be seen only in the skipper's mind's eye as he pottered around from Southend to Brighton. And there were the names of women, the kind of names you would only give to girls in wet dreams.

It wasn't only the names that were the boat-owner's equivalent of Dunroamin and Mon Repos. Through the net curtains in the cabin windows Pax scoffed at the teak veneer and dralon and plastic brass. Some of the bigger cruisers had patio doors opening onto the rear deck.

"Shall I lay the table on the patio dear? – No, darling, we'd better move into the lounge. There's a Gale Force Eight springing up."

He did not spare the serious boats from face-saving mockery. A long racing yacht was being washed down by its tanned crew, sluicing off the salt of the North Atlantic. A bearded man in overalls with a booze-red face was pouring pitch onto the deck of an old Thames sailing barge. A Whitstable oyster boat was being fitted with a new wooden tiller. They were just as much a symptom of ostentatious consumption as the others. They were unnecessary and irrelevant, like the dock itself with its tarted-up warehouses. It was all an expensive luxury, a tourist trap living off the crumbs of the Tower of London next door.

Pax looked at his watch. It was time to go back to the bank. Wallowing in bitterness he turned his back on the boats and walked towards the Tower. He trod in a dropped ice-cream and collided with a little boy on a bicycle. This jerked him out of his reverie. Otherwise he might not have noticed Nick and the hairless Carlo trotting down the steps to a pontoon on the other side of the pool.

Carlo led the way. He walked with a jaunty stride, fluttering his hands by his sides as though he were singing to himself. His polished head shone in the sunlight. Nick followed with his hands half in the pockets of his City Gent's coat, elbows sticking out at the back. They looked as though they were heading for a large, seventy-foot cruiser, bristling with aerials and radar, at the end of the pontoon. Did they have a rendez-vous with a mysterious tycoon?

Pax mingled with a gaggle of German tourists who were milling by the chain fence at the edge of the quay taking pictures of the boats. Camouflaged among them he could spy on Carlo and Nick without being seen. They stopped short of the cruiser. Carlo took Nick's sleeve and pointed at a speed-boat. It was a large power boat, the kind that usually has a number painted on the side and advertises cigarettes or con-traceptives. Even without those decorations it was flashy. It was painted bright red with a silver stripe down the side. The nose was pointed and rose out of the water. The back swept up to the housing for its massive engines. The manifolds were painted silver and ended in a battery of exhausts.

They went on board and sat down behind the windscreen. They were having a heated discussion. Nick began to wave his hands about. Finally they shook hands.

They left the boat, Nick walking dangerously backwards along the pontoon so he could continue to admire it. Pax slipped away from the Germans and walked briskly out of the dock, putting on a funny walk in case Nick looked up and saw him.

What was Nick up to? Who was the unsavoury Carlo?

She switched off the alarm clock and lay staring at the ceiling for a few moments. Out of habit she counted the cracks in the ceiling illuminated by the yellow light of the street lamp. Her eyelids grew heavy again. Gritting her teeth she swung her legs out of bed before it was too late and she slipped off into sleep again. She sat on the edge of the bed, shoulders hunched, waiting to feel dizzy.

"This is madness," she whispered, and forced herself to stand upright.

Pax stirred behind her, sprawling his arms and legs over her side of the bed. His mouth lolled open and she resisted the temptation to shut it. She resented that he was still asleep. Let him lie there ugly.

She padded over to the window and peeped through the curtains. The Square was quiet and empty. The first light of day struggled against the bilious glow of the lamps. Cars drove fast along the main road, their headlights on, bringing her a sense of wonder that anyone else should be up at this time. She had not seen the dawn since Sarah had given up her early morning feed. Then there was the consolation that she could go back to bed until it was really time to get up.

She put as many of her clothes on as she could without taking off her nightdress. Pax's old tracksuit bottoms, rugby socks, tennis shoes, bra. That's how nuns got dressed, so Jesus would not be shocked. Finally she whipped off her nightdress and groped for the T-shirt and sweatshirt she had left at the foot of the bed the night before. Still she shivered.

She groped her way to the bathroom and splashed water on her face. Against her better judgement she looked in the mirror and looked quickly away again. "There are women," she thought, "who take their make-up off before they go to bed at night."

She tiptoed past the children's room and down the stairs, avoiding the creaking step. The kitchen, like the rest of the world at that time of the morning, was bleak and hostile. She was starting to feel sick. She put the kettle on for a cup of tea and found an arrowroot biscuit in the tea caddy to nibble.

"Snap out of it, Thea. This is your new life. Get used to it."

Out of the cupboard under the sink she heaved a bulging plastic bag decorated with the name of the health food shop in the village. Bending down so early made her dizzy. She dumped it on the table and took out bags of wholemeal flour, bran, sugar, lard and salt. She scrabbled in the drawer at the bottom

61

of the cooker for a baking tin and in other cupboards through-out the kitchen and the dining room for bowls and spoons and scales. From behind the toaster she retrieved the recipe torn out of *The Guardian*.

"Why am I doing this?" she asked herself as she tried to focus on the blurred and dancing newsprint.

It was fully light outside when she had finished. The sink was piled with dishes. The bag of salt was on its side. The work surfaces, floor and the front of her clothes from neck to toe were covered in a fine white dust. Little blobs of grey dough clung to the hair at her temples like fungus. She looked down with loathing at the small baking tin standing in the epicentre of the chaos. She picked it up and threw it into the oven as if she never wanted to see it again.

She sipped her lukewarm tea. The worst was yet to come. Willing away her headache and fighting back the urge to lie down on the sofa she rinsed her hands and went downstairs and unlocked the front door. Praying that none of the neigh-bours would see her she sauntered outside and round the corner into the street. When she was out of sight of the windows in the Square she broke into a half-jog, half-trudge. She slowed down to a walk at alternate lamp-posts to catch her breath and hitch up Pax's tracksuit bottoms and then doggedly trotted off again in pursuit of the New Woman.

Pax was dragged out of sleep by the insistent ringing of a bell. He groped for the alarm clock, pressed all the knobs and shook it but still the ringing continued. The smell of burning made him open his eyes. Fire Alarm! Struggling into his dressing gown he was about to rescue his children when he realised it was the front door bell. He blundered downstairs and blinked at the vision on the doorstep.

Her face was scarlet. Her hair was plastered to her head with sweat and wholemeal dough. She was leaning on the door frame, her forehead against the bell-push, sucking in air with the sound of old bellows.

"What the hell are you doing?"

62

She staggered past him and crumpled to the floor, her face pressed against the carpet.

"My face. My face is on fire."

"Are you all right? Thea! Speak to me. Do you have a pain down your left arm?"

He groped for her pulse. She lifted her face and wheezed from the bottom of her chest. "The bread. Save the bread."

He looked desperately round him and then on the doorstep and down the garden path.

"In the oven, you fool."

Smarting from the insult he stomped upstairs leaving her to die in the hall. For a few moments he stood aghast on the threshold of the kitchen. Strewn with ingredients and piled with utensils it looked as though a temperamental chef had gone berserk. The Joy of Cooking. The Horror of Cleaning Up. Taking off his dressing gown so it would not be contaminated he retrieved the oven gloves from the top of the fridge and took the bread out of the oven. The tin was black and the contents a very dark brown.

"Is it all right?" croaked Thea as he dropped it with a thud on the draining board. "Why didn't it rise?"

"Is this all? Out of all this?" he asked with a theatrical wave of his hand.

"You needn't eat any. It's for the children. Eat well to grow well."

She wetted a tea-towel under the cold tap and spread it over her face. Peering through the cloth she shuffled back into the dining room and sat down at the table. Her thighs were shaking uncontrollably. Pax left her to get dressed, her head cradled in her arms and the cloth covering her head.

When he came down again Thea was sitting on a stool at the sink. Thomas and Sarah were eating cornflakes at the dining room table. Between them was the loaf, sitting on a wire tray. It looked like a small iron brick.

"Hey Dad. Look what Mum's invented."

"She's waiting for you to cut it."

He picked up the breadknife and tapped the crust. It gave a metallic ring. He put it onto the breadboard and began to cut.

The teeth of the knife made no impression. He hunched his shoulders and pressed down hard, sawing in short, sharp cuts. The knife broke through and revealed a soft, nutty centre.

"It looks lovely, dear." He picked up the first slice, took a large bite and chewed.

"What's it like, Dad?"

He made it to the sink just in time. The contents of his mouth exploded into the dirty bowls like a splatter of shrapnel. He grabbed for a cup, filled it with cold water and gulped it down. Thea ran from the kitchen and up the stairs as fast as her wobbly legs could carry her.

When he came back from taking the children to school she was sitting at the table writing a letter. She had pushed the remains of breakfast to one end but there was no sign of the bread. She was scribbling furiously. In front of her was the *Guardian* recipe. He stood behind her and read what she had written.

"I don't think it will stand up in court, darling."

"Then they'll have to settle out of court. Damages. Mental distress."

"I'm not sure you'd find a lawyer to take it on."

"Then I'll go myself. I'll sue. I'll sue. I want a written apology printed on the front page. I'm going to the Press Council and the Ombudsman. They're not getting away with this."

"How about the European Court? The Court of Human Rights."

"Whatever it takes."

"It was only a misprint."

"Then they should be more careful. They have a social responsibility."

"What did they say when you phoned them?"

"God, they were rude. They said that no-one else had complained. They said I should have realised it was a mistake. I said that was a disgusting attitude to take. I thought they were supposed to be left wing and caring. They showed a callous disregard for human weakness. I was going to get my recipes out of the *Telegraph* in future."

"Wasn't that a bit strong?"

"I know. I lost my temper. I got silly."

He picked up the recipe. Two pounds of flour. One pound of salt.

"What should it have been?"

"A teaspoon of salt. How was I to know? I've never done it before."

She scooped up the paper and pencil and threw them across the room. He put his hands on her shoulders and started to massage but she shrugged him off and went over to the sofa. With a deep sigh she turned her face to the cushions and fell immediately into a deep sleep. Pax went upstairs and brought down a blanket to cover her with.

"There has to be another way," he said to her as she slept.

❊ Chapter Six ❊

It was a shock to see a stranger on the *Swan*.

Pax was on the quayside gazing down at her while in his mind's eye he tacked into Casablanca harbour against a gentle south-westerly breeze.

At least he *thought* it was a south-westerly. He couldn't remember if winds were described by the direction they came from or, like public transport, the direction they were going. The Edinburgh train went to Edinburgh and the Barnet bus went in the direction of Barnet, even if it actually went no further than Finchley bus station.

The direction was important because if the wind was coming from the south-west he wouldn't need to tack into Casablanca harbour, he would be blown in a straight line, as far as he could tell from Thomas's school atlas.

Then the problem was how you stopped when you got to the jetty. If the wind was against you, he supposed you just pulled the sails down at the right moment and let the momentum carry you on to the mooring. But if the wind was behind you, all he could think was that you threw an anchor over the back and hoped for the best. They should have big fenders like dodgem cars or new Volvos in case you came into the parking space a bit quickly.

There was a lot to learn.

Be that as it may, he was sailing in a gentle breeze towards Casablanca harbour, sipping a Bacardi, sheeting in this and belaying that, the children fishing happily over the side, Thea down in the galley filleting freshly-caught fish, Annabel sun-bathing on the foredeck, when a man in a red sweater climbed out of the cabin into the cockpit, stood up from his crouching position and cracked his head on the boom.

66

"Landlubber," muttered Pax.

The intruder sat down on the bench by the tiller, rubbing his head. "Serves you right," thought Pax. Until now he had suppressed the thought that the *Swan* belonged to someone else.

"Shit," he said, to express his sudden disillusionment.

Without thinking what he was going to do when he got there, he walked to the end of the quay, stepped over the chain with its dangling sign, "Private Boat Owners Only", walked down the ramp to the floating pontoon and strolled along to the *Swan*. The wooden path under his feet rocked and he could see dark water through the slats. "Stand By To Repel Boarders" kept running through his head.

"Nice boat," he said, in the same way he would have said "nice day" and hoping it was what you said to private boat owners.

The man in the red sweater looked up at him, glumly. He was a tall, thin man with a long, thin face. He reminded Pax of a stick insect, quite the wrong morphology for a sailor who has to look lively in and out of the cabin and up the rigging and in and out of hammocks.

"A wonderful little boat," he said with forced enthusiasm, as if he were talking about some other craft and not the one that had just inflicted severe damage on his skull. "She needs a coat of varnish but otherwise she's as right as rain."

The varnish was peeling here and there. Where it was not peeling it had stripped off altogether, leaving grey, weathered patches. Nothing that an hour or two with sandpaper wouldn't put right.

"I bought her a year ago. An old couple were living on her up in Richmond. They'd been moored under a willow tree for twenty years."

Pax had to readjust his mental image of the *Swan* like fiddling with the controls on a television. He had imagined her battling against the choppy waves of the North Sea or coasting through the swells of the Bay of Biscay on her way to the Mediterranean. In fact she had been a floating granny-flat riding out nothing more than the wash of passing pleasure boats.

"What happened to them?"

"They swallowed the anchor."

What did that mean? Did they die in their hammocks or fall overboard?

"Come on board," said the stick insect man in a way that suggested "if you must" at the end of his invitation. "Take a look forrard."

As he put his foot on the peeling varnish of the bench in the cockpit, Pax knew he was making a fateful, historical step. He felt he was casting off into the unknown, a new world that he had only inhabited before in his imagination. He wished he were not wearing his Houndsditch Warehouse brogues. He should be wearing seaboots.

There was a narrow strip of grey teak deck between the cabin and the side. There was no outside rail, only a wooden rail along the cabin roof which he clung to as though they were battling against a brisk headwind. Never mind. It would be more embarrassing for the entire tourist population of Saint Katherine's to shout "Man Overboard."

He stood on the foredeck and looked up to the top of the mast, tapering into infinity like Jacob's ladder. Thin ropes ran up the side of the mast and were fastened round wooden hooks at the bottom with intricate knots. The stick insect man was looking at him so he gently pulled one of the ropes and nodded, knowingly.

The deck seemed much smaller when you were standing on it than when you looked down on it from the quayside. It was covered in fine green mould. At the front was a chunk of galvanised metal with hinged flat bits, attached to a chain and tied down on the deck with string.

"What's that?" he asked, poking it with his toe.

"The anchor."

He felt foolish. He had lost all the points he had earned from his nods and knowing looks and rope-tugging. He thought all anchors looked like the decoration on blazer buttons.

A round spar ran from the base of the mast to the point at the front of the boat where it passed through a round metal hoop. It looked as though you pushed it out when you were sailing.

The name bowsprit came back from books about sailing ships.

He walked back to the cockpit, holding on to the cabin rail. The cockpit was low and broad, with seating enough for at least six. The floor was teak, stained with oil and mould. Around the louvred doors were carvings of grapes and birds. Pax wanted to say how pretty they were but doubted if it was a nautical thing to say.

"Look at the carvings. Aren't they pretty?" said the thin man.

He opened the cabin doors and pushed back a sliding hatch in the cabin roof immediately above the door so that you could go down the steps into the cabin without bending double. On the right was an alcove with a filthy-looking stove. On the left was a small sink and draining board. Above the sink was a spice rack with a pokerwork inscription proclaiming it was a gift from Margate.

Inside the cabin some meagre light came in from the grimy portholes and a skylight. It was not high enough to stand up straight in. The floorspace was taken up with a table covered with a red gingham plastic table cloth. On either side of the table were benches covered in green dralon. The walls of the cabin were varnished wood, hung with pictures and ornaments and souvenirs from holidays. Most of the places depicted were landlocked – Switzerland, the Grand Canyon, Stratford-upon-Avon. If you live on a boat you take your holidays inland. On the white-painted ceiling were fixed three flying ducks made of pink china. Above the portholes ran a pink plastic-coated wire for little chintzy curtains. It smelt of tobacco and damp and embrocation. It didn't feel like a boat. It felt like Mavis in miniature.

In his imagination the interior of the *Swan* had been a murky, ill-defined region. Apart from hammocks strung up from the ceiling he had found it hard to visualise what it would look like. He had driven out of his mind the interior of a Bluebird caravan but there was nothing to replace it. He had certainly not visualised the interior of a bedsitter in an old people's home.

A very low doorway went through into a second cabin under

the foredeck. Immediately on the right was a folding door into a small cupboard housing a lavatory bowl. It had not been used for some time. It seemed doubtful if an adult of normal proportions would be able to sit on it without serious injury. It was flushed with a hand pump whose pointed handle lay in wait for misdirected bums.

The rest of the cabin was filled with coils of rope and jumbled sails. The owner was obviously not very tidy. Pax would have folded up the sails like sheets in an airing cupboard.

There were no hooks for hammocks. The couches on either side of the table in the lounge – sorry, the cabin – must be beds. He shuffled past them to get out into the cockpit.

"She's registered as a British ship. I can show you the registration certificate. This is a little piece of Britain, you know. You can sail into any foreign port and show them the book and the British consul has to come and help you if you need it. Registered Port of London." He made it sound like bad news.

Pax doubted if the services of the British consul were required in Richmond under a willow tree. He was no more confident about the help offered by the consular service to the owners abroad of British-registered granny-flats. It didn't do much good if your Cortina broke down on the continent and you waved your log book around. You were better off with your AA membership card.

"She's a great little boat. She's a purpose-built yacht but modelled on a Dutch fishing boat. Very handy in shallow water. She draws about two and a half feet so you can take her to places you couldn't take an ordinary yacht. You could go to Geneva in her, you know."

Geneva? Pax tried to conjure up a map of Europe. The last time he had looked, Geneva was in the middle of landlocked Switzerland. Was the Swan amphibious?

"Through the canals. She's flat-bottomed and you can lower the mast. You could take her through France right up to Lake Geneva."

New information was coming thick and fast. A British-registered fishing boat for the canals of France. Tacking into

Monte Carlo from the direction of Paris. A sheltered little inlet on the Grand Union Canal. It wasn't America's Cup territory but Thea might take to it more willingly at the beginning. He could tell her that the flat bottom made the boat more stable because it sat flat on the water. It might even be true.

"What are those wooden things sticking up on the side?" he asked, pointing to the flat boards he had assumed were stabilisers.

"Lee boards. If the wind's coming from your port you put the starboard one down. If it's coming from the starboard you put the port one down. If you don't know what you're doing you put both of them down. It's because you haven't got a keel to stop you being blown sideways."

"What about the engine?"

The stick insect turned a small key sticking out of the side of the boat where he was sitting. There was a whine and a rumble and a cloud of blue smoke from behind the rudder. The cockpit vibrated with the chuntering of a diesel engine. Next to the key was a red handle. He eased it back and the engine slowed down.

"Perkins four thousand. Right as rain. You won't waterski but she'll do six knots, believe me."

"Where is it?" asked Pax, looking round for a radiator grille or some other clue.

"You're sitting on it."

Pax stood up and cracked his head on the boom. The other man looked at him but said nothing. He opened the top of the bench and pointed, unnecessarily, as even Pax could recognise an engine when it was running. He nodded knowingly at a revolving rubber belt. It was the only part he could see. It seemed to be going round all right.

The engine was switched off. Pax remained standing. He wanted to go somewhere private to rub his head without being seen. He had probably outstayed his welcome. The tour of the boat had been entirely unexpected, a seafarer's custom he had never heard of. Obviously if someone came up and said, "Nice boat," you were expected to whip them off on an inspection of the premises, like when the relatives come round to your new

71

house for the first time and look expectant when they've had a cup of tea and you wish you'd made the beds.

"Well, what do you think of her?" asked the stick insect, gloomily, as if he were waiting for bad news.

"Wonderful boat. Right as rain. I've been looking at her for weeks. She's a bit different inside from what I had imagined."

"Where did you see the advertisement?"

"What advertisement?"

"The one in *Exchange and Mart* or *Yachting World?* This is the twentieth week."

Pax rubbed his head very hard. The bruise was beginning to swell. The boat seemed to be rocking more than before. He knew what was coming and felt a nervous twitching in the abdomen.

"I didn't see an advertisement. It was just a social call."

"Well she's for sale. And if I don't get my price by the end of the week I'll have her out of the water and lay her up at home."

The mast head made tiny circlets in the blue sky. The *Swan* moved up and down restlessly in the ripples. The ropes up and down the mast made a gentle slapping sound. Through a gap in the warehouses he could see Tower Bridge being raised, as it was raised so often in the old days to let the tall masts through. A breeze touched his cheek and riffled his hair.

Tourists stood on the quay, licking ice-creams and pointing at the boats. Among them were men in dark suits and ties, ten minutes' walk away from their offices. They were looking at him standing in the cockpit of the prettiest boat in Saint Katherine's. They were wondering who it was down there, about to hoist the spinnaker and cast off the sheet anchor and tack out of the dock to the river and the open sea.

He heard himself say the fateful words. They seemed to come from a great distance. It was as if the Pax he knew wanted to disassociate himself from them, chew them back, these first words of adventurers and lovers. "Can I have your telephone number?" he said.

"We have to put an offer in tomorrow for Romona Terrace."

Thea scraped baked beans off the plate she was holding.

Some went onto the kitchen floor, some went on top of the lid of the pedal bin, some went into the black plastic bag.

Pax concentrated on arranging the cups and glasses in the top of the dishwasher. Loading it was his primary domestic skill. He told himself to stay calm.

"What the hell for?" he snapped.

"Because otherwise the executors of that old couple are going to put it up for auction. If we make an offer now, we'll probably get it cheap."

"Not cheap enough so we can afford it."

"I thought you could get a bigger mortgage."

"Not big enough. We would have to put our entire savings into it. We'd have nothing at all put by. That would eliminate the possibility of paying the children's school fees if we wanted to." It was one of his best arguments. He hoped he hadn't used it too soon. He rolled back the top tray and began to work on the plates underneath.

"I'm going to work to pay for those. That's my contribution," she said blithely, wiping the dining room table. Scraps of fish finger and mashed potato scattered on the carpet.

"Listen, Thea, I wonder if we're doing the right thing. I know you want to get out of this house because it's too small and like a goldfish bowl. And you want a real sort of house with separate rooms and a proper kitchen. And the downstairs where the downstairs ought to be and not on the first floor. And the upstairs where the upstairs ought to be and not scattered around."

"That's not why I want to move. I couldn't care less about the house. I just think we need a new start. I need a new start. That's why I'm going out to work."

She took a carpet sweeper from behind the louvred door and began gleaning scraps of baked bean and fish finger from the carpet. She succeeded only in laying a neat trail of last night's supper crumbs.

"That's just my point. We ought to be looking for a new dimension to our lives. If we buy Romona Terrace we limit our options for the next twenty years. For God's sake, don't let's burn our boats."

73

That was clever, to bring the subject round to boats. He straightened up from the dishwasher and set the dial. It was time to deliver the impassioned speech he had been rehearsing in his mind for a week. Thea rinsed the milk bottles while he fiddled with the red pointer on the wire bottle-holder.

"How many pints for the morning?" he asked.

"Three."

"We're in our thirties now. If we buy Romona Terrace we'll spend the best years of our lives making it into an Ideal Home. By the time we've finished the kids will leave home and we'll sell it. And what have we done with our lives? Is that what it's all about?"

"I think there's another empty bottle on the step."

"Do you really want to grind away the next twenty years in an office? Voluntarily? I'd give my right arm to get out of mine. Look at us. Young. Healthy. Attractive. At least to each other. We have more to get out of life than a pine kitchen and a through lounge."

"Wait. I want to put a note out for eggs."

"The world is so wonderful and exciting. There's so much to see. So much to do. Look at all the countries we've never been to. Look at all the people we've never met. We should be doing something interesting and useful. Not this drudgery."

"Can you see if we've got enough cornflakes?"

"We say we're doing it all for the children. That's just an excuse. They won't thank us for it. How many times have we despised our own parents for their humdrum, selfish lives. Limited horizons. Frittering their lives away on keeping up with the neighbours. Scraping to buy a new lounge suite. Thea, let's not do it to ourselves. We deserve something better than a prison in Romona Terrace."

He was standing with his arms open wide, spanning the narrow kitchen, one hand holding the basket of milk bottles. He felt sheepish. Thea tied a knot in the top of the bin-liner.

"So what do you suggest?" she asked.

"I think the first step is to stay here and have something else that would broaden our lives a bit."

"A country cottage?"

74

"Sort of. Perhaps a bit more mobile than a country cottage. The trouble with country cottages is that they stay in one place all the time. The same old scenery every time you look out of the window."

"Now you point it out, I suppose it is one of the features of a country cottage. It does tend to stay in one place. Some people would even say it was an advantage. At least you know where to look for it on a Friday night."

"I'm being serious."

"Oh God, I think you are. I know what you're getting round to. I don't believe it. You give me the big speech about liberty and unselfishness and a new dimension. And what does it lead up to? You want to buy a caravan. You want to spend our life savings on a caravan to park in the drive so we can spend our bank holidays frying baked beans and fish fingers in the middle of the motorway. If that's your Brave New World I'll stick to Romona Terrace, thank you very much."

"You're wrong. You're quite wrong. I wasn't thinking about a caravan at all. I've seen this fantastic boat. Honestly, Thea, you'd fall in love with it. It's wooden and pretty and we could all sleep on it. It would take us all away."

"A floating caravan. You want us to buy a floating caravan. We've had this conversation about boats before. The last thing I want in my life is a dirty, leaky, floating death-trap. Think again, Pax Brown."

"I see."

"Don't forget the note about the eggs," she called as he went down the stairs.

75

❧ Chapter Seven ❧

The telephone woke them at three o'clock in the morning. Pax pretended to be asleep. He did not want to answer it. Telephones in the middle of the night meant someone had died. He wanted Thea to be the first to hear the news and break it to him gently. She nudged him.

"Answer it before it wakes the children," she whispered.

"It's on your side of the bed. You answer it. It's probably a wrong number."

Thea picked the receiver off the hook, pulled it across her so the cradle fell on the floor with a crash, and held it to his ear. It was Annabel. She was sobbing and incoherent. He repeated phrases back to her to make sure he understood them. He promised to drive down to Orpington straight away.

Thea had buried her face in the pillow with her hands over her ears. Pax got out of bed and walked round to the other side to put the cradle back on the bedside table and replace the receiver. Out of habit he let the receiver dangle to untwist the flex. He sat on the bed and touched her shoulder.

"He's dead, isn't he?" she said.

He offered to telephone her parents in Spain but Thea said she would do it herself in the morning. There was no point in breaking bad news in the middle of the night. The shock would be bad enough in the light of day.

"Annabel has to go down to Southend to identify the body. I think that's what she said. I told her I would go with her. But I don't want to leave you alone."

"No. You have to go with Annabel. For Nick's sake."

Nick was clearly past caring but this was not the right time to be realistic. Annabel could not be expected to go on her

76

own. It was an excuse for a morning off work that he'd never used before.

"I don't know how long it takes to drive there and back. If I'm not back before breakfast can you phone the office for me?"

"What was he doing in Southend?"

"Annabel had no idea. He told her yesterday that he was going out on the river in a friend's speedboat and that he'd be back by evening. He didn't come back and he didn't phone so she's spent the whole night worrying. Then she had a message from the River Police in Southend. They said they'd picked him up in the Thames. She could come and identify him there and then or wait until he was brought back to London."

"Nick drowned. I don't believe it."

Pax went into the bathroom. Drowning was indeed a surprise. While he was peering he reflected that there were many other more likely ways for Nick to have met his end. Car accident, heart attack, shooting, stabbing, poisoning, hanging, *crime passionel*, all these and more were on the cards but not plain and simple drowning. Perhaps he didn't drown by himself. Perhaps he was helped. He thought of the hairless Carlo and shuddered, not only because he had come to the end of his pee.

He ran the razor over his chin without bothering with lather and rinsed his face with cold water. His face looked puffy with sleep. How does a drowned person's face look? He let his jaw sag and his eyes stare vacantly.

He went back into the bedroom wondering what to wear to claim the corpse of a brother-in-law. Sombre but not formal. He found a pair of dark-grey trousers among the jeans and a white office shirt. It would be cold in the early morning so he wore his thick guernsey. He was shivering already. He kissed Thea on the forehead. She was lying on her back, staring at the ceiling, expressionless. Perhaps she too was trying to imagine what it was like to be drowned. She was dry-eyed. The shock would come later.

"Where are the car keys?"

"In my handbag."

He didn't bother to ask where her handbag was. He started the search at the top of the house. The house was an alien thing at half past three in the morning. The lights were too bright, the proportions had changed, it was too quiet inside and outside. He went into each room with a quiver of apprehension, half expecting to see Nick sitting in a chair with dripping clothes, his face already nibbled by fish, seaweed clinging in neat rows to his transplanted hair. By the time he had found the handbag and taken the keys out he had to tell himself firmly to get a grip on himself. The rest of the night was going to be difficult enough without peopling it with phantom relatives.

He went back upstairs to say goodbye. She clutched his arm and made him promise to drive carefully and not go near the water. He made her promise to fetch Thomas into her bed to keep her company. He told her how he understood how awful it was for her. Finally he asked if she had any indigestion tablets. Getting up in the middle of the night always made him feel sick.

He let himself noiselessly out of the front door by putting the key in the lock and turning it instead of slamming the door shut. He didn't want to wake the children or the neighbours. He then kicked over the milk bottle basket, sending one bottle clanking over the step and down the path. The dog next door started to bark. The car needed three flogging bursts of the starter before it would start. Then it stalled because he didn't want to wake the Square by revving the engine.

To hell with them. It's not every day someone drowns.

He drove fast to Nick's flat in Orpington. He drummed impatiently on the steering wheel every time he had to stop at a red light at a deserted crossroad. He had never driven round London at this time in the morning and he was surprised how much traffic there was. How many of them were on their way to dead bodies, he wondered. He hurried not because of Nick, who now had all the time in the world, but because of Annabel. She sounded very upset. The longer she was alone the more distraught she would be.

He remembered the first time she had come to the house. Nick had brought lilies and their first words had been about cemeteries and funerals and death. She had said that she didn't like death. He would have to be very understanding and considerate.

She would open the door and fall into his arms. Her soft, blonde hair would smother his face. He would feel her wet cheek against his and her long lashes would tickle him. He would kiss her under her perfect ear to show that he understood her grief and knew how to console her. Her long, firm fingers would press into the back of his neck. He would hold her tight. He would feel her lithe body sobbing against his, yearning for his warmth and strength. He would feel her firm breasts pressed against his chest, her flat stomach against his abdomen, which he would suck in like he did when he walked around in swimming trunks. Her legs would gently buckle and he would support her, her thighs pressed against his. She would abandon herself to her grief in his arms and he would feel strong and protective and manly. And virile.

She must have been watching out for him. She opened the door before he rang the bell. She looked surprisingly composed. If she had been weeping, the evidence had been cleverly disguised. She was wearing a soft, dark-grey cashmere sweater and a black woollen skirt. He opened his arms for her to fall into but she just handed him her leopard-skin coat to hold while she made sure she had her keys in her handbag.

"It's sweet of you to do this," she said, as if he was giving her a lift to the supermarket.

He could not think of anything to say as they drove through suburban South London. It began to drizzle and he concentrated on driving. He would have liked to be consoling but she gave no outward signs of distress. "Brave girl," he thought, although she looked more irritated than sorrowing. She spoke first as they reached the motorway.

"I've never seen a dead body."

"Neither have I. I'm sure they look like ordinary bodies. Just a bit paler."

He was not so sure on this point. He tried to assemble in his mind all the facts he knew about dead bodies. Rigor mortis made them stiff, but that shouldn't affect their appearance.

Did they turn green, or was that only in horror films? The word waxy came to mind. Undertakers put make-up on the faces and someone had to close their eyes and bind up their jaws.

"Won't he look different?" she asked.

"I'm sure he'll be the same old Nick. Just a bit less lively."

"He won't look all swollen and waterlogged will he? I told him his face was getting puffy."

"I'm sure he won't. Look, you needn't see him you know. I will."

"I read somewhere that drowned women float on their backs and men on their stomachs."

He didn't know what to say. He began to feel angry that the whole business had been kept from him all these years. People were dying every minute. Dropping in droves all over the country. Yet here was a grown man in his thirties who had never seen a dead person. In the old days you went round for a look at the body when someone died but not any more. Death was embarrassing now. The undertakers whipped the body away and disposed of it as if nothing had happened.

"What do I have to do, Pax? I've never had to cope with anything like this before. Will I have to take his clothes back? I suppose I'll have to comb his hair. He was so sensitive about his hair. It really is too much."

He reached out and took her hand. He felt her long, pointed nails and soft palm. Thea's were scaly and the nails broken with housework. He squeezed her fingers and rested the back of his hand on her thigh. To console her. "Poor old Nick. He was quite a character. I remember the first time I met him when Thea took me home to meet the family. He was bald and fat in those days and wore glasses."

She took her hand away and rummaged in her handbag. Pax thought she was looking for a handkerchief but she brought out a packet of cigarettes.

"He wasn't bald and fat. How could you say that?"

"Sorry. It was just a passing phase. Puppy fat. And he only had temporary baldness. It all grew back again."

"He didn't wear glasses either. He wore contact lenses be-cause free-fall parachuting had distorted his eyeballs. I made him give up sky-diving when we started to live together."

Pax had to disguise a snigger as a sniff. Thea had told him all about her brother's fear of heights. And about his tonsils and his adenoids and his squint and the tubes in his ears and his ingrown toenails and fallen arches and undescended testicles that made Nick the fat little boy in the corner of the playground with one lens of his spectacles taped over with sticking plaster, watching the others play football.

"Did he tell you about the SAS?" he asked.

"As much as he was allowed. He was wounded in Muscat. They aren't allowed to have medals, you know."

He squeezed her thigh. There was no reaction. She sucked deeply on her cigarette and stared through the squishing wipers. He felt pins and needles coming on but kept his hand where it was.

Good old Nick. Sky-diver, SAS, what else had he told her?

"He looked up to you and Thea, you know. He called you the salt of the earth. He envied your stability. He was too restless to make that kind of life himself. He never grew up."

Nil something or other. Do not speak ill of the dead. Let her keep his image intact. She needed an impetuous, overgrown schoolboy to mother. Within a year or two he would be a hero. There aren't many heroes and lovers around, so dead Nick will have to stand in. Poor conniving, boastful, shallow, unprincipled, insecure and dead Nick. Dead on the slab, seaweed in his hair, water dribbling from his nose, mud in his ears.

Pax shuddered and took his hand away from her thigh. His arm was now completely numb. His fingers felt as though they had been inflated with an air pump. He shook his arm, waiting for the pins and needles to strike.

A dead arm. Like Nick's. Was he in some kind of limbo now, waiting for the pins and needles to come back to his stiff and swollen limbs? When the last trump came there would be millions and millions of people jumping up and down trying to get rid of pins and needles in their resurrected bodies. Nick would be there, his irises a natural blue, his eyeballs perfectly spherical, everything else perfect to match. The boat and the

81

water and the suffocation and the struggling and the terrible pain would fade like a dream.

At least he knew what death was like. He had met at last what had been lying in wait for him since his first cry in the midwife's hands. There were no secrets any more for Nick. He knew all there was to know. He had answered the only two questions in life that really matter:

What will it be like to have sex? What will it be like to die?

The first question had dominated Pax's waking hours until he was twenty years old. It overshadowed all the other problems of the first part of his life. Does God exist? Why is there evil in the world? What is the purpose of life? These were trivial questions compared with the first one.

Having sex didn't mean that he stopped thinking about it. It still dominated his thoughts. He wondered if he was getting enough, whether it was the right quality, why other people seemed to be getting more of it. But the mystery was no longer there.

The second question remained. What was it like to die? There was always the possibility that you never found out. By definition you can't experience being extinct. If Nick was truly and totally dead, he couldn't know what it was like.

"Oh, Pax, I just remembered. I just sent off a cheque to the Squash Club for his annual subscription. Do you think I can stop it in time?"

He took his eyes off the road to look at her. He could see her face in the undipped beams of the oncoming vehicles. Her eyes glistened as if they were wet with tears. They were even more lovely than usual. He wanted to kiss them, press his mouth against the closed lids, feel her long lashes against his lips, to tell her that everything was all right.

Would she do that for Nick as well? Would she kiss his cold, dead eyes? Presumably someone had already closed them like they do on films, both at the same time with thumb and forefinger. It looked pretty easy to do. The eyelids seemed to roll down without any problem. On the films you never saw them struggling with the eyeballs, cursing them for not shutting properly, leaving the body with one eye closed and the other jammed open for eternity in a deathly wink. In real life perhaps they sprang back up again like a roller blind that won't stay down.

"Don't worry about the Squash Club, Annabel. I'll look after it when we get back."

Actors on films don't have that trouble. The script says they just put their hands on the top of the eyes and they close. Scripts also say that all they have to do to blow out an oil lamp is give a little puff over the top of the chimney and the whole room is plunged in darkness. In real life you know the bloody flame won't go out. You singe your hair leaning over the chimney. You blow lampblack in your eyes. You burn your fingers on the glass lifting it up so you can spit on the wick. It's the same with dead eyes. In real life they don't stay shut. Ah! That's why you weigh them down with pennies.

"Do you have any change in your handbag?" he asked.

"I don't know. Why?"

"No reason. Just in case."

Excuse me. Anyone got change for 50p? I've got this body . . .

Who would close his own eyes for him? Would Thea do it or a pretty nurse or one of his own children? Perhaps it wouldn't be necessary. Perhaps he would be burnt to a crisp in a fire or a nuclear explosion or scattered over a two-mile radius around Heathrow.

"Should I have brought pyjamas for him? He can't stay in his wet clothes, can he?" she asked.

"I'm sure they'll be dry by now."

She had a point. What do you get buried in? Russian politicians and murdered gangsters wore dark suits and white shirts. Did everyone have to wear a lounge suit and tie to their own funeral? He would be just as happy in his denim shirt and favourite jeans. It was more difficult for women. Should they wear evening dress or a well-tailored suit or a nice summer dress? Pyjamas and nightdresses seemed more appropriate for eternal rest.

One of the few facts he knew about death was that the Department of Health and Social Security gave you a grant for a shroud. He had no idea what you did with it. Did you wear it over your clothes or next to your skin instead of clothes? It was probably made of polyester fabric. He couldn't bear nylon next to his skin. It made him sweat and gave him a rash.

It was very difficult to appreciate that if they put a nylon shroud on him he wouldn't notice. He wouldn't even know. They would do all sorts of things to his body and he wouldn't be there to mind.

But where would he be? Everyone's got to be somewhere. He began to feel panic. He moved his hands up the steering wheel into the quarter to three position they taught you at driving school. He wanted to see his hands as he drove, reassure himself that they still belonged to him.

"Do you think they'll want his kidneys?" asked Annabel.

"I think they like them while they're still warm. The same with the heart and the liver. We can ask, if you like. Do you think he'd mind?"

"I don't think so. He'd probably like to think that a little bit of him lives on somewhere in someone else. He always liked to feel he was indispensable to other people."

Certainly when he was alive Nick was preoccupied with putting parts of his body into other people's.

"I think they can take the eyeballs when they're cold. You needn't mention about them being distorted by parachuting."

They passed the sign for the Southend turnoff and he moved over into the left lane, slowing down and indicating although there was no-one behind them. He didn't want to go to Southend. He wanted to drive on through the night with this beautiful woman until the whole nasty business was over. He could feel her becoming tense. She too was probably thinking about how she would react. He tried to think of something to say that would distract her from her own feelings.

"There may have to be an autopsy," he said.

Pax imagined his own body on the slab. Naked with a modest cloth across his privates, like Jesus taken down from the cross. Eyes weighed down with 2p pieces. He is looking down from the ceiling at himself.

Thea has gone home to look after the children and find the

life insurance policies that live in the sideboard drawer under the cutlery tray with the birth certificates and the guarantee for the dishwasher. She has left him alone with the pathologist. He has a white coat and a white operating cap and a white mask so you can only see his eyes. His own body is white and cold and stiff. It doesn't twitch when the pathologist takes off the loin-cloth. It doesn't flinch when he places the tip of a scalpel just underneath the breastbone.

Pax on the ceiling looks down and wishes he has hands to hide his eyes in.

The scalpel slices down in one deep cut through the layers of skin and fat from the breastbone to the pubic bone. There is no blood because the heart that pumps it has stopped. There is a glimpse of dark liver and greenish guts. The pathologist then makes another cut from armpit to armpit to make a gaping Y. He puts down the scalpel and rolls back the flap of flesh over the chest up under the neck. He takes a quick look at the larynx which is sticking to the underside of the flap. Then he rolls back the long flaps on either side of the first cut he made. There are the lungs and the heart and the intestines.

Pax on the ceiling remembers the times he had cut up chickens and turkeys and is sorry.

The pathologist picks up an instrument that looks like a wire-cutter and snips the ribs from the bottom up, starting at the sides and passing up where the nipples used to be and ending at the collarbone. With two hands he tears away the breastbone and the ribs with a ripping, sucking sound.

Pax is glad he has no stomach to feel sick in.

Laid bare are all the bits he used to worry about. All the parts he used to look up in the medical dictionary. He recognises them from their shape and location in the line drawings in the pocket *Gray's Anatomy* and the *Dictionary of Symptoms* but their colour and consistency are a shock. They look like the entrails of any other animal hanging up in the butcher's. The pathologist pokes around in them. He then snips them out, one by one. Liver, pancreas, gall bladder, spleen.

The Pax on the ceiling begins to get interested. What exactly did he die of?

He groped in his pocket for the indigestion tablets. He felt sick and his palms were sweating. He breathed deeply, gasping for air. He could smell formaldehyde in the air but he knew it was his imagination. He slapped his cheek to remind himself that he was not in the ceiling but still more or less implanted in his own body. He was about to see someone else's corpse on the slab.

"What's the matter?" asked Annabel.

"Nothing. I just thought I felt a mosquito," he replied, rubbing his cheek.

Pax drummed his fingers on the scarred wooden counter, waiting for the duty officer to appear. Annabel sat with her leopard-skin coat around her shoulders studying the framed chart of the Thames Estuary on the wall. She smoked impatiently. If he had not known what a turmoil of emotion she must have been suffering, he would have said she looked bored.

After he had read the rabies posters and a few notices to mariners about wrecks and buoys he pinged the bell again. At last they heard footsteps and Pax mouthed to Annabel to be brave. She nodded and yawned.

The duty officer was a beefy middle-aged man with grey hair. Pax looked at his ham-like hands and wondered how many corpses he had fished out of the river on the end of a standard-issue boathook. Dealing with waterlogged bodies had clearly convinced him of the emptiness of the tittle-tattle of normal social intercourse. When Pax explained they were relatives of Nicholas Smith he simply grunted, lifted a bunch of keys from a board behind the counter and pointed at a frosted glass door behind them.

Pax helped Annabel to her feet and held her arm. She leaned on him as they walked down a green-painted corridor behind the shambling policeman. He jangled the keys in front of a metal door that opened onto concrete steps leading down into a basement. The walls and the ceiling and the steps were painted the same shade of hospital green. Their footsteps echoed, like going down into a cold church crypt.

86

When they reached the bottom of the stairs Annabel let go his arm. She threw her shoulders back and pursed her lips. Pax admired her courage. They all looked waxy in the light of the fluorescent tubes but not half as waxy, he reminded himself, as the other inmates of this terrible cellar.

The policeman fumbled with his keys again in front of another metal door with a number five stencilled in black. Were they worried about body-snatchers? Murderers tampering with the evidence? The policeman pushed open the door and held it open. Pax stepped forward to go in first. His knees were shaking and his chest was suddenly tight. Annabel held him back.

"Let me see him first," she said, taking a deep breath. He squeezed her hand as she pushed past him.

Her scream echoed in the corridor. Pax had never before heard the primal scream of terror and despair before the absolute nothingness of death. It chilled him to the marrow. He felt dizzy. He wanted to run away from the hideous sight that awaited him.

The policeman rushed into the room to help, letting go of the door which slammed shut behind him. Pax struggled with the keys that were still in the lock and pushed it open.

Annabel was lying on the floor, unconscious. On one side of her knelt the grey-haired policeman. On the other side knelt Nick, patting her face. Pax felt distant and faint. He wasn't in a morgue at all. He was in a cell.

The Bible doesn't say if people were pleased when Lazarus came back from the dead. When the excitement of seeing him walk out of the tomb had subsided it must have been a bit of an anticlimax after all the worry and grief they had been through. And what about Lazarus? He had to go through the whole dying thing a second time, perhaps next week or next year. He couldn't have been very enthusiastic about the prospect. One death-agony per life is enough. Nor does the Bible say if Lazarus told everyone what it was like on the other side. If he had, he would have saved the rest of us a lot of worry.

Pax hoped that Lazarus got a better reception from his loved ones than Nick. When Annabel came round she sat on the hard wooden bed next to Pax, holding a mug of strong, sweet police tea. She looked dazed and fragile. Nick kept repeating it was really him and not a ghost but this didn't seem to make her much happier.

Later on Pax would tell Thea about his relief and joy that her brother wasn't dead after all. At the time he felt only resentment and disappointment. He had screwed himself up to confront a dead body and feel all the emotions of bereavement and now all the adrenaline had nowhere to go but in the direction of his complacent, conniving and now criminal brother-in-law. Nor would he tell Thea about his frustration that he couldn't put his arm around Annabel and squeeze her thigh to help her get over her shock.

"Why aren't you dead?" she asked.

Nick fidgeted and hesitated and nodded conspiratorially in the direction of the beefy policeman who stood in the corridor by the open door. "They've got some silly idea I've been smuggling. Complete nonsense. You know me, Pax. You think it's nonsense, don't you?"

He was wearing tight jeans, an open-necked yellow silk shirt and the kind of shiny anorak with stripes down the sleeves that people wear to make believe they're rally drivers or ski champions. A gold medallion dangled on his hairy chest. Nick had an unerring sense of costume. When he got dressed that morning he might well have had felony in mind. From what he knew of his career and saw of his present circumstances Pax thought it perfectly on the cards that he had been smuggling.

"I was thinking of buying a boat for you, love, and I wanted it to be a surprise. Carlo lent me one to try out."

The hairless Carlo. The power boat at Saint Katherine's. The business with the antique gold coins. Partnership.

Annabel looked over to the policeman in the corridor. He was manicuring his fingernails with a cell key. "What kind of boat? This is the first I've heard of it. What gave you that idea? I hate boats. And where's the money coming from? You haven't got enough money to buy a boat and I'm not buying one for myself. I'd rather have a set of saucepans than a boat."

88

Nick tried to calm her with *molto piano* gestures.

"So I went out on Carlo's boat for a trip round the bay. Then I see a fishing boat that looks as if it's in distress. Just bobbing up and down in the swell and nobody fishing and people waving at me. Now you know me. I can't turn my back when anyone's in trouble. Besides, it's the law of the sea, isn't it? I go and see if they need help. What else could I do, Pax?"

"Generous to a fault, Nick," he muttered.

"There was nothing wrong. They were just fiddling with the engine. They start it while I'm talking to them and they push off. They were Belgians, I think. Or they could have been French. Anyway, it's getting late and I steam off home at twenty miles an hour. Suddenly I see I'm being chased by this other boat. A race, I say to myself. Fine by me. I'll give you a race. So I open up the throttle and away we go. Real power boat stuff. Just like the old days."

"You never told me you raced power boats," accused Annabel.

"Assault boats in those days, love. No moon. Hostile beach. You know the sort of thing. Anyway, how was I to know this boat's a Customs and Excise boat? All I can see is the bow wave and the spray. They're blathering away on the loud hailer but I can't hear a thing because of the noise of my own boat. All the time I'm concentrating on not hitting a piece of driftwood or a buoy or something."

Nick was crouched in front of them, holding an imaginary steering wheel. The policeman had stopped doing his nails and was looking down at his boots, straining to hear. Annabel had stopped looking cross and was looking interested.

"So there we are. Steaming along nicely. They're beginning to catch up with me. Then I see this little tanker coming the other way. I know I have to keep to the right. Rule of the road. So I swerve in front of his bows and round the back of him. The Excise men do the same only they hit a buoy and decide to pull out of the race. Their boat sank, you see."

"Was anyone hurt?" asked Pax.

"They were lucky. The tanker lowered a boat and by now there was a helicopter overhead."

"So you went back to help, I suppose. Unwritten law of the sea and all that."

"I would have, Pax, I would have. You know me. But I noticed I was running out of fuel. No sense in having them rescue me as well. They were being looked after. What could I do? So I carried on up the river and tried to find somewhere to tie up and get petrol. I went down this little creek. While I was wondering where I could fill up and phone home to tell you I was all right I was surrounded like Bonnie and Clyde with boats and helicopters. It's all a terrible mistake." He laughed nervously and looked over to the door. The policeman was studying the back of his beefy hand.

"What do they say you were smuggling?" asked Annabel. "Not drugs. Please say it wasn't drugs. I couldn't bear it if it was drugs."

"It wasn't drugs. It wasn't anything. I wasn't smuggling. Don't you believe me? Don't my own family, my own loved ones believe I'm innocent? Where can I turn?"

"Hold on. No-one said anything. But if you're not being accused of drug smuggling, what are you being accused of?" asked Pax. He had a horrible suspicion that he already knew the answer.

Nick paced up and down the cell and stopped where he was between the policeman and Pax. He looked hard at him while he spoke and twitched his eyebrows up and down in a frantic signal whose meaning soon became clear.

"They searched the boat and what do you think they found? Gold coins. A little bag of gold coins. I have absolutely no idea how they got there. They were wrapped in an oilskin bag in the bilges. Perhaps Carlo knows something about them. I don't."

Pax took a deep breath. Gold coins. Should he come out with it right now in front of the policeman? He saw Nick's pleading look and lowered his eyes.

"Were they antique gold coins, Nick? Collector's items?"

Nick's eyebrows jiggled furiously. "I don't know what sort of gold coins they were. They wouldn't even let me see them. They asked me if I had a VAT receipt for them. How could I

90

when I didn't know I had them? I told them to look in the bilges."

"But why would anyone want to smuggle gold coins?" asked Annabel.

Nick opened his mouth to say something but remembered his innocence and shrugged. Pax was putting two and two together.

"Because there's Value Added Tax on gold coins in this country. Fifteen per cent. If you can get hold of coins without paying the tax you can pretend you've had them under the bed for twenty years and sell them at a clear profit."

"Fifteen per cent profit isn't worth the risk of smuggling, is it?" asked Annabel. She had a good head for figures even under stress.

"If you smuggle them out of a country like France where they have exchange controls and strict rules about holding gold you can treble that profit. There are plenty of people who would pay for their assets to be smuggled out of Mitterrand's socialist paradise. Does that sound right, Nick?"

Nick shrugged, glumly. "How the hell should I know? I don't know anything about that sort of thing. Ask Carlo."

"Carlo's out of the country by now, if he's got any sense," said Pax.

"Now don't worry, Annabel. It will all be cleared up soon," said Nick. "I come up before the magistrate this morning and he'll give me bail and then we can talk about it. I didn't do anything, I promise. Trust me?"

"Why wouldn't they give him bail?" asked Thea.

They had a bad line. Pax was torn between shouting so she could hear and whispering so that the queue outside the booth would not. On the other side of the entrance hall of the magistrates' court Annabel sat smoking impatiently.

"It's probably a decoy," he whispered loudly. "They know Nick is innocent but they want to give the real smugglers a false sense of security. Or they want to worry the person the coins really belong to in the hope that he will do something to give himself away."

"You think he's innocent, don't you Pax?"

Pax did not have to answer that. The pips went. "I've got no more money," he lied, and hung up.

He was very tired. The events of the past few hours had been a strain. After their allotted fifteen minutes with Nick in his cell they had gone in search of the transport cafe recommended by the ham-handed policeman. Nightworkers and truck drivers devoured Annabel along with their dripping sandwiches and sausages and chips. At least it was warm behind the steamed-up windows. Annabel used her mug of tea as a hand-warmer rather than a beverage.

He had telephoned Thea with the good news/bad news from the cafe. She sobbed with relief for the duration of two 10p pieces before he could tell her that he would stay in Southend with Annabel to see what happened in court and drive her home.

When they had outstayed their welcome at the cafe they drove aimlessly up and down the sea front. It was cold and drizzling and there was nowhere else to go. When the car warmed up they parked in a car park by a silent fairground with the engine running.

"We're like two lovers with nowhere to go," said Pax.

Annabel opened her eyes, yawned, and went back to sleep. Not sure how to proceed he switched on the radio. He took refuge in the inanities of morning radio until he too dozed off.

At nine o'clock Annabel shook him awake. He had a stiff neck. While she put on make-up he hobbled through the drizzle to a phone box on the promenade to call Doreen, his secretary. He told her he had to appear in court as a witness. He asked her to track down all the copies of an internal memo he had written to Gilbert Pinkish, the Branch Manager, recommending an account relationship with a company called Collectors' Coins Ltd.

Annabel called her solicitor, who said there was no point in his postponing the hearing so he could be present. Nick was bound to get bail. He should simply say nothing to the police or the court.

Everyone thought Nick should get bail except the magistrate. In defiance of public opinion he sided with the police. He agreed that this dangerous malefactor who had already wrecked a taxpayers' customs boat, wasted a great deal of public money and was linked with an international gang of criminals, was dedicated to the downfall of society as we know it by evading Value Added Tax. He made it sound as if the Mafia, the IRA, and the KGB all had a share in Nick's bag of gold coins. Nick could not be released on an unsuspecting public without a VAT receipt.

They met again in the cells below the court, zoo cages smelling of urine and disinfectant. He would be moved up to London later in the day. Pax would have to phone the court later to find out which prison he was being remanded to. Nick was slumped on his bench, glassy-eyed with shock. "Bugger," he was muttering to the floor, "bugger." It was the first time Pax had seen him lost for words.

"Oh God," said Annabel, as they walked up the stairs from the cells, "it's like when we used to leave Monty in kennels."

They drove home in silence. Pax was too tired to think or daydream or take stock of his feelings. He concentrated on not falling asleep at the wheel. Annabel dozed, lolling in her seatbelt. He looked at her from time to time. The seatbelt over her chest emphasised her lovely breasts and her jaw sagged so prettily and her little, snuffly snore was like a sleeping puppy's. They could be coming back from a stolen weekend in Paris or Brighton, alibis at the ready, sated with each other.

She invited him in for coffee and something to eat. It was less than eight hours since he had picked her up that morning but they had gone through so much together in that time. They had shared bereavement, unbereavement, shock, scandal and breakfast. Surely these were grounds for greater intimacy.

He followed her into the kitchen. Stripped pine and red enamelled saucepans. He helped her off with her leopard-skin coat. She made instant coffee and they took it into the living room. He felt scruffy and unwashed on the pure white flokati and the white leather sofas. She put the tray down on a glass and chrome coffee table, pushing aside the incriminating copies of *International Currency Review* and *Power Boat Owner*.

93

Pax moved round behind her and as she stood up grasped her arm and pulled her round to face him. He wished he'd cleaned his teeth. He ducked his face down towards hers. He expected a slap or a kick or for her to wriggle out of his embrace.

She put her arms round his neck and kissed him full on the lips. He tasted coffee and lipstick and his own bad breath. His tongue probed between her lips and she held him tighter, pressing her fingers into the back of his neck. Their tongues met and her fingers caressed his scalp. When they ran out of breath she pushed him gently away.

"Thank you Pax. You were wonderful. I don't know what I'd have done without you. You were so strong. I'll be back in a minute."

He heard her go down the corridor past the kitchen and then the sound of water running. He gulped his coffee and sat on the sofa. Nick had almost provided his first corpse. Was Annabel about to provide his first affair? He closed his eyes and tried to think of Thea but she obstinately refused to appear.

All he could think of was whether Annabel meant them to do it on the white leather sofa.

He woke up with a travelling rug over him and a cushion under his head. Everything about him was white and chrome. "I'm in the morgue," he thought, and jumped to his feet. This made him dizzy and he slumped down again on the white leather sofa. He remembered where he was.

It was half past five. Because he wore an old-fashioned watch and not a digital he could not tell if it was the middle of the night or the afternoon. Judging by the bad taste in his mouth it could have been either. He stood up slowly, still clutching the rug like a security blanket, and went to the window. The view onto the deserted gardens at the back was no help. It was grey and drizzling. Dusk or dawn.

Annabel. His first affair. He couldn't remember a thing about it. Disorientation or guilt. Amnesia. Like after a car accident. The last thing he remembered was kissing her passionately over the coffee cups. Then she had gone to the

94

bathroom, promising to be back in a minute. What had happened then? He had a vague recollection of her coming back in a silk kimono, open to the waist, ready to fall on him with strangled cries of passion. Had that really happened or was it his imagination?

He looked on the white leather sofa for tell-tale stains. There was only a damp discoloration the length of his body. He got down on his hands and knees on the flokati. It was immaculate.

He was still fully clothed. White shirt and thick sweater. His trousers were still done up, the belt buckle on the last hole but one. And the clincher: he was still wearing socks. Even at the height of passion or intoxication he knew he would have taken his socks off.

He went down the corridor calling her name. There was no answer. There was a television in the kitchen. He switched it on and discovered that it was the afternoon. That much was certain. He ran back into the living room to put his shoes on. He had to find her. He would seize her by the hand and drag her back upstairs and take her on the flokati to make amends for falling asleep.

She was nowhere to be found. He ran out into the street. There was no sign of the yellow Jag. Where had she gone? Did she have a flat of her own? Was she on a modelling job, flaunting her ears to lascivious advertising men? He would wait for her upstairs until she came back, even if he had to stay for days. And then he would give her what for. But the front door had slammed and he didn't have a key.

Fortunately his own car keys were still in his trouser pocket. There was no choice but to drive home to the bosom of his family.

❊ Chapter Eight ❊

He was still awake at one o'clock in the morning. Thea's naked arm was across his chest but he didn't push it off. Its weight was comforting in the dark and a reminder of their love-making.

He told himself that he couldn't sleep because of his long siesta on Annabel's sofa that afternoon. Regret for what he didn't do would have been nearer the truth. Another opportunity missed. Another might-have-been. He would never know what it would have been like. He could still feel her lips on his, mingled with the after-taste of Thea's.

It had been an unusual day. Most days were filled with things like going to the office, getting the car mended, taking clothes to the cleaners. This day he had been confronted with death and adultery and the translation of a brother-in-law into a brother-out-law. But he had been an onlooker to it all. Surely life wasn't meant to be a spectator sport.

Nick was a crook and a con-man. A pathetic character, a self-made failure. Pax did not want to step into his shoes. Particularly where he was now, in some dark, stinking prison cell. But he *did* things. They may have got him into trouble but at least he could say he put something into his life and got something out. Meanwhile Pax booed and cheered from the grandstand and daydreamed of doing it better.

Soon it would be too late. Assuming he made his three score and ten he was half way through his life already. Or he could have a year or a week or a day to go. The dark was getting closer. He pushed Thea's dead arm away. It was making him feel hot and breathless. He had to think of something quickly before gnawing remorse and anxiety turned into a panic.

Tomorrow. Tomorrow he would be a man of action. He

96

would do something. Drifting and dreaming were over. With this new determination he closed his eyes and drifted off into dreams of boats and money and the dead bodies of men and the live bodies of women.

Pax woke up late. Downstairs he could hear Thea shouting at the children to go and get dressed. She should have brought him a cup of tea in bed by now. One of the little bonuses of lovemaking was that she was nice to him the morning after. He could usually look forward to little kindnesses at least until lunchtime.

There was no point in rushing as he was already late for work. Having had the day before off with a fictional sore throat he might as well pay an imaginary visit to the doctor to make sure he was fully recovered. He went downstairs in his dressing gown. The table was already cleared. The only signs of breakfast were on the floor. There was probably enough down there in the way of cornflakes, half-eaten egg, toast and marmalade to make a square meal if he could be bothered to get down on his hands and knees.

Thea came upstairs into the living room, rising from the depths like Aphrodite. Pax pointed out the likeness but she was in no mood for frivolity. She was late, she had a lot to do today and she had had no time to get herself ready. Somebody, emphasising the word somebody, had turned off the alarm that she had set for half past six. Pax shrugged. He might have done it unthinkingly when he realised he was still awake at one o'clock in the morning. It was much harder to get to sleep if you knew you were going to be woken up again in five hours' time.

"Did you like last night?" he asked, trying to nuzzle up to her as she stood at the sink wiping a pair of black high-heeled shoes on the dishcloth.

"That was last night. Today is today. I've got to go to school with the children, go to the cycle shop to have the push-chair mended, go to the estate agents to put an offer in for Romona Terrace, go to the courthouse to see the Probation Officer, go for an interview for that secretarial job and be back home

97

before lunch to pick Sarah up for a home dinner. So I don't have much time to be chatty."

She pushed him away and sat down at the table to put her shoes on. She was wearing the black dress she wore when she gave up work eight years ago. There was now plenty of room in the bust but the material was tight and wrinkled round her hips. She hadn't worn the shoes since they last went to a wedding. They were old-fashioned and scuffed but they were the only ones she had which would go with the dress. There were bulges around the tops of her thighs as she bent over to fasten the straps. She struggled with the buckles and Pax knelt down to help her.

"Even my bloody feet have got fat," she snapped.

She hadn't had time to wash her hair which hung limp and badly parted. She hadn't had time to pluck her eyebrows, sprouting with abandon after previous prunings or put the stinging cream on her faint moustache. All she had done was daub green eyeshadow unevenly on her eyelids.

But she was still good looking and he had always been more of a face man than anything else. Where her face was lined it was with laugh-lines at the corners of her eyes and lips. A touch of make-up was enough to hide the faint frown-lines on her forehead. She could still excite him with darting, provocative glances from her perfectly green eyes. Only these days she was less often in the mood to give them.

She balanced on the unfamiliar heels and went to the kitchen sink, walking stiff-ankled like a child in its mother's shoes. Pax stood up, ignoring the lemon curd that had stuck to his knee from the carpet. He watched her piling the breakfast things under the running tap and felt a prickling in the back of his throat and behind his eyes. He put his arm round her shoulders. She did not seem to notice. He thought of pulling her away from the dishes, mop in hand, and kissing her on the lips. Would she stay stiff in his arms? Would she turn her mouth away because she had just put lipstick on? Would she put her head on his chest and hug him round the waist? Was she asking to be loved or left alone? After ten years of living with her he could not answer this simple question.

98

The smarting of compassion turned slowly into self-pity. Why couldn't she give him just one signal of what she really wanted? He deserved sympathy and understanding as much as she did. He needed someone to put an arm round his shoulders too. He needed tenderness and love. Why didn't she think about him sometimes? He took his arm away from her shoulders.

To hell with it. Today he was a man of action. He seized her by the shoulders and spun her round. She looked very miserable. Kissing her and petting her suddenly seemed too trivial.

"We have to break away from this life," he said. "It's destroying us bit by bit, every day. Let's make a new start."

"That would be lovely," she said, shaking out the bits of egg-shell Sarah had put into a milk bottle. "Can we just get the children off to school first?"

"I'm serious. We can't go on like this for the next forty years. If we live that long. I don't know which would be worse, to live like this for forty years or not to live at all. Do you see what I mean? Let's do something different before it's too late."

"You'd better get dressed first. You're not going to get very far in your new direction just in your dressing gown."

She wiped her hands on the tea-towel and examined her chipped and peeling nails that she had meant to varnish at half past six that morning.

"You're not taking me seriously, are you?" he snapped, snatching away the tea-towel and wiping his knee. He couldn't stand the sticky feeling of the lemon curd any longer.

"What on earth do you think I'm doing this morning? I'm going out to get a job, increase our income by half, start a new career and move us into a decent house. If that's not breaking away from our present way of life I don't know what is, except packing up and emigrating."

"Darling, what you're doing is wonderful. But it's all in the same direction, isn't it? What we need in our lives is something completely different. We need to do something that's just, I don't know, a dream."

"I tell you what. You stay at home in your dressing gown

and do the dreaming for us while I carry on changing our lives. But first could you help me find my handbag?"

Pax offered to take the children to school. He was going to the Bank Auditors' Associated Annual Conference in Stratford-upon-Avon. He did not have to be there until the late afternoon but he had told the office that he had to catch the early morning train. He had looked forward to pottering about the house in his dressing gown for the morning, but Thea's speech the day before about doing the dreaming for them in his dressing gown had taken the pleasure out of that little plan.

What if he never came back from Stratford? What if he kissed them all goodbye and never saw them again. That's what his own father did. Pax was five at the time. He remembered it well. His father finished his tea, declined the last slice of Battenburg even though it was the end with all the marzipan on and said he was going out for a bit. He kissed Pax on the forehead, put his coat on in the hall and was never seen again. Just like that.

"I'll take the children to school. You see, I won't be coming home tonight." (Or any night. I'm going round the world.)

She looked up from the sink with an expression of mingled surprise and gratitude. "That would be lovely. I've got another interview at half past nine and Thomas has a class assembly. You'd better hurry up. Thomas has to be there at five to nine."

Didn't she hear what he said about coming home? He was sure she had forgotten he was going away to Stratford. He had forgotten himself until Doreen reminded him when he phoned in to say he had a sore throat.

"Make sure you put the milk bottles out. If you let them build up he doesn't take them all and then they lie round on the step for days. I shan't be here." (I shall be on a banana boat steaming out of Harwich.)

"Sarah has to take two days' dinner money. I didn't have any change yesterday. Can you find my handbag?"

"I said I won't be coming home tonight." (You can have everything. All I need is my passport.)

"Here it is. One of the children must have put it under the

100

sofa." She stood up and brushed the lint off her black dress.

"Will you be all right on your own?" (You'll never see me again.)

"I think I can manage. Don't forget that Thomas has to take his library book back."

"I shall be gone for some time." (Ever and ever.)

"Hurry up and get dressed. They have to leave in five minutes or you'll miss the first bell."

He kissed her on the forehead, for practice.

"There's no time for that now. Go on, get that dressing gown off."

It never even crossed her mind that he could walk out on her. Just like that. She did not believe that he would throw up everything and start a brand new life on his own. The trouble was, neither did he.

"Where are my shoes?"

"There's still egg on your ear."

"Where did you leave your gym bag?"

"Sarah's hidden my satchel."

"Where did you leave them last night?"

"Let's go."

"We'll be late."

"Get off."

"Pissoff."

"Hurry up."

"Mummy will be angry."

"Where is Mummy?"

"Gone to the shops."

"You didn't wash your hands. I can still see the marmalade."

"Whose shoes are they?"

"Mine."

"Then who should know where they are?"

"If you take your cardigan off again I'll smack you."

"I don't want to wear my hair slide."

"I haven't got a snack."

"We have to take the exact dinner money."

"Has anyone seen the car keys?"

"Whose car keys are they, Daddy? Then who should know where they are?"

"We'll have to walk."

"Pissoff."

And so the three of them joined the procession of little children being pushed, pulled, bullied and cajoled to school by their dishevelled mothers and fathers. First Thomas was thrown into the riot of his playground. Then Sarah was wheeled another half mile to her playgroup in the church hall. The wheel of the push-chair only fell off once.

"Are you Sarah's farver?"

"Yes."

"Your Sarah gave my Elvis a black eye yesterday. I had to take him to the doctor's."

"I'm terribly sorry."

"He's all right now. Aren't you Elvis."

"Oh good."

"And anuvver thing."

"Yes?"

"When I told her off she told me to pissoff."

"Oh dear."

"It's a church playgroup isn't it? They get enough language at home."

"I'm sorry."

"Never mind. Come on, Elvis, get your bum off of that pram and into school."

"Bye-bye Sarah. Now don't forget, be kind to the other children."

"Pissoff."

"I shan't be coming home tonight."

"Will you come back ever?"

"Why?"

"You didn't give us our pocket money."

"Is that all?"

"Elvis's father went away for ever."

"Did Elvis mind?"

"No. His mother lets him watch telly all the time."

102

"Bye-bye Sarah."

Class assembly was a concert given by a class at morning assembly in front of the rest of the school. Parents were invited. Thomas was dressed as a daffodil. He had to sing the first verse of *All Things Bright and Beautiful*. He forgot the words.

Pax shuddered and remembered his own knicker-wetting terror. The applause like the sound of smacked bottoms, the humiliation of forgetting the words like waking up in a wet bed, the sea of grinning faces like the moon-headed giants who chase you down unending corridors in bad dreams. Do this. Do that. Say this. Say that. Perform. Training for Life. Wear your mother's cut-down dress, your father's outsize cap, tie a tea-cloth under your chin, take off your trousers, wear this crêpe paper. You are a shepherd or a daffodil or a bear or, worst of all, a grown-up.

It was almost as agonising for the teachers. They knew they were on trial too. Parents wanted some proof that they were doing their job of kneading the clay they had been given and pressing it into the right mould. They hovered and pointed and mouthed the words. They were as anxious as the children for it to be over soon and not to be "let down". The parents were anxious too. They wanted reassurance that their children were capable of aping their mothers and fathers, that they would grow up like themselves.

Pax watched Thomas forget his words and wanted to press him into his arms. He blushed and fidgeted and put his finger in his mouth until he was prompted. Pax put his elbows on his knees and his face in his hands until it was all over.

Out in midstream he cuts the engine and raises the sails. He points the bows downstream towards the sea. On the lockside there is a crowd of adults and children, a school outing. They say to each other how pretty the *Swan* looks with its new varnish and crisp white sails. They clap their hands but the smacking sound is soon lost on the wind as she sails away. Thomas and Sarah peep out of the cabin.

"Can we come out now?"

"Yes, come on. You'll never have to go back there again, I promise."

The rest of the children are taken back to school. In the classroom they write about the *Swan* in News. They get out poster paints and paint a picture of it to take home and stick on the wall or the door of the fridge. It has two white sails the same size and a red flag at the top of the mast and above the blue water is an enormous yellow sun.

The teacher writes underneath, Y is for Yacht.

❋ Chapter Nine ❋

The name of the stick insect man in the red sweater who owned the *Swan* was Harry. He was waiting at the dock at lunchtime.

"Just thought I'd take a quick look over her again if you don't mind. Help to make the mind up."

"You've been over her three times already. I'm not dropping the price any more. Someone else came to see her this morning. He's very interested at that price. He's coming back this afternoon with a deposit. He knows a lot about boats. He says it's a bargain and I'm a fool to sell it. This is your last chance."

"I'm going away on a business trip for a couple of days. I'll let you know when I come back," said Pax.

"It'll probably be sold by then."

Harry had never been so eloquent. Normally he was mono-syllabic. Of course the story about the man coming back with a deposit was rubbish. A well known sales ploy. But Pax wanted to believe he was telling the truth. He wanted Harry to keep talking, to give him more reasons to buy the *Swan* there and then. He wanted Harry to tell him what a good investment it was, how the family would love it, that the reality of owning it would be like the dream of owning it.

He sat down in the cockpit and looked up at the mast making lazy circlets in the sky, a hypnotist's pendant. Like an actor speaking the lines someone else had written, the lines he had been rehearsing for three weeks, he listened to himself negotiate with Harry.

"I can't afford that but if you came down just a bit . . ."

The British Registry of Shipping is on the top floor of the Customs House in Lower Thames Street. The facade is un-adorned and severe, granite-faced like the customs men in the green channel: "Nothing to declare? A likely story." Harry led the way. He carried the *Swan*'s registration book, a small folder bound in blue cloth in which was glued a large sheet of yellow paper that folded up like a map.

Pax carried his cheque book in his inside pocket, touching it every few paces to make sure it was there. The price agreed with Harry was the same as the deposit on Mavis.

Somebody had to make the break. Somebody had to save them from the suffocating coils of suburban domesticity.

Behind them walked another Pax, the same one who lurked on the ceiling of the autopsy room watching the other being gutted like a taxidermist's specimen. He was filled with horror at what was about to happen, but also curiosity.

A wide, sweeping staircase led up from the cold marble entrance hall of the Customs House to the registry. The walls were decorated with Notices to Mariners, plain white pieces of paper printed with ominous warnings of fresh dangers to sailors. Wrecks, buoys, dredging works, unexploded mines. In about half an hour Pax would be master of a British-registered vessel, a mariner prey to the hazards of the seafaring life.

At the top of the stairs they went into a large, rectangular hall. Around the edges were deep wooden counters whose clerks were dwarfed under the high plastered ceilings. Some of them scuttled around the room bearing piles of papers while others sheltered behind bastions of files. Everyone in the room except a languid, uniformed attendant was busy paddling against the tide of paperwork. An ornate clock above the door reminded them that time waited for nobody either.

They filled out an Admiralty Bill of Sale with details of themselves and the *Swan*. Pax's hand shook when he signed it. It shook even more when he signed the cheque and handed over the Romona Terrace deposit money to Harry.

He thought he would feel excited, the same kind of excitement he had felt when he followed Annabel up the stairs to her flat or down the green painted corridor to Nick's dead body. But all he felt was an ominous foreboding.

The other Pax looked on. He could see no reason for feeling anything else.

106

They shook hands on the steps. It was too late for Harry to cash the cheque, he would have to wait until nine thirty-one the next morning. He seemed to have grown even more elongated as he strode away, an enormous burden lifted from his narrow back.

Pax walked back to the bank to pick up his suitcase. He did not have time to see the *Swan* before he left for Stratford. He would have to keep it locked in his imagination for another two days before he could hold it in his hands, feel it under his feet.

Pip . . . Pip . . . Pip . . . Pip . . . Pip . . . Pip . . . Clunk.

"Darling, I'm calling from Euston Station . . . The train leaves in two minutes . . . You know the boat I was telling you about . . . The one in Saint Katherine's . . . It's all ours darling . . . Yes, ours . . . Yours and mine . . . I bought it for us . . . all of us . . . Hello? . . . Hello? . . . Darling say something . . . I'll explain when I get back . . . Thea, are you there? . . . " Click.

He lay fully clothed on the bed. The phone at home was still engaged. Thea must have left it off the hook. It was very unreasonable of her to behave like this before he had had time to explain.

"What if there's an emergency?" he asked Hamlet. Hamlet was engrossed in Yorick's skull. The painting was by a "local artist". It was an appropriate epithet as his style had obviously been inspired by the pub signs of the neighbourhood. "What if it was a joke? How could I tell her I hadn't really spent the Mavis money? She'd be all upset for nothing."

But it wasn't a joke. He had written the cheque and given it to Harry. Harry would be on the bank's doorstep tomorrow morning demanding the contents of their joint savings account. There was still time to stop the cheque of course. It would be Thea's fault if he didn't stop it because she wouldn't speak to him and persuade him to.

"She probably thinks I'm a coward not to tell her face to face. She probably thinks I arranged it so I would be away for two days," he soliloquised to the silent Hamlet on the wall. "I couldn't help it. I was busy. I nearly missed the train. It was bloody good of me to phone her from the station. I wanted her to know as soon as possible. I could have kept it a secret."

Hamlet leered at the skull. It was the size of a football. Yorick must have had a big head. The local artist had tried to achieve a resemblance between Hamlet's face and the skull. This gave them both an inane, Halloween-pumpkin expression.

She had slammed down the phone before the money ran out. He didn't have the right coins to try again and the train was leaving. He couldn't try again until he reached the hotel. "I don't think she's being fair. It's her fault if she won't let me explain. She thinks I ran away to Stratford. I mean, I tried to discuss the boat with her, didn't I? She wouldn't listen. She thinks the boat is a craze, another daydream. But I'm fed up with dithering around. I'm fed up with just getting older and no further. How many years have I got? You have to *do* something while you have the chance. Right or wrong. She'll thank me in the end, you know. She'll wake up one day and see that she's been frittering away her life worrying about houses and schools and summer holidays and real life has passed us by. I don't want to be Nick. I don't want to be like Nick. But at least he *does* things. You can't shilly-shally and piddle and dawdle for ever can you?"

Hamlet had no answer to that.

He looked at his travelling clock. The opening session of the conference would soon be over and it would be time for cocktails before dinner. The rest of the night was free. To-morrow there would be speeches all morning and a panel discussion in the afternoon. The conference ended at teatime.

That meant he could have a lie-in in the morning, potter round Stratford and have a long lunch before joining his fellow auditors at the concluding session before tea. He had made sure that the transcripts of the speeches and minutes of the panel discussions would be available before they all left. He could skim through them on the train on the way home so he could tell people at the office what it was all about and dictate a summary to send off to Head Office.

Damn Thea. She was selfish and inconsiderate. She was

108

spoiling what should have been a pleasant couple of days off work. He should have been relaxing and getting used to the idea of being a shipmaster and mariner. Instead he was being henpecked at long distance.

He picked up the *Swan*'s certificate of registry from the bedside table. Its blue cloth binding had white stains. Had the sea broken over the bows, forced its way through the hatches and into the cabin, gone into the captain's locker where he kept the ship's papers with the rum and the yellow-fever flag?

He unfolded the certificate. The paper was thick and yellow. On top it said in large, black letters, "CERTIFICATE OF BRITISH REGISTRY". Underneath, in less bold type, were the words "Particulars of Ship". He savoured the words, read them out loud to his lugubrious friend on the wall.

She was described as "Sailing and Auxiliary Motor Ship – Single Screw. Rigged – Gaff Cutter. Stem – Curved. Stern – Lifeboat. Build – Carvel. Framework – wood yacht."

Carvel-built and gaff-cutter rigged, curved stem and a lifeboat stern. How could he have lived so long and be so totally ignorant of what those words meant? He rolled them lovingly round the tongue. He put the book down on the bedspread and tried to memorise them in case the subject of boats came up over dinner.

He looked up at poor old Hamlet. If he had had a new boat he wouldn't have wasted his time brooding over dead bodies. There was too much else to do, too many new things to learn.

"I, the undersigned, Registrar of British Ships at the Port of London hereby certify that Pax Brown is the Master of the said Ship."

He felt full of emotion. He stood up from the bed, straightened his tie and looked in his pocket for his comb. He remembered the night before his wedding, contemplating the wedding ring. Now he felt the same sense of tremulous excitement mingled with grim foreboding. He looked at the blue, stained book on the bed. Again he was embarking on a relationship with a strange, unpredictable creature for which he felt completely unprepared. The *Swan* represented a new life, new hopes, the translation of daydreams into reality. Once he stepped on the teak deck and rigged the cutter up into the gaff and turned the curved stem in the right direction and straightened out the carvels he would cruise off at six knots an hour into the unknown. The blue book on the bed was the passport to the world that awaited him there.

At the same time there was the same sense of the irrevocable that had haunted the wedding ring, the parachutist's knowledge that there is no going back. It was more than the normal doubts about whether his feelings were genuine and deep. There was a pervasive undercurrent of guilt, a premonition of punishment for what he had done. Was it because he had demolished Thea's own dreams, however misguided, of a new life?

He couldn't even ask her. She'd left the phone off the hook.

He put the comb back in his pocket, brushed the dandruff off his shoulders and checked his flies. There was only one thing to do with feelings of excitement and foreboding, whether you had decided to take a wife or a mistress or a boat, and that was to drown them in alcohol.

The atmosphere in the Falstaff Room was charged with false jollity. Auditors are like policemen and football referees and other guardians of public morals. When they get together they try to convince each other that they can have a good time too. The false bonhomie was made even more unnatural by the complete absence of women. Feminists had chosen more interesting battlegrounds than computer fraud.

Pax collected a gin and tonic at the bar. He circulated according to the position of the dry roasted peanuts, nodding and smiling to those he knew. Occasionally he was caught in a cluster of acquaintances and tried to steer the conversation around to ships and the sea but without success. Finally he gave up, found a window in the corner where he could look out on the placid Avon and waited for the warm glow of his third gin and tonic to clear his mind of nagging premonitions.

Dinner in the Mistress Quickly Suite was mercilessly predictable from the prawn cocktail through the grey roast beef to the *poire belle Hélène*. After each course he tried the telephone only to hear the callous pips of the engaged signal. He began to worry that she might be ill or the house had burned down or a gang of rapists were holding her and the children to ransom. He promised himself to be really angry at her childishness. This was no way for an adult to behave.

After dinner he went for a walk into the centre of town. He felt bloated and drunk and thirsty. Stratford's logo is the swan. The live variety swam around the river even at night. Pictures of swans on pub signs and hotel signs and "Stop Littering" signs and public convenience signs mocked him as he passed. He was supposed to be happy, dammit. He had broken away with his own swan, shown his independence. All he could think about was that housebound little woman who had left the phone off the hook.

He went back to his hotel room. There were three miniatures of scotch in the mini-bar and he emptied them into a tumbler with a little bottle of Perrier. He would try the phone just once more. If it was still engaged he would not try again. Ever. He would call at the house for his clothes. Say goodbye to the children. Go and live on the boat he had bought.

Having screwed himself up to this decision he was taken aback when Thea answered. He couldn't think of anything to say. She said "hello" several times.

"It's me. I'm in Stratford. I've just had dinner." He burped to prove it.

"That's nice. I'm just going to bed. Did you have a nice evening?"

He was not taken in by the sweetness of her words, the carefree nonchalance. If she was in a normal mood she would be moaning about the children and listing the jobs she wanted him to do when he got back.

"Listen, Thea. I can stop the cheque in the morning. I really can."

"That's all right, dear. You go ahead. The agent said they would probably have accepted our offer but I told him this afternoon that we were withdrawing it. We had other plans. And I've cancelled those people who were coming back for another look at our house. You know, the cash buyers. They sounded disappointed."

"Listen to me. I said I would stop the cheque in the morning."

"And I said you're not to. I've cancelled the agent. I've no right to interfere in your life."

"How did you have time to tell the agent? By the time I phoned from the station he must have been shut."

"He was just leaving."

"Why did you leave the phone off the hook?"

"I wouldn't have done a thing like that. One of the children must have taken it off. Well, goodnight darling. You'd better get to bed if you've got the conference tomorrow. I'll get some sailing books out of the library for you."

They mouthed loving words to each other. It was a very bad sign when she called him "Darling". He put the phone down and gulped half the contents of the tumbler. He suddenly felt horribly sober.

Harry would not be pleased. They would have to go back to the registry together. He would threaten to sue him. Breach of promise. It would be an uncomfortable half-hour.

He took the blue book out of his inside pocket. He weighed it sadly in his hands and then put it in the top drawer of the bedside table where he could not see it. He drained the glass and let it drop out of his fingers onto the carpet. He undressed, letting his clothes lie where they fell. Naked he stood in front of Hamlet.

"Sorry old man. Couldn't carry it off. All a bit of a fiasco. Bit of a coward, I suppose."

He got into bed and closed his eyes. He began to feel dizzy and surrendered to the whirling maelstrom of lights in his head, hoping he would not dream of skulls or sailing ships.

He woke up feeling sick. He lay quietly in the dark at first, hoping the nausea would go away. He promised his stomach that he wouldn't move, that he would treat it more considerately in the future, in the hope that it would not assume an independent existence and drive him to kneel on the bathroom

112

floor. Gingerly he stretched out his arm to the bedside light, switched it on and screwed up his eyes until he was used to the glare. He turned them away from the picture on the wall. Yorick only exacerbated the feeling of imminent doom that precedes the stomach's violent rebellion.

It was only one o'clock. He had spoken to Thea barely an hour before. In eight hours' time he would phone the bank and stop the cheque. He dwelled on the idea, hoping it would avert the punishment that was building up in his abdomen.

After half an hour he swung his legs gingerly over the side of the bed and sat up. He shuffled carefully to his suitcase and rummaged among his socks for indigestion tablets. He munched them in the bathroom, sitting down with his head in his hands and his pyjama trousers round his ankles. They made him feel worse. He succumbed to the temptation of trying to remember what he had had to eat the night before, waiting for the spasm in his stomach when he named the culprit. It seemed that gin and dry roasted peanuts were chiefly to blame followed by three large brandies and the table's entire ration of after-dinner mints. He cursed his greed.

He needed a drink. Water was too bland. He craved Coca-Cola. Wasn't that supposed to settle the stomach? He stood up and hobbled out of the bathroom, his pyjamas round his ankles. He didn't dare bend over to pull them up. He felt like the wolf in the story whose stomach was full of stones which the mother goat had swapped for her kids.

He took a bottle of cola out of the mini-bar. It was cold in his hand. He held it against his forehead which brought on a fit of shivering. He bent down slowly, feeling the contents of his stomach edge closer to his mouth. He looked for the bottle-opener in the top shelf of the fridge among the swizzle sticks and beer mats and cheese snacks which did nothing to quell his rising gorge. It wasn't there. It wasn't on top of the fridge under the bar tariff and the laundry list. It wasn't hanging down from the side on a chain. He shuffled back to the bathroom but there were two empty screwholes behind the door where the opener should have been.

He squeezed the bottle tighter. The contents had become an

elixir, an instant cure. He had to have it. He knew people who always had an opener in their pocket or on their key-ring. He envied them now. He looked at his pallid reflection in the mirror. The dazed, listless eyes pleaded for action.

He held the bottle tightly in his left hand and positioned the jagged top against the front of the washbasin. There might be enough of a lip to catch the top if he banged down hard enough with his right hand.

Later on he was to wish that he had thought of another method of opening the bottle or at least found a more defined edge than the rim of the washbasin. He began to have misgivings even as he brought his right hand smartly down towards the basin. By then it was too late. There was no going back.

His right hand knocked the bottle out of his left hand. The jagged edge of the bottle-top gashed the second joint of each finger and the base of the thumb. His left arm jerked instinctively upwards and outwards and he banged his funny bone on the wall. The bottle landed on the big toe of his left foot with an audible crack.

The reaction was immediate. His left leg jerked up so that his kneecap cracked the underneath of the washbasin. Reaction piling on top of reaction, his left leg drove hard down towards the floor where the cola bottle had smashed to pieces on the tiles. Feeling the sole of his left foot spiked with broken glass the leg once more jerked upwards and gave his kneecap a second go at the washbasin.

There was plenty going on while all this was happening to his left leg. Without the expected resistance from the bottle which had slipped from his grasp, the heel of his right hand smashed down against the edge of the basin. He had no training in karate and the encounter did more damage to his hand than the ceramic.

The sudden pain in his wrist sent his right hand flying upwards to meet the underneath of the glass shelf above the washbasin. It broke in half and disintegrated on the floor with two tooth-glasses. Blood poured from the back of his hand.

At this point Pax lost his composure. He screamed. Not so

much with shock and pain but in protest at the malevolence that had sprung from nowhere.

He also lost his balance. He clutched at the basin, wrenching it sideways as he fell. Although it was securely fastened to the wall the treatment it had received from his flailing arms and legs did not come into the category of normal wear and tear. With a crunching sound it came loose from the wall and accompanied Pax on his slow motion fall towards the bath, scoring a wide graze down his right shin and trapping his right foot.

His scream was cut short when he hit the back of his head on the bath. He lay stunned on the broken glass and blood and cola, sprayed by the water spurting from the broken pipes in the wall where the basin used to be.

"If this is death," he thought as he lapsed thankfully into unconsciousness, "at least I don't feel sick any more."

❊ Chapter Ten ❊

His first thought when he woke up in the clean, white room was the pathologist's slab. The wave of panic subsided when he found that although he could not move his head or his limbs he could blink his eyes and hear himself breathe.

A second wave of panic washed over him when he saw the large mound under the bedclothes where his legs ought to have been. They had been amputated. He could feel pain and twitch the muscles but he knew that was just an illusion created in his brain. He still had his arms. He could see them lying heavily-bandaged on the white counterpane. He closed his eyes and thought of Douglas Bader.

Thea was his first visitor. She hesitated to touch any part of his body and kissed him on the nose. She sat down by the bedside and gave him a wintry smile.

"Hello Thea. Tell me the worst." He forced a brave voice.

"Don't talk so loud. They can hear you in the corridor."

She broke it to him gently that he was still in possession of his legs. He took the news well. He had spent the last half an hour constructing a new life around a pair of artificial limbs and a trolley with little wheels that he would push along with rubber knuckledusters. In his relief there was the tiniest trace of disappointment.

In fact there was nothing much wrong with him at all. He had a black eye, mild concussion, a swollen knee, hairline cracks in his big toe and a bone in his right hand, a sprained ankle and various lacerations and bruises. For a man who felt lucky to be alive there wasn't much to boast about.

"Why did you do it?" asked Thea. There was less sympathy in her voice than he felt entitled to.

"There comes a time when you have to call a halt. Take

116

stock. Make a stand. Life's a struggle, Thea. I felt trapped. We are all trapped. I had to start somewhere. I had to break out."

"But why the bathroom? Why did you have to break out of the bathroom?"

"What bathroom? I'm talking about buying the boat."

"I'm talking about the bathroom in the hotel. The one you wrecked last night. Why did you do it?"

"Do what? I didn't do anything. I was done to."

"They want to know why you went berserk in the bathroom."

So that was it. It was all his fault. A martyr to his own misfortune. They were trying to pin him down again. Even his own wife had turned against him. There was no point in explaining. There was no point in explaining anything.

"I was attacked. I was attacked when I went into the bathroom. I put up a hell of a fight. It was no holds barred. Life or death."

"Oh God. Who attacked you?"

"A bottle of Coca-Cola."

Thea burst into tears and rummaged in her handbag for a handkerchief.

There was no going back. He was Master of the *Swan*. By the time he had woken up in hospital it was afternoon and Harry had been to the bank to cash his cheque.

The bathroom marked a turning-point. It had prevented him going back on his decision. The onslaught of sanitary ware had changed his life.

It was the punishment he had been anticipating. Now he had atoned he felt free of guilt and ominous foreboding. Premonition had turned to admonition. It was a warning to make the most of his life before the unforeseen struck again.

He tried to explain this to the psychiatrist. She nodded and took notes and stared at him through gold-rimmed spectacles.

"Why are you looking at me like that? Why don't you accept what I tell you at face value? I'm telling you the facts. Why don't you believe me? You think I went mad in there, don't you? You think it was an overdose or epilepsy. You think I

117

tried to kill myself don't you? My God, if I was going to slash my wrists I would have sat in a hot bath and used a razor blade. Or I would have put my head in the plastic laundry bag. Or I would have put the cord of my dressing gown over the shower rail and tied it in a noose. Or I would have strolled off the balcony. But I would not have broken a Coca-Cola bottle at one in the morning and slashed at my wrists and missed!"

This outburst earned him another day under observation with mild sedation.

On his second day in hospital the hotel management sent him a basket of fruit and a letter politely requesting some several thousand pounds to cover the cost of repairing the bathroom. He bought a flat metal bottle-opener from the hospital shop, decorated with a swan, and sent it back to the hotel with a charming note explaining the incident was entirely their fault. However, as a goodwill gesture to the next occupant of his room he was enclosing a little souvenir of his stay in hospital, the bill for which would be sent to them in due course.

His colleagues at the bank sent him an arrangement of pink carnations. He was touched that someone had remembered the section of the Personnel Policy and Procedures Manual that sanctioned floral tributes not exceeding the value of twenty-five dollars to employees and employees' spouses on the occasion of a birth, bereavement or hospitalisation.

"Dear Gilbert," he wrote. He doubted whether Gilbert Pinkish knew about the flowers but felt he could not address his bread and butter letter, "Dear Procedure Manual." He wanted to work for the bank for another few months until the *Swan* was shipshape and he had learned to sail it. The annual pay-rise was due in May and he did not want to jeopardise it. ". . . I was touched by the flowers and the heartfelt sympathy of all my colleagues at the branch . . ." He promised to be back at work as soon as possible but hoped that the lift door was wide enough for a wheelchair. At the same time he was careful to imply that the seriousness of his injuries might call for extended sick-leave.

On the afternoon of the third day he lay fully dressed on his bed waiting for Thea to pick him up in the car. She had driven back to London immediately after her first visit and they had only spoken on the telephone for a few minutes since then. They had kept the conversation on the neutral ground of health and weather, studiously avoiding the topics of Mavis and the *Swan*. The truce would probably last until that evening when the children had gone to bed.

He mulled over his tactics. He had to build up a reservoir of sympathy. To the doctors he had exaggerated the pain and discomfort in his hands so that they did not take off his slings and bandages. He would keep them on as long as possible. His left leg was in plaster up to the thigh. With his hands immobilised he couldn't hold his crutches. As long as he couldn't walk or hold a pen or open a file he couldn't go to work. He couldn't even dress himself. He was banking on his apparent helplessness to bring out Thea's mothering instincts. She mustn't find out that in private he could already slip his hands out of the slings and walk perfectly well without crutches.

He was not usually a good malingerer. He had spent many hours browsing in medical dictionaries in the City library in rainy lunch-hours after mornings of excruciating boredom, looking for convenient illnesses. A convenient illness was one whose symptoms were invisible, treatment unknown, recovery guaranteed, prognosis excellent and gave you a few days off work, like the flu that most people in salaried employment feel entitled to when they have used up their holiday.

In the search for a convenient illness he had toyed with peptic ulcers, the milder wasting diseases, mystery viruses, glandular conditions and other disorders which demanded frequent rest but which the medical dictionary claimed did not affect the length or quality of life. Too often his eyes wandered down the page to the cancers and other horrors which made him snap the book shut and decide not to tempt fate but enjoy the good health which condemned him to another afternoon with the ledgers and the procedure manuals.

True malingering needs stamina and mental toughness. He tried to get the best out of his sick days. If he had spent the weekend in bed with a cold he would take Monday and

119

Tuesday off to compensate, on the principle of never being ill in your own time. Or he would make every effort to go to work when he felt ill so that when he took the time off that the sickness justified he would be well enough to potter around the house or go to the cinema. In short he managed his sick-leave like many other people but he failed the test of a true malingerer. That is, to take sick days off when you feel completely healthy and still feel healthy at the end of them. If he phoned up the office in the morning with an imaginary sore throat, sure enough by the end of the day he would have a real one.

But now he could indulge in a condition which, in return for only a modest amount of discomfort, would ensure him at least three weeks off work. He was not tempting fate because fate had already done its work without being invited. He could take his time with a clear conscience.

He would use that time to turn himself into a mariner. He would become Master of the *Swan*.

Thomas and Sarah had made a large "Welcome Home Daddy" poster for the living room wall. It featured their father as the victim of every natural disaster conceivable by a five-year-old and a seven-year-old. It looked like a Breughel painting of hell. Featured in the middle was the hideous fate of being done to death in a hotel bathroom. It was all depicted on the pale green lines and perforations of the computer print-out he smuggled home from the office for their artwork. The catalogue of personal misfortune also featured the entire international loan portfolio of the bank. It seemed an appropriate combination and he insisted it stay on the wall.

Thea was very attentive. She installed an armchair and a footstool in front of the television. She had hired a wheelchair and an invalid table from the Red Cross. She cut up his food and brought him drinks with a straw. But beneath this display of solicitude there lurked something sinister. She was calling him "darling" like you would call someone "fascist" or "child molester".

"Aren't you coming over here to eat?"

"No thanks, darling, I ate with the children."

"Aren't you coming to watch the news?"

"I heard it on the radio in the car, darling."

"Shall we turn off the television and chat for a bit?"

"I've got the ironing to do, darling."

"Listen Thea, if it's about our boat . . ."

"Your boat, darling. You do just as you please."

"I'll get rid of it. I'll put an ad in the paper tomorrow."

"But you only just bought yourself a boat, darling. You're not tired of it already are you?"

"Thea, I refuse to let you make me feel guilty."

"I wouldn't want you to feel guilty, darling. Why should I?"

"But I bought the boat for us. For the family."

"What a lovely surprise, darling. I'm sure we'll all enjoy it."

"Let's go to bed. Let's have a cuddle and talk about it."

"I've made up a bed for you in the playroom, darling."

"What's all this? Where are you sleeping?"

"In my own bed as usual, darling."

"Are you playing funny games?"

"It's so much easier for you, darling, than trying to get up the narrow stairs with your leg in plaster and your arms in slings."

"Stop being ridiculous. And I've been away for days. Don't you feel like, you know . . ."

"You're not much use like you are, darling. And I might kick you in the middle of the night. You're much better downstairs."

"But I want us to be together."

"That's nice, darling. But you have to practise being on the boat on your own, don't you. Can I give you a hand down the stairs?"

"I don't care what you say. I'm coming upstairs to sleep in my own bed."

"You can try, darling, but I promise you I shall lock the door. And if you make a noise, you'll wake the children. Now come on, I'll give you a hand downstairs."

"Don't you lay your hands on me. You're a shortsighted, malevolent, unadventurous, unromantic, bourgeois, *bijou*-dwelling bitch."

121

"Goodnight darling. Sleep well. Careful going downstairs. We don't want you to fall overboard, do we?"

He loathed the playroom. He avoided it whenever possible. It was at the back of the house on the ground floor. The cork tiles were stained with poster paint, glue and crushed crayon and covered most of the time with the contents of the child-height toy-cupboards that stood empty round the walls. Above the cupboards were festoons of computer print-out, daubed and scrawled and signed by Thea like entries for a cereal packet competition: "Sarah, Age 4."

The way to the back garden was through the playroom. You either had to mince your way carefully through the mess or take giant strides regardless of the crunching sounds under-foot. Their predecessor had covered the garden with green concrete. Pax thought this was a great idea. Thea had made some half-hearted attempts with flower-pots and strawberry barrels to alter the resemblance to a school playground but had only succeeded in making it look like a better class of car park.

Thea had made up his bed in a corner of this shrine to chaos and mess. With ostentatious moans and grimaces he made his way downstairs on his bottom, spurning her hypocritical help. Inside the playroom he slammed the door behind him, got to his feet, ripped off his slings like a beggar coming home from work and fell on the bed fully clothed. Above him, on the bank's payroll print-out for last October, a hideous stick man with a swollen green head and crazed eyes looked down on him. It was signed "Daddy by Thomas Age 6."

"I'll show you," he muttered.

The next morning he pretended to be asleep until the children had gone to school and Thea had gone for another job inter-view. He couldn't face her false attentiveness. He made himself breakfast and then scoured the bookcases for something nautical to begin his mariner's education. The closest he could get was *Treasure Island*. It was not very technical but better than nothing.

He had got as far as Blind Pew delivering Black Spots when the doorbell rang. He ignored the first five rings but then deduced from the caller's persistence that his presence in the house was known. He hoped it was Thea who had forgotten her key. He looked forward to pretending he could not open the door because of the bandages on his hands. He stood up from the sofa, hobbled downstairs and put his arms back in their slings.

He peered through the opaque glass of the door. He could see it wasn't Thea but a man. He took his arms out of their slings again and opened the door. Despite the warmth of the spring day the man wore a long tweed overcoat, a scarf up round his nose and a deerstalker hat pulled down over his eyes. He wore dark glasses. Before Pax could ask him who he was collecting for the stranger pushed past him into the hall and slammed the door.

Pax tried to push him back but a shooting pain went through his right arm and he tottered backwards on his plastered leg. The stranger grabbed his other arm to stop him falling over. He was about to scream for help when the villain whipped off his dark glasses. It was Nick.

"Christ. How did you escape?"

He had not escaped. He had applied for bail again when he was moved to London and this time it was granted. He had been released on the same day that Pax had gone to Stratford.

"Why didn't Thea tell you? I called her three days ago when you were in hospital."

"Thea isn't telling me anything these days. There's a bit of a frost around the house."

"You should be in mine. It's like the bloody Arctic."

They went upstairs and made coffee. Nick stayed away from the windows.

"O.K. Why are you walking round like Blind Pew delivering Black Spots. You gave me a terrible shock down there. I thought I was being mugged by a blind man in my own home."

"Incognito, old boy. You know, the Press, *Private Eye*, nosey neighbours. When you come out of jail you're sensitive about that sort of thing. At least until you've proved you're innocent."

"Do you think you'll be able to do that?"

123

"Come on Pax. Not you too. It's a fine thing when even your closest relatives think you're a crook. I'll have a perfectly good explanation for the whole thing."

"What about those accounts for Collectors' Coins Limited that you asked me to open at the bank?"

"You didn't open them did you?"

Pax told him that the accounts had not been opened and that he had destroyed all evidence of them as soon as he got back from the police station in Southend. Nick sagged back in his seat with evident relief.

"Listen, Pax, that was all a coincidence. They had nothing to do with the coins in the boat. You must believe me. But you have to admit that if anyone found out that we'd talked about them they might jump to the wrong conclusion."

"Why didn't you phone me if that was what you were worried about?"

"I think I'm being watched. Clicks on the telephone. Wrong numbers. Strange cars parked in the street. They might be watching you too. Anyway, enough of my problems. Tell me about this boat of yours."

Pax told him about the *Swan* almost apologetically but Nick was surprisingly positive about the idea. He thought it was the best thing he could have done.

"I thought you were a power boat man. Traditional boats not fast enough for you," said Pax.

"Power boats have their uses but there's nothing to beat the beauty of a fine old yacht. The water, the wind, the wood, the canvas. Time stands still, old boy. Scudding before the breeze, one eye on the compass. Freedom of the seas. Lost in the sea and the sky. It's so *elemental*. Great idea."

"Thea doesn't think so. I've half a mind to sell it again."

"Then resist. Stick to your guns. How can you give up an opportunity like that? Listen. You hang on to that boat of yours and when this trial business is over we can take her down to the open sea. Across the Channel even. Believe me, once you've tasted it you'll never look back."

"I'm not sure I'm ready for the open sea yet. I've got a bit of homework to do first."

"Then we'll forget about the open sea until you get the hang of it. We'll cruise around the Thames Estuary. Up into the Essex marshes. Safe as houses, old boy. Hundreds of little creeks. Old ports in the marshes, all silted up. Enormous skies. Flat horizons. Acres of waving reeds. Hundreds of birds. Smugglers' tales. Your boat is flat-bottomed so it can go where most other boats can't. A lot of the little creeks are shallow and dry out at low tide. We'd be on our own. Then you can run her gently onto a mud bank and sit there while the tide goes out. Cook up a meal. Open a beer. Smoke a pipe before turning in for the night beneath the stars. That's the life. You stick at it, old boy. Never mind Thea."

"I don't smoke a pipe," said Pax and realised he was sounding like Thea. Perhaps he resented someone else intruding into his daydreams.

"Have you given her a good going over since you got back?"

"Haven't had a chance. She makes me sleep in the playroom."

"I mean the boat."

"I haven't seen her since I bought her. I went straight up to Stratford and then back here. I'm supposed to be an invalid. Otherwise I'd have to go back to work."

"That's terrible. If I had bought a boat you wouldn't be able to keep me away. I'd hire native bearers to carry me there if necessary. How are you going to learn to sail her?"

"I just thought I'd do the theoretical work first."

Nick picked up *Treasure Island* from the sofa and threw it down again. He reached for his coat and his deerstalker. "Come on. Let's go. I want to see this boat of yours."

"But Thea . . ."

"Never mind her. We'll be back home before she knows. Let's go."

Nick helped Pax drape a raincoat over his shoulders and button it at the neck. He put on his own long coat, scarf, deerstalker and dark glasses. He carried the wheelchair downstairs and unfolded it in the drive. Then he pushed Pax out of the Square and round the corner to a side street where he had parked his bright yellow Jaguar.

125

"If this is incognito, what would we have to do to draw attention to ourselves?" asked Pax.

❊ Chapter Eleven ❊

It was not how he had imagined coming aboard his first command. The worst moment was when he found himself with one plastered leg on the pontoon and the other in the cockpit while the boat swung away from the side. He became emotional at the prospect of sinking like a stone with plaster of Paris sea boots.

He sat in the cockpit to get his breath back and tried to get it into his head that he was the skipper of his own sailing boat. One of his oldest dreams. There was nothing to stop him hauling up the sails, casting off fore and aft and setting a course for the open sea. Nothing to stop him except an almost total ignorance of anything to do with sailing.

It wasn't the first time he had been aboard her but somehow, now that she belonged to him, she looked different. He noticed things he had never noticed before. Little hooks and eyes for holding the cabin doors open. The name of the boat-builder engraved on a small brass plate tucked under the lip of the rail that ran around the cockpit. A small brass cleat on the boom above his head. He also noticed the blemishes for the first time. The black stains on the wood where the damp had got under the varnish. A crack in the mahogany of a locker lid. He studied her and knew her in the same way that he had looked at sleeping Thea's face the first time he had woken up in the same bed.

"I like the indoor swimming pool," said Nick, peering into the cabin.

Water was lapping almost to the top of the benches. A cushion bobbed in between the table legs.

"My God. What are we going to do?"

"We'd better do something or you'll be the proud owner of a string of bubbles. Where's the pump?"

Pax did not know where the pump was. He had never seen the pump. There had been no talk of pumps. He wouldn't recognise a boat pump if he was sitting on it. He was gripped by horror and panic made worse by his impotence. He wanted to get off, catch a number twelve bus back home and forget he ever had anything to do with boats.

Nick began to lift the cockpit seats and peer into the lockers underneath. Then Pax had a flash of inspiration. He remembered that every time he saw Harry on the boat he would be sitting on the right hand side of the cockpit cranking away with a handle. He had never thought to ask what he was doing.

"Here. Is this it?" he exclaimed triumphantly, brandishing an aluminium handle with a black plastic ball at one end.

"That's part of it. Now find the hole to stick it in and you're home and dry. So to speak."

At the bottom of the locker was a black plastic box screwed to the boards. Out of the box protruded a metal socket. Pax stuck the handle in and pushed it backwards and forwards as he had seen Harry do from a distance. He was rewarded by a sucking sound, a gurgling, and soon a spasmodic stream of dirty water from the side of the boat into the dock. He had found the pump.

After five minutes he had to hand over the work to Nick. Even without his injuries his arms and shoulders would have been aching. It took Nick another fifteen minutes until the pump gasped and the handle became light as it sucked only air. Nick was breathless. Perspiration ran down the grooves of his hair transplant.

"Quick. We'd better take a look down there before it fills up again."

With Nick's help, placing his legs for him, Pax inched down the steps to the cabin and sat down, elbows on the table. It smelt mildewy and damp. Harry had left the pictures and the ornaments. The first thing to be done was to take them down and varnish the wood panels. The ceiling was painted white. It was grimy and needed stripping and repainting. Nick had a different idea about the renovation priorities.

"So what did the survey say?" he asked.

128

"Survey? What survey?"

"You mean you haven't had a survey?"

"Christ, Nick, what a stupid question. If I say 'What survey?' doesn't that indicate that I haven't had a survey done? The chances are very high that if I had had a survey I would have known what you were talking about when you first asked. How many people do you know who could have their property surveyed and then not know what a survey was? Use what meagre and shifty intelligence you have."

The next few minutes were taken up with reviewing Pax's heated statement. Pax retracted his hasty remarks on the quality and honesty of Nick's intelligence, thanked him for his hard work at the pump, recalled the warmth and closeness of their relationship over the years and excused his outburst on the grounds of anxiety about the boat, his state of health, the traumatic experiences of the past few days and the deteriorating relationship with his wife. He didn't think it was a good idea to mention his consuming desire for Annabel as he still needed Nick's help to extricate himself from a boat with a propensity to fill with water.

They went back to the survey. Nick explained that it was conventional to have a surveyor take a look as he would if he had bought a house. "He might even find out where the leaks are coming from."

"But that will be expensive, won't it? Look how much it costs to have a house done."

"My dear Pax, you know the old saying. Sailing is like standing under a cold shower all day tearing up ten-pound notes. You haven't even started yet. First there are the mooring fees. How much are they?"

"A lot."

"Insurance?"

"Insurance? What insurance?"

"You mean you haven't got it insured?"

"Christ, Nick, what a stupid question. If I say 'What insurance?' doesn't that indicate that . . ." He cut himself short. They didn't have time to go through all that again.

"Then you ought to have her out of the water once a year to

have the bottom scraped and antifouled."

"Antifouled? What's that? And please don't say 'You mean you haven't had her antifouled yet?' "

"They have a special paint that stops the weeds growing on the wood. If that happens, the roots eat away at the planks and the bottom falls out."

Pax shifted uneasily on the bench and eyed the floorboards.

"Revarnishing and repainting will cost a lot in materials alone. Treble it if you want someone to do it for you. The sun and salt water eat away at the varnish and you have to re-do it once a year. Then there are the bits of rope and tackle that wear out or rot or get lost that you have to replace. But I'm sure you've worked all this out already."

Pax nodded dishonestly. He was getting a cold, heavy feeling in the abdomen. He had not given any thought to the expense of owning a boat beyond the initial purchase.

"Then there's the engine. Diesel isn't it? Annual overhaul. Regular service. A new set of batteries every couple of years and they are expensive. The fuel's dear as well if you get it at the marina pump."

"It costs as much as maintaining a house."

"And that's if you do the work yourself. That will take you most weekends between March and October. The trouble with having a boat is that you never have much time for sailing."

"I'll have to get another job to afford it," said Pax, glumly.

"You could always think of it as your little flat in the City. You're close to the office. A nice little *pied-à-mer*. You could get up to all kinds of mischief in here."

"The thought never crossed my mind," said Pax, thinking of Annabel.

"But we've only been talking about the running costs. Before that you'll have to sort out the problems, stop the leaks, take the varnish down to the bare wood and build it up again, check the seams, recaulk the decks, cut out all the rot, replace the tackle and the ropes, buy all the extra gear. You'll need a dinghy, a lifejacket, a compass, a radio, an echo sounder, a radar cone, lifebuoys, navigation lights, flares, safety harness. All that will cost you what you paid for her."

130

"I know all that," Pax lied, "but it's not just a hobby. It's a change of life."

"Even changes of life need money. You need a little bit on the side to pay for all this."

"Who do you want me to open bank accounts for now? I thought we'd finished with all that."

"I have nothing in mind at all. I was just speaking generally. I was only suggesting that if any little offer turned up you would be glad of the money."

Nick bent double and crawled through the narrow doorway into the front cabin. It was heaped with sails and ropes. There was no panelling so the bare planks of the hull were visible. Pax waited in the main cabin, doodling in the grime on top of the table, grateful that his legs prevented him from meeting face to face the rotting planks and leaking seams.

Take an architect round a house, a gardener round a garden, a mechanic round a car and they look for faults and flaws like a pig after truffles. Pax suspected that Nick didn't know much more about boats than he did but he certainly displayed an expert's exhilaration when he found something wrong.

"Seams are leaking," he crowed from the bows, "and the water's been pouring down from the top deck. The deck planks round the edges are probably rotten. The head needs looking at. I think the ceramic's cracked and the seawater valve needs replacing."

"The head of what?" asked Pax.

"The head. You know, the head."

Pax gritted his teeth and clenched his fists as tightly as the dressings would permit. "No, I don't know."

"The loo, the bog."

He had heard the expression "going to the head" before but had thought it was slightly rude.

Nick emerged from the forecabin dusty and grimed. Without a word and looking serious he pulled the back cushion from the bench to expose the cabin wall of varnished plywood. He found a seam, inserted his fingernails and gently pulled. There was a wrenching, tearing sound and the whole of the wall came away.

131

"Hey, watch it!"

"Couldn't help it, old boy. Whatever it's nailed into is probably rotten."

He had exposed the planking. He pointed out the stains where the water had come through the seams and trickled down from the deck planks above. He pressed one plank with his fingernail and left a deep imprint. Pax remembered the balsa wood he used for models of boats when he was a boy. Nick gave a tug at the partition between the kitchen part and the main cabin. It split with a sharp crack.

"That'll need replacing."

"It will now," said Pax.

Nick pushed the table to the front end of the cabin and bent down to lift up the floorboards. They were rectangles about a foot square that lay on what Pax would have called joists in a house. In between the joists was oily black water. Pax couldn't see how deep it was. It looked as though it went right down to the bottom of the dock and he began to feel uneasy.

"Should that water be there?" he asked plaintively.

"That's the bilges. You've got to have some water there, keep the planks nice and tight. Look, it's only about three inches deep."

"Do you think the wood underneath is OK?" asked Pax, hopefully, like a terminal patient trying to look on the bright side.

But Nick would not give him comfort. "Can't tell until you have her out of the water. I wouldn't want to go poking down there now. Do you remember the story about the boy who had to keep his finger in the dyke?"

By the time Nick had finished his examination of the cabins and the galley they were a shambles. Pax's comparison with a customs search after a smuggling tip-off was not well received. Nick was not gentle while he helped Pax back up into the cockpit.

"Well at least the woodwork up here looks all right," said Pax, grasping at straws.

Nick did not answer. He lifted the seat to open the locker where the pump was housed. He picked up a rusty screwdriver

132

and pushed it with ease, like a skewer through a sponge cake, through the side of the boat from the inside to the outside, just above the waterline. Pax was furious at this wanton vandalism.

"Better to find out now than three miles out to sea when Sarah throws a tantrum and kicks a hole in the side of the boat," replied Nick with cold and overwhelming logic.

Nick continued to prod around the cockpit like a nervous cook unable to decide if the joint was done yet. Sometimes the screwdriver met a solid bit and left only a pock mark, sometimes it sank effortlessly through the wood. In retaliation for the comment about the customs search Nick began to recite under his breath the saga of the Jumblies, the creatures with green heads and blue hands who, in spite of all their friends could say, went to sea in a sieve.

"And you're making it like a bloody colander. Please stop perforating my boat with that screwdriver," erupted Pax.

"If you insist," said Nick, looking hurt and throwing the screwdriver down on the floor of the cockpit. "How about the engine?"

Pax thought he was on safe ground. All Harry did when asked the same question was turn the ignition key in the side of the cockpit above the locker that held the pump. No, Harry had not walked off with the key or hidden it somewhere inside the cabin but when Pax turned it there was nothing but a derisive click. Nick whistled tunelessly through his teeth and gazed up at the mast, the offended expert waiting for the ignorant to grovel. Pax looked desperately at the three gauges built into the side of the locker that housed the engine. They told him nothing and he clicked the key again in desperation.

"Batteries connected?" condescended Nick.

They were not. Pax fiddled clumsily with the terminals until Nick took over. Pax turned the key again and was rewarded with a flogging, grinding sound as the starter motor turned and a cloud of black smoke from the waterline at the stern enveloped them. Next to the key was a silvery lever with a red handle which Nick pronounced was the throttle. They tried it in various positions but always with the same result – a *rallentando* flogging sound and the smell of old tyres burning.

"That's why it's called a throttle. It chokes off the bloody engine," muttered Pax despondently.

"Is the fuel cut off?" asked Nick. It was obvious that he regarded such technical questions as purely rhetorical. This only added to Pax's feelings of inadequacy. Nick opened the engine locker and jiggled with various cables and levers, muttering about fuel-injection and pre-ignition. He asked which was the fuel tank. There were two brass screw caps set in the seats, one at the stern and one near the engine. Pax pointed optimistically at the one nearest the engine. Nick unscrewed it, put one eye close to the hole, picked up the screwdriver from the cockpit floor and dipped it in. He sniffed the liquid that dripped from it when he pulled it out and tentatively tasted some on the end of his little finger. He looked at Pax with a world-weary, tolerant expression. "Either your engine is very cheap to run or this is the fresh water tank. Shall we try the other one?"

The tank in the stern was for fuel. There was plenty of diesel in there and Nick pronounced that the fuel line was not blocked. Pax tried the key again, determined to flog the engine until it started or the battery ran down. He was rewarded when on what felt like its final, asthmatic cough the engine caught with a sudden roar and a small mushroom-cloud of smoke from the exhaust. Nick throttled back the engine.

"We don't want it shaking itself through the bottom of the hull do we?" he shouted above the noise.

They opened the engine locker for inspection. Pax watched the fan belt going round and round and nodded wisely. Nick touched various parts of the engine with the back of his hand, like a mother with a sick child, explaining that you had to watch out for the temperature. Pax did not ask whether it was supposed to be hot or cold and made a mental note to get a book out of the library on engines as well as navigation, practical seamanship, knots and splicing and boat-restoring.

They closed the locker and sat down to enjoy the vibrations when Nick noticed that they were pulling hard on the mooring ropes that attached them to the pontoon. They were in forward gear. Unless they found the gear control or cut off the engine they would soon find out if the mooring ropes were rotten too. They rummaged in the lockers and found a handle like the pump handle which you put through a slit in the side of a locker and pushed into a socket which controlled the gears.

"How many gears are there?" asked Pax.

"Two. Forwards and backwards."

It was time to go. Thea would soon be back home and he did not want to give her the impression that he was fit enough to go out to work. He turned the key to stop the engine but it carried on running. He turned the key backwards and forwards, jiggled it around, took it out and looked at it. Nick explained that the ignition on diesels was not electric and the only way to stop it was cut off the fuel supply. He opened the engine locker and tugged on a cable.

"You've got plenty of work on your hands, old boy. But I think she'll do," said Nick when the engine had choked into silence.

"Don't patronise me, Nick. I can see it's a floating disaster. Thea was right." He looked down at his plastered feet and felt an irresistible sadness creeping over him.

"Listen Pax. Don't give up now. She's the prettiest boat in the dock. All she needs is a little time and money. You find a boat-builder to have a look at the bottom. Have the engine serviced. And when my trial business is over we'll have a little trip downriver. And then if you're not convinced, you can sell her again."

"What fool is going to buy her?"

"You did," said Nick.

He tried to cheer Pax up with an outline of the Bigger Fool Theory, usually applied to the stock market but also relevant to vintage cars or antiques or boats. The theory states that however stupid you were to buy something there is always a Bigger Fool around the corner to buy it off you.

"But sooner or later you have to come to the Biggest Fool of All. Perhaps that's me," said Pax.

"Don't you believe it. I'll just take a look on the foredeck and then we'll go home and start phoning a few shipwrights."

135

Why was Nick so interested in the *Swan*? Pax remembered Thea saying that Nick never did anything unless there was something in it for himself.

Nick walked carefully on the deck, holding on to the mast, as if he expected the planks to give way and send him plummeting into the cabin below. He bent down and started picking at the black rubbery caulking between the teak planks and pulling it away in long strings.

Pax's despondency began to change to resentment. He looked at the wreck Nick had made in the cabin, the holes punched in the side of the cockpit with the screwdriver, the spilt diesel fuel on the cockpit seats. He had come to the boat this morning and seen nothing but its beauty. Nick had stripped it down to leaking seams and mildewed planks. The *Swan* was a woman at the end of her prime. Nick had washed off her make-up and stripped her down to her thermal underwear and after this humiliation was doubtless thinking of sending her out on the streets to work for him.

He was now looking up at the masthead, tugging at the ropes that ran up the side of the mast and through a couple of pulleys at the top. Pax decided it was time to put an end to these indignities.

"Leave it alone," he called.

Nick gave a final sharp tug. The rope parted half way up the mast. The end in his hand coiled back and hit him in the face. He teetered backwards towards the edge of the deck, his arms flailing to keep his balance. Behind him were the oily waters of the dock, thick and poisonous. There was no safety rail.

Pax knew that it was accidental. He knew the *Swan* was an inanimate object, an assembly of wood and metal and fibre. He knew that sailors call boats "she" out of tradition, that they have no life of their own, no will, no feelings, including feelings of resentment and revenge.

Just as Nick recovered his balance at the edge of the deck the block which was fastened to the other end of the rope fell from the top of the mast and hit him right between the eyes.

Nick parked his yellow Jaguar in the Square. He took the

wheelchair out of the boot and unfolded it by the front passenger door. He was dressed only in his deerstalker, his overcoat and sockless brown brogues. His bare legs were pale and hairy. He helped Pax struggle into the chair, piled wet clothes in his lap, and trundled him up the Browns' drive to the front door. Thea was looking down on them from the kitchen window.

She looked smug when she brought them hot coffee to go with the brandies they nursed. They sat side by side on the sofa. Pax ached with the exertions of the morning. Nick sat disconsolate with a blanket over his shoulders, still wearing the deerstalker, a large plaster covering the wound between his eyes. They sipped their drinks and stared morosely into the middle distance, sole survivors of a natural disaster.

Pax explained. He described in detail Nick's perfect backflip into the murky waters of Saint Katherine's Dock. There was not much of a splash because of his classic entry into the water, feet following head. It was more of a heavy plop followed by a column of water rising in the air.

That might have been the last anyone saw of Nick alive if the rope he had snapped had not wrapped around his wrist as he waved his arms in the air. Pax hobbled and crawled as best he could to the foredeck and pulled in desperation on the rope, dragging Nick to the surface. He managed to reach down and grab his hair long enough to keep his face out of the water until help arrived. A boatman walking on the hull of a barge from a dinghy fished him out.

"You grabbed his hair?" asked Thea, looking inquiringly at Nick.

Nick nodded morosely and took off his deerstalker. There was a bare patch the size of Pax's fist in the middle of his transplant.

"You poor darlings," she said.

Pax reached out for her hand and she kissed him on the forehead, the Judas kiss of a hostile woman.

Thea went on her own to the parents' wine and cheese at Thomas's school. Pax said it would be bad for his legs. He

137

would stay and babysit. Thea was glad she did not have to keep up appearances by being polite to him in public. She was very polite to him in private but that was a different matter. That was malevolent politeness.

The party was in the hall where they had assembly. Thea took her Tupperware box of cheese and pineapple cubes skewered on toothpicks to the food table and gave it to Olivia's mother. She took them out and patiently stuck them onto a cabbage head with the solemnity of black magic. There had obviously been some confusion on the committee. The table was groaning with severed punk heads bristling with pineapple and cheese. Alexander's mother had only a small tin of sausage rolls to serve and Damian's mother was doing her best to feed the five thousand with two mushroom quiches and a running camembert. Thea accepted the vociferous thanks for her contribution and moved on to the drinks table where Benedict's father was dispensing acrid red wine from two-litre bottles.

"You're Thomas's mother, aren't you? I'm Maggie's mother. Maggie says you've got an old beggar with bandages and crutches living in your playroom. I think that's wonderful. We should all be so Christian. We have a bible meeting in our house every Wednesday. Would you like to come and talk to us about it?"

Thea sidled away, muttering about evening classes on Wednesday and having to help cut up the quiches.

She got James's father to refill her glass. Dominic's mother almost knocked it out of her hand.

"I hear you're moving in to Romona Terrace. That's lovely. I bet you're excited. They're lovely houses. I wish we could move into something like that."

"We're not moving. I told the agent today we were withdrawing our offer. We decided against it."

"Oh dear. Is there something wrong with it?"

"No. But my husband has decided we're going to live on a boat."

"What? And go round the world?"

"When he's learned how to get it out of the dock, yes."

"Golly. You must be brave."

Thea waved her empty glass to no-one in particular on the other side of the room and mouthed a meaningless message. "Be back in a minute."

Alice's father waved and made his way through the knots of parents towards her. He worked in advertising and thought he was attractive. He liked to dance with his hands on your bottom.

"Hey, I hear you've bought a boat. That's fantastic. That's really fantastic. You must be really thrilled. What sort is it?"

"I don't know."

His attractive smile faded. "Oh God. Have I blown it? Was it meant to be a surprise?"

"It was a surprise all right."

"But you're supposed to know."

"Yes I'm supposed to know. I got a phone call."

They were joined by Richard's mother, who was known to be having an affair with Alice's father.

"Thomas's mother's got a boat but she doesn't know what sort it is," said Alice's father.

"It's made of wood and it's got a mast. That's all I know."

"Haven't you seen it yet?"

Dominic's mother recounted the news to Anna's father.

"I had a wooden boat once. Never again. Too much trouble and expense. Good luck to you."

By now the word was spreading and there was quite a gaggle of boat experts around Thea.

"We didn't know you were a sailor."

"That's wonderful. Congratulations."

"You'll have to go to navigation lessons."

"You must have been planning this for a long time."

"The children will love it."

"So many people waste their money on cars and houses."

"I'd love a boat."

"Aren't you lucky."

"Aren't you wonderful."

"You must be so thrilled."

"Thrilled."

"Thrilled."

139

"Thrilled."

As an alternative to screaming how much she loathed boats and boating and anyone connected with boats she escaped to the loo. When she came back she skulked by the wall bars, swigging wine.

When she got back home she found she had forgotten the key. Pax had to let her in. They stood looking at each other on the hall mat. Her eyes narrowed into small slits. Her lips disappeared into a thin line. "Whose father are you?" she spat, and pushed past him to stomp up the stairs.

❊ Chapter Twelve ❊

A friend of Nick's knew a good marine surveyor. His report arrived in a brown envelope. Pax ripped it open in the hall and hobbled back to his bed in the playroom.

"A shallow draught gaff-rigged yacht with twin lee boards. Carvel planked of African oak on solid oak fashioned frames. Iron spike fastened. Fitted with a teak deck laid fore and aft caulked and payed."

"Thea! Where's the dictionary?" He shouted upstairs.

"What dictionary?" She shouted downstairs.

"*The* dictionary. The English dictionary that tells you what the hard words mean. And how to spell them as long as you know how to spell them in the first place so you can look them up."

"Are you sure you don't mean the Australian slang dictionary? The Gaelic dictionary we took to Ireland? What about all your medical dictionaries you hide under your side of the bed? You think I don't know they're there."

"Please, Thea, do you know where the English dictionary is?"

"I'm in the kitchen. It's not here with me."

"Well it bloody well ought to be. You might look up the difference between simmer and boil. And braise and burn. It would do you a lot more good than all those cookery books."

"Please stop shouting from down there. Come up if you want to talk to me."

So it continued until they both had a last word and both slammed a door. Pax found the dictionary pressing flowers under a couple of bricks in the garage. He sat on his bed in the playroom and brushed squashed daisies from the Mensurable to Mesenteritis pages. They left a perfect yellow and white print of a daisy on the definition of Meretricious.

He and Thea would have to communicate in writing. It was the only solution. The simplest spoken words led to a row. He would write long notes with difficult words like meretricious and hide the dictionary. It would serve her right.

He already knew what caulking was but he looked it up to make sure. It meant that the gaps in between the deck planks were stuffed with string. Payed didn't mean that you had finished the Hire Purchase instalments but that they were smeared with pitch or tar or rubber as a defence against wet. He remembered Nick pulling up long strings of black stuff from the foredeck.

Now came the first bad news. He could imagine the surveyor rubbing his hands and smiling and nodding like an expert over his first truffle.

"Five planks starboard side and four planks port side rotted and in need of renewal."

The water tables were rotted. The port lee board was rotted. The gunwhale strakes were rotted. The sheer strakes were rotted. The top strakes were rotted. The inner berthing board was rotted. The cockpit supporting structure was rotted.

And so on. And so on.

Finally, the rudder pintles were slack. He looked up pintles (Pin or bolt. OE Penis) and threw the dictionary on the floor with the same dull despair that he threw the *Dictionary of Symptoms* on the floor when he had a stomach-ache. The case was hopeless. The choice was a terminal decline or an expensive operation that would give a few more years of life. Wouldn't it be better to put the *Swan* out of her misery now?

He put the report back in its brown envelope. He was stupid to have opened it, as he had been stupid to steam open the envelope from the specialist to his doctor when he was having trouble with his ears. He interpreted the jargon to mean he had a malignant brain tumour when in fact he just had inflammation of the inner ear.

He was a fool, meddling in things he didn't understand. He would never go to Saint Katherine's again. He had thrown their life savings away on a folly, a whim, a leaking, rotten hulk. Thea had been right. He would confess as much. He would go upstairs to the kitchen, hobble over behind her while she pretended not to hear him and kiss her on the back of the neck. He would say he was sorry.

He would show her how he could walk perfectly well on his plaster. He would show her how he slipped his arms out of the slings and bandages. He would go back to the bank on Monday. He would ask Gilbert Pinkish for a raise. He would ask for promotion. He would buy Thursday's *Financial Times* and apply for any job with better pay and prospects.

He would build up their savings again and put them in her name. He would go round to the estate agents with her. He would put the *Swan* in *Exchange and Mart* right now by telephone. He would put postcards in all the newsagents' windows. He would not rest until she was off his hands and he had recouped at least some of the money.

He would be a good husband and father. He would take the children to museums and the library and read them an improving story every night instead of gabbling a Mister Men book in half a minute. He would go to all their concerts and open days and volunteer for the Parents' Committee and collect jumble for the jumble sale and serve on the cake stall at the Bring and Buy.

He would not leave his underpants lying round the bedroom floor. He would rinse the shaving cream and little black bristles from around the basin, he would not leave wet towels lying on the bed. He would be a wonderful person to live with.

He would tell her all this in the kitchen and beg her forgiveness and ask to move back into the bedroom. He would abandon false pride. With a bit of luck they would seal their reconciliation by making love before the children came home from school. It would be the first time since a week before he went to Stratford. There was a lot of pent-up emotion waiting to burst out. A stirring erection promised the rewards of turning over a new leaf.

Adjusting his trousers he made for the playroom door, enjoying the growing excitement of penitence and lust.

Everything would be laid bare. He took a deep breath and clumped along the hall to the stairs.

"Thea, love, can we talk?"

Pax woke up from his doze in the rumpled bed and stretched luxuriantly but carefully, to avoid the cold wet bits. It had all gone more or less according to plan. After some initial resistance in the kitchen, to test whether his offer of reconciliation was genuine, they exchanged warm, slobbery kisses, wet with tears, and rushed upstairs. Since it was so long since the last time it was all over much too quickly but triumphant and glorious while it lasted. Thea had got dressed quickly and left to fetch the children from school leaving him with a soft kiss on the lips.

It was now time to take stock of what he had promised.

His confession had not been as totally frank as he had planned in the playroom. He had kept a little of his guilt to himself. There was no point in telling her how despicable he was if he meant to turn over a new leaf. That would have been counter-productive. There was no doubt in his mind that his firm purpose of amendment was sincere. It just had to be modified slightly to be practical.

He promised to go back to the bank on Wednesday, not Monday. He needed time to organise things and go to the doctor for a check-up. He did not demonstrate how he could take his bandages off as well as the slings. He limped on his plaster more than was strictly necessary.

With a heavy heart he recalled his promises. Not going near boats again was the easiest to fulfil. He was glad of the excuse. None of his encounters with boats so far had been happy ones. They had brought him worry and expense. Nor did he worry much about putting their savings in Thea's charge. She was not yet liberated enough to spend them without asking his permission.

What worried him most was the image of the New Man he had drawn for Thea while he caressed her bottom. He knew from previous experience how dispiriting it was to get to work on time, wear a clean white shirt every day, ask for raises, read

144

the job advertisements every Thursday and generally attend to his career and prospects. It wasn't the effort he minded, it was the pointlessness.

But it was his duty. Responsibility to his wife and family. He had promised. He closed his eyes and tried to recapture the feelings of tranquillity and fulfilment that follow sex and New Year's resolutions. He wiggled his toes, stretched his legs and rolled over for another doze, gathering strength for the New Life he had promised. He was boobytrapped by a patch of wetness and opened his eyes.

On the floor by the bed was the brown envelope from the surveyor. With the wry smile of a reformed smoker picking up a packet of cigarettes he reached out and picked it up. He took the survey out of the envelope and read it again to reinforce his determination. He would rid himself of the millstone that was threatening to drag his family, his career and life savings into the oily depths of Saint Katherine's Dock.

"A shallow draught gaff-rigged yacht with twin lee boards. Carvel planked of African oak on solid oak fashioned frames. Iron spike fastened. Fitted with a teak deck laid fore and aft caulked and payed."

He read through all the descriptions of rot and cracks twice, to rub it in. But then his eyes strayed over other parts of the survey which he had so far ignored.

It was true that nine planks in the hull needed replacing but the rest were in good shape. The stem had a crack but the transom was good. He wondered what a transom was and decided to look it up in the dictionary. Purely out of academic interest as he had no intention of going near a boat again.

The rudder was good. The stern gear was good. The deck was good. The grab rails were good. The forehatch and skylight were good. The hog, clamps and breast hooks were good. The space under the sole was good. The stern sheets were good. The iron-work was good. The mast and spars were good.

And so on. And so on.

"*Summary*: This vessel is a very pretty boat in generally

145

good condition and in our opinion well worth renovating and repairing."

He carefully folded up the report and put it back in the brown envelope. Of course he couldn't go back on his word. He had made a solemn promise to Thea and to himself. There was no question of trying to keep the *Swan*. All that was finished.

But on the other hand there was no point in being hasty. He had several thousand pounds invested in the *Swan* and he wanted to get as much back as possible. He owed it to them both. He mustn't do anything rash. There was obviously more to her than the first reading of the survey showed. There were a lot of good points about her. Hog, clamp and breast hooks for a start.

If he had some of the work done she would be much easier to sell. He was bound to get the money back. The least he could do was get an estimate. Of course he wouldn't go near her himself. He would do it all by telephone. It was one thing for the reformed smoker to pick up a cigarette packet. It was another thing to take out a cigarette and roll it between his fingers and ask what on earth he saw in smoking in the first place.

He didn't want to go near the *Swan*. He was finished with that silly daydream. A very pretty boat in generally good condition. Who cares?

❊ Chapter Thirteen ❊

Doreen was full of sympathy when Pax went back to the office. She gripped his arm with her fat fingers when he got out of the lift and steered him to his chair.

"Ooh, Mr Brown, you can walk much better than we all thought."

He exaggerated his limp and wished he had brought walking sticks. If Doreen thought there wasn't much wrong with him it would be all over the bank by lunchtime. He twisted his face into a stoic wince as he sat down.

She had made a special effort with her appearance. Her long mane of straggling black hair had been heaped on top of her head like an enormous worm cast. She had found a new shade of purple eyeshadow. She was dressed in a small pink marquee that stopped short at her impressive knees. Over her shoulders she had flung with contrived abandon a red check Arab head-cloth he had brought back for her from Bahrain. On her left breast was pinned an upside-down watch like nurses wear.

"Did someone give you a new watch, Doreen?"

"Ooh no. It was my mother's. It was lying round on the dressing table at home. I'll go and get you a nice cup of tea. And do you want an aspirin for the pain?"

She came back with his mug and a large brown paper bag which she put on the floor by his feet.

"Look what I found for you, Mr Brown. It's a get well present from me. For your poor legs."

With a flourish she whipped the paper bag off a footstool upholstered in gold dralon with red sequins embroidered into the brocade fringes. She pushed it in front of the file drawer of his desk. He sat looking at it, trying to think of something to say.

"You put your feet on it," she said, helpfully.

With his hands he lifted each leg in turn and deposited it on the stool. "Doreen, you shouldn't have. I'm very touched. I wish my wife was as considerate."

She bit her lip and fussed with her Hashemite gingham. "I know what it's like, Mr Brown. I too have suffered. I once had a riding accident and broke both my legs."

He tried to fit Doreen and a horse into the same mental image. He bit his lip before he could ask who fell off who. Before he could say anything else Doreen swept out of the room, overwhelmed by her own confession.

He launched into his work with unaccustomed vigour. It was not that he was refreshed by his absence and his good resolutions. His efforts were dedicated to scouring the bank for any evidence that he had recommended opening accounts for Collectors' Coins Limited. He began by asking Doreen for his own personal memo files and her own correspondence copy files.

"But you've never gone through those before, Mr Brown. You're the auditor."

"*Quis custodiat custodies*, Doreen. We must practise what we preach."

He sprang a surprise audit on the files of the credit department, the cash department, the customer services department. He even looked at Gilbert Pinkish's files after he had made sure he was out for the day. These were the thinnest of all. Replies to lunch and cocktail invitations and invoices to canary fanciers' magazines, charged to the bank. When he was asked what was going on he raised an eyebrow and muttered about the Auditor General and the Clerical Systems Procedure Manual. Finally he scanned the computerised files and ledgers of the entire bank.

"I'll be in the Terminal Room, Doreen."

He didn't like that phrase. It reminded him of the little rooms at the end of cancer wards or the unspoken chores of the Battersea Dog's Home.

"You mustn't work too hard, Mr Brown. First day back. You'll tire yourself. Would you like one of my pick-me-ups?"

148

She rummaged in the pharmacopoeia of herbal remedies she kept in the bottom drawer of her desk. He graciously accepted a concoction of arsenic and sunflower seed and carob disguised as a dog's chocolate drop. He hoped this would satisfy her protective urges before she made a grab for his pulse and squinted at her upside down watch.

"You haven't lost something, have you Mr Brown? I know it's not for me to say, but I don't ever remember you being so thorough. Are you looking for something special? Perhaps I can help. There may have been something while you were away. Why don't you tell me?"

Oh shit. She suspected something. She was right. There could be something he had overlooked. But there was no way he could tell her what he was looking for. It would be all over the City by the middle of next week. He laughed a shrill nervous laugh that was meant to be a deprecating chuckle.

"I'll be in the Terminal Room, Doreen," he said as firmly as he could.

He was still worried that he had overlooked something. Was there some little paper, some note on a record card that would lead back to him? He waited for the police to call. Helping them with their inquiries. He was a relative, he needed money, he'd spent all his savings on a boat. What better motive, Milud? Had it not been for his alert and public spirited secretary . . .

"Thanks for all your help, Doreen. You know, I think your pick-me-up worked. I don't know what I'd do without you. And that's such a pretty dress."

Pax invited Nick to lunch at a discreet little restaurant he knew on the fringe of the City. This part of town was for the small fry, the scavengers who followed the sharks that cruised in the world's largest pool of financial expertise. Office supplies. Twenty-four hour printers. Rubber stamp manufacturers. Seedy restaurants.

"Used to come here for a read in the old days. Made a change from the lavatory."

Pax spoke wistfully, as though the carefree days when he

149

could sneak off with a book were gone. He poured them some water out of a chipped carafe. Nick looked round doubtfully. The moulting flock wallpaper looked as if it had taken on a life of its own, feeding on the scraps. The linoleum floor had died long ago. The only other patron was an old man in an ancient black overcoat, now green. He probably wore it all day in his grimy, unheated office, shuffling tattered invoices.

"*Vaut le détour*, certainly,' he said. He didn't have the usual meaning in mind.

"I thought we could have a quiet chat about, you know, the coins business and so on," said Pax.

Nick allowed a knowing smile to spread over his face. He started to put his elbows on the table, saw the state of the table cloth and changed his mind. "So that's it. I wondered why we were being so secretive. The thought had crossed your mind, purely *en passant*, that my brilliant and expensive defence lawyers were going to bring up at the Old Bailey the complicity of a certain international banker and financial genius. Am I right?"

Pax lapsed into a shifty silence while the waitress waddled over to their table with two plates of "Stroganoff". She was a large woman with a round face and ham-like hands covered with eczema from washing up. She plonked the plates on the table.

"Ah. The *plat du jour*. Which *jour* did they have in mind, do you think? Last Wednesday?"

"I did wonder, Nick. I mean I wasn't worried. I just wanted to make sure."

He hid his awkwardness by stabbing into his meal. It looked like the inside of a frozen steak and kidney pie. Out of courtesy Nick picked up his fork and toyed with a gobbet.

"Have no fear, Pax. I haven't mentioned a word. Not a dicky bird, old boy."

Pax concealed a sigh of relief and tucked into his stroganoff. Nick watched with amazement while he cleared his plate of the reconstituted soyabean and the nameless plasma in which it floated. But then, Pax liked baked beans and fish fingers too.

"I was only thinking of Thea and the children."

150

The waitress waddled over, brandishing a dog-eared, brown-stained menu card. She threw Pax's empty plate on top of Nick's with a squelch and scooped up the unused cutlery.

"Sweet, dearies?"

Pax chose treacle tart. Nick opted for cheddar cheese on condition it was an individual portion still in the manufacturer's wrapper.

"You're very lucky to have a family to think about, old boy. Nice home. Steady job. Sometimes wish I had."

Pax took out of his mouth the treacly spoon that he had been sucking upside down and looked at Nick in surprise. This was a most uncharacteristic sentiment. The prospect of the trial must be disturbing him.

"But Nick. You have a wonderful life. Your own boss. No ties. Deals. Projects. Excitement. Annabel. Most men I know would give their eye-teeth to live with a girl like Annabel."

Nick shook his head and gazed at the future in the chipped carafe. "Annabel. I don't know what I'm going to do about her. She's driving me mad. I've never been so frustrated."

Pax said nothing. He waited agog, neglecting his treacle tart.

"It's her bloody ears. Do you know she spends two hours a day bathing them and massaging them and oiling them. It's an obsession. She walks round the house with this big pair of pink fluffy ear-muffs. And the worst thing is she won't let me near them. I can do anything I like with the rest of her body. Believe me, anything. And I do. But she won't let me touch her ears." He scrabbled unsuccessfully with the little red strip on his cheese wrapper. "I lie awake thinking about them, Pax. The things I've imagined doing with them. You wouldn't believe."

"Forbidden fruit, eh?"

"I don't know what I'll do if I get sent down. I couldn't bear it if she left me. Before I've, well, you know what it's like."

"You think you've got problems? I mean, Thea won't even let me . . ."

"Please, Pax. That's my sister you're talking about."

"Sorry. You were saying."

Nick threw the unopened cheese on the table. "I just don't know how I'd ever keep her."

151

Pax waved to the waitress and reached inside his wallet pocket. He brought out his luncheon vouchers, wrapped with a rubber band, and started counting them out on the table-cloth.

"You mustn't worry, Nick. We'll all stick by you. And so will Annabel, I'm sure."

"Thanks, old boy. And thanks for lunch. I needed cheering up."

Out in the street they shook hands. Pax headed in the direction of his office until he was out of sight and then doubled back in the direction of the library. He needed something to take his mind off Annabel's ears and her nose and her lips and the rest of her delicious person. Nick walked in the opposite direction until he too was out of sight and then doubled back in the direction of the City. He looked at his watch. There was still time for a spot of lunch.

Pax went to the trial. He decided it would look more suspicious if he did not go. Thea went and so did Annabel. She looked dressed for divorce in black silk with pink trimmings. He sat between them. Nick was dressed in dark suit, white shirt and what from a distance could have been an Old Etonian tie. He smiled at his family when he came into the dock. Pax trembled when the charges were read out and Thea had to hold his hand.

Nick was sentenced to three years in prison for conspiracy to defraud Her Majesty's Government of the value added tax on a million pounds' worth of gold coins. His accomplices had been arrested on their return to France and were about to stand trial for evasion of exchange control. With the political pendulum in Mitterrand's France swinging away from Liberty towards Equality, the rich were trying to get as much as they could out of the country before it was Fraternally redistributed.

In giving sentence the judge echoed the regrets of the police that other accomplices in Great Britain had not been apprehended. The police had not discovered the method by which the proceeds of the sale were to be collected and transferred to his French accomplices. They were still trying to trace the bank

152

accounts he must have opened.

Pax felt faint. Thea winced as he squeezed her hand tighter.

The judge noted there was no evidence of theft. There was every intention of paying the original sellers of the coins. There was enough profit in buying them in France at below market, selling them in the United Kingdom without VAT and charging a commission for the transfer of funds to Switzerland. The gross profit was nearly fifty per cent.

The judge also noted the accused's evident regret. He had seldom seen such sincerity, humility and a desire to reform combined with an unchanged plea of Not Guilty. But there was also the question of the missing money. Apart from the bag of coins found in the accused's power boat there was still almost a million pounds in gold coins unaccounted for.

A plea of Guilty and the surrender of the missing money might have obtained a more lenient sentence. As it was, there was still time for a change of heart and the recovery of the coins to be taken into account when parole and remission were being considered.

After sentencing, Pax went down with Thea and Annabel to the basement under the court. It was divided by wire mesh and metal bars into narrow cubicles where the day's bag was collected. At the end of the afternoon the prison van came for them. One by one the convicted men came down and sat on narrow benches in the cages with their knees on their elbows, staring at the floor. The first-timers tried to get used to the idea that they could not just get up and leave when they felt like it. The old-timers settled back into passive compliance with the system.

Annabel saw him first. She was let into his cage. She was very composed as they talked together in whispers, sitting side by side on the narrow bench as though they were in church. When she left she kissed him on the lips, leaving a red smudge.

Thea was next. She too put on a brave face, like someone at a funeral, promising to explain everything to their parents in such a way that they would not die of shame. She kissed him on the forehead. That's where you kiss dead people, thought Pax. Then it was his turn to go inside the cage.

"Cheer up, old son. It's not the end of the world. It really isn't so bad after you've got over the initial shock. The first week and the last week are the worst."

This was Nick talking. Pax looked even glummer than the prisoners. He nodded and forced a smile. This was even worse than visiting people in hospital, longing for the bell to go.

"I've gone through the worst bit already. That was when I was on remand before they gave me bail. I was in a tiny cell with a child rapist and a stockbroker who'd chopped up his in-laws with a machete. I didn't sleep a wink for three nights in a row. Three men and a chamber pot locked up together for twenty-two hours a day. No wonder I was constipated."

"That's terrible," murmured Pax, trying to drag himself out of his melancholy for Nick's sake.

"You know the only thing I'm not looking forward to?" Nick whispered so that Pax had to bend his head down towards him. "The medical. I hate people looking up my bottom. Must be something from childhood. They search you for drugs up there, you know. Once that's over I shall be all right."

Pax was lost for words. What do you say to a man who doesn't like people looking up his bottom? "You stood up to them in court," was the best he could do.

Nick formed his face into the expression of penitence and injured innocence that had so impressed the judge.

"The only thing I really objected to was the way the police blackened my character. I had half a mind to change my plea to Guilty but I wouldn't give them the satisfaction. If I'd done that they would have pestered me about the money."

"Three years seems a lot just for stealing money from the government. It's not that you did anything really wrong."

"I should have raped a couple of little girls. You only get a year for that. Evading value added tax is much more serious. Still, with remission for good conduct and parole I shall be out in twelve months."

"That's wonderful. It will fly by."

"I'll just have a couple of weeks in Brixton or Wandsworth or somewhere like that. Then I'll be sent to an open prison.

You read books and play football all day. I might even write a book. It's no worse than boarding school. So listen, Pax, you buy a calendar and a pencil and tick off the days for me. And when I'm out we'll take our little trip down the river. I'm counting on it."

"The *Swan* will have rotted away by the time you get out. She's in a terminal condition even now."

"Nonsense. You'll have hardly finished the varnishing."

"I'm getting rid of her. I'm serious this time. I promised Thea I would put her in *Exchange and Mart* just as soon as they finished repairing the hull."

"You mustn't do that. For my sake."

"Why for your sake?"

"I'm going to have a lot of time on my hands in the next few months. A lot of time staring out of the window at the grey sky. A lot of time reading old library books and sewing mailbags. I'll wonder what you and Thea and Annabel and my friends are doing. I shall hope they know what to do with the freedom they have. I shall hope they aren't frittering away their lives dreaming they were somewhere else, like me. When they lock me in my cell for the night at six o'clock I shall think of you and the *Swan*."

"But that's what I used to think at the office. I sat in front of the ledgers and files and thought that someone somewhere else was doing something interesting like windsurfing or collecting butterflies or lying on a sofa reading a book. And then I bought a vintage wooden sailing boat with a carved rudder and brown sails so I could sail away into the sunset. And what do I do? I sit and worry about the rot and the leaks and how I'm ever going to get out of the dock."

"That's because you're a romantic. What makes people romantic is the desire to be somewhere else."

"In that case prisons and banks are full of romantics."

The warder ambled over and pointed his keys of office at Pax as a signal that his time was up.

"Look after yourself," said Pax, resisting the impulse to kiss him on the forehead.

"Plenty of people to do that for me, old boy. Take care of

Annabel for me. Between you and me I think this whole business has been a bit of a shock for her. I'm not sure how she'll feel about me when I get out."

Pax promised to look after her. They shook hands. He walked back through the lines of cages trying to keep his eyes off the expressionless faces of the other prisoners. At the foot of the stairs leading up from the basement he looked back at Nick. He sat with his elbows on his knees, staring at the floor.

As they walked back to the car park from the law courts Pax remembered Nick's last wish and put his arm round Annabel. When they got to the car she kissed him lightly on the lips. Thea didn't seem to notice.

Chapter Fourteen

The simple answer was that he needed money. In the long term he needed enough for a new house, a boat and two private educations. In the short term he needed enough to pay for the necessary repairs on the *Swan*.

First he had to buy time. He went to the local lending library where they kept back numbers of *Exchange and Mart* and *Yachting World*. He found the advertisements for the *Swan* that Harry the stick insect man had put in. He hesitated between stealing the entire magazines and ripping out the relevant pages. In the end he opted for wholesale theft and a promise to bring them back as soon as he had shown Thea.

"Look darling. I've put the ads in the paper for the *Swan*. She'll be gone by next week."

As a second demonstration of good faith he went to the estate agent himself and asked to be put on their list again. More brown envelopes began plopping on the door mat with the brown envelopes from the Gas and the Electricity and the Water and the Boat Insurance and the Marina Office. Normal antipathy towards brown envelopes turned into loathing.

He started a standing order with the football pools. He checked to see if he still had their premium bond certificates. He calculated the surrender value of his life insurance and decided that even their full redemption value at maturity wouldn't pay for more than a three piece suite and a fortnight in Spain.

With a heavy heart he scoured the job advertisements in the Thursday *Financial Times*. The jobs he was qualified for paid no more than he was earning already. They certainly wouldn't support his chosen lifestyle. He would also have to work a lot harder than he did now. The advantage about staying in the same job for some time is that you get to know the minimum amount you have to do in order to survive. If you move you have to do everything until you find out what is really important and what can be left to fester in the in-tray.

He replied to a few of the advertisements for jobs he was not qualified for but which paid a lot more. A Midlands engineering firm wanted a Finance Director. A management consultancy was looking for Senior Associates. An international bank wanted a Corporate Finance Executive. He would let the forcefulness of his personality, the freshness and vitality of his ideas, the persuasive fluency of his arguments substitute for lack of experience and qualifications. In those precious minutes in bed in the morning before getting up late for work he practised mentally his interview style. He would captivate them all.

The euphoria of being a Finance Director or a Corporate Consultant lasted until coffee time. He would drive round in a BMW, wear a mohair suit, fly first class. But then reality nudged itself into the picture. He would have to work much harder for a start. No more pottering off to the loo with a spurious file under his arm and a paperback in his pocket for a good read. No more dummy appointments so he could go to the cinema in the afternoon. No more leisurely lunch hours to wander round the dock on a sunny day.

It was all very well telling your boss that you wanted to be evaluated and rewarded by your results. In his experience when pay rises came round that was the last thing he wanted to be rewarded by. And when would he have time to spend on the boat that he was working so hard to afford? The whole point was to work less hard and get more money for it.

It was nevertheless a blow to his pride that the recruiters felt the same way. No-one wanted to interview him.

Gilbert Pinkish flicked a grain of canary seed off his sleeve and looked at Pax over the top of his half-moon spectacles.

"You want a personal loan to repair a vintage wooden boat?" he repeated incredulously. "But you could buy a brand new one for that amount of money."

158

Pax took a deep breath. He had come to the conclusion that the only solution to the short term problem of making the *Swan* seaworthy was to borrow the money for the repairs. He had no great confidence in Nick's Bigger Fool Theory. He reckoned that in her present state nobody would buy her.

The alternative was that by the time she was on the water again Thea would have seen the light and learned to love her. It was not impossible, just as it was not impossible that he would land a part-time Finance Director's job at twice his present salary.

But who was going to lend him the money? First he made a thorough analysis and cash flow projection of his personal financial situation. He found that, taking the market value of the house into consideration and balancing out his assets and liabilities, he was worth exactly zero. Because of life insurance he was worth a few thousand pounds dead but the precondition was for the moment unacceptable.

He read the advertisements in the newspaper for unsecured loans through the post, no questions asked. But the limit was five hundred pounds. He walked into a couple of finance companies but they wanted a second mortgage. This was impossible as the house was in joint names. He could always forge her signature but the risk was too great. He did not want to sleep in the playroom again.

The most obvious step was to ask his own bank but how was he to explain? They always wanted to know the purpose of the loan. The bank would give unsecured personal loans to buy a car or furnish a house but they always wanted a receipt. Pax knew because he had to audit them. He knew all about the Chief Dealer's yellow and black leather three-piece suite, the Senior Cashier's *Dolce Vita* bathroom with simulated gold-plated taps, Gilbert Pinkish's centrally heated and air conditioned purpose-built canary-breeding shed.

He thought of forging a receipt. Or buying something conventional like a chrome and brass dining table and matching chairs and then returning the goods to get his money back. It wasn't worth the risk. For ten times the amount he wanted dishonesty was possibly worth it. For relatively small amounts

159

honesty was the best policy. Still, he couldn't imagine Gilbert Pinkish taking a rosy view of employees buying dilapidated boats.

He was right.

"I didn't know you were a sailor, Pax."

"A well-kept secret, sir. A little bit of luffing and jibing on the side, you know."

He decided on a tone of man-to-man bonhomie rather than the abject supplication he really felt. He had a couple of mildly dirty jokes up his sleeve if necessary. But Gilbert did not rise to the bait. This was serious talk about money. The life-blood of human existence.

"That's a lot of money," Gilbert said gratuitously.

"Depends who you are. Small change for a lot of people. Arab sheiks, dope peddlers, bank managers . . ."

Gilbert pursed his lips. Pax read the alarm signal. Never be flippant about money to a bank manager. Out of the window he could see the blank stone wall of the Bank of England.

"Seriously though sir, this is a very viable proposition. The boat has been in the family for generations. Museums all over the country would love to get their hands on it. It's got oak carvings from the *Fighting Temeraire*. But we've decided to sell it. You see, Gilbert, it just isn't prudent to commit to the expense of maintaining her. And with my commitment to my career and family, I just don't have the time. So I need to have her thoroughly overhauled before I sell her. Take a look at the survey and valuation."

He handed over the desk a photocopy of the surveyor's report on the *Swan*. He had spent an hour the previous evening after his secretary had gone home experimenting with the different golf-ball heads of her typewriter. He had found a type that almost exactly matched the type on the survey. This enabled him to add to the bottom of the report a valuation approximately five times what he had paid for the boat.

His heart pounded when he saw Gilbert reading it. His palms grew moist, his collar tight. His future and the future of the *Swan* depended on it. Gilbert pursed his lips again, leaned back in his chair, and put his thumbs in his waistcoat pockets.

"Well, Pax, it's very unusual but I suppose we can go along with it. We'll lend you the money for six months. That should give you time to sell it. And let us see the boat-builder's estimate."

"That's wonderful. Thank you very much."

"And what are you going to do with your spare time when you've sold it? Buy another one?"

"No fear, Gilbert. Actually, I was thinking about canaries. What do you think of Norwich Fancies . . .?"

Pax took a block of frozen spinach out of the freezer compartment and brushed the frost off the instructions.

"I hope Nick likes the open prison. At least he's out in the country. It was a scandal keeping him in Brixton for a month. You'd be prosecuted for keeping animals like that."

Thea stabbed the eye out of a potato with excessive vigour. She had read an article about the importance of Sharing In Human Relationships. They were jostling each other in the narrow kitchen preparing Sunday lunch together.

"Of course it's terrible. It's meant to be. We all talk as if he'd won a fortnight at Butlin's. He's been sent to prison for breaking the law of the land. It's a punishment."

"But he's your own brother. You can't wish that on your own family."

"He didn't think of that when he got into his mess. What about Mummy and Daddy? We still haven't told them. Nick says he's going to tell them himself but he's too ashamed."

"I hope he doesn't. They'd only come back from Spain and stay with us."

"I think we're wrong to try and take it in our stride. Anyone would think he'd just gone into hospital. What are we coming to when it's considered normal to break the law?"

"What do you want us to do? Disown him? Move away from the neighbourhood?" He was touching on a sensitive subject. Romona Terrace was still for sale. "What if it was me in prison? What would you think then?"

"That's a silly question."

Pax cut open the packet of frozen spinach with a breadknife.

161

The question was not totally silly. As he considered his worsening financial situation the only solutions seemed to be criminal ones. It was only a question of time before she found out that he had borrowed from the bank to pay for the repairs on the *Swan*. And that the advertisements in *Exchange and Mart* were a year old. Then the fat would be in the fire. He needed a lot of money very quickly.

"What would you tell the children if I did go to prison?"

They had told the children that Uncle Nick had gone to Australia. They had discussed long into the night what they would tell them. It had been easier to tell them about Sex and Death. Where Daddy puts his willy and what happens when the tired old body runs down like your little clockwork mouse, dear, seemed simpler and less emotional than the topic of Uncle Nick in the slammer. They would have asked tiresome questions in public and bragged about it in the playground.

"Well my mummy's brother is in prison for robbery and murder and treason so there. Harly larly loo la."

. . . After all it's only a white collar crime and it's not even really criminal, just breaking the rules a bit and no-one got hurt did they, if he'd mugged an old lady in the street he'd have only got six months and if the police spent their time on things that really mattered everyone would be much better off, I mean it wasn't even the sort of thing where innocent people lose their life savings and in any case smuggling is traditional isn't it, part of the heritage and it's such a scandal to put basically honest people in with murderers and burglars and real criminals, that's how you breed them . . .

It's a lot easier to be broad-minded when other people's relatives are doing porridge. But then, at the stroke of midnight, they hit on the answer. We are honest and broad-minded and we don't mind the children knowing about it but what about Uncle Nick? He is the person we have to think of. He might be embarrassed if he thought the children knew. For the sake of Nick's feelings we'll make up a story.

Pax suspected that Uncle Nick couldn't care less if the children knew but it was a good excuse for not telling the children so they wouldn't blab it round the neighbourhood.

"Wake up, Pax. What are you dreaming about? Annabel's here."

He had watched the yellow Jaguar turn into the Square and stop in the parking spaces on the other side. She had combed her hair in the driving mirror. When she got out of the car her red dress rode up to the top of her thighs. She slammed the door with a flourish and flounced across the grass in the middle of the Square, swinging her handbag.

He was still holding the knife in one hand and the packet of frozen spinach in the other. He couldn't feel his fingers and green juice was dribbling down his wrist. It looked like gangrene on top of frostbite. While Thea went downstairs to open the door he dropped the brick into boiling water and covered the saucepan with a plate. He tousled his hair with his fingers into what he hoped would be an attractively carefree coiffure and teased a provocative little kiss-curl over his fore-head.

The red dress was low-cut and she wasn't wearing a bra. Instinctively he looked for the faint line around her hips that would show if she was wearing pants. She was, but no tights. She swept her blonde hair away from her face and threw her handbag onto the sofa.

"I need a drink, Pax. A large gin and tonic. Prison gives you a thirst. All those randy men. I'm surprised they don't all pole-vault over the walls. They wouldn't need any equipment."

"I didn't know they had visiting on a Sunday morning," said Thea in a tone of voice that heralded the immediate collapse of Law and Order.

"If you go regularly to Church a relative can come too, once a month. He's put himself down as a Catholic. They have the shortest service."

"That must be very uplifting for you both," said Thea. She resented Nick's choice of Annabel as principal relative. It denied her the opportunity to overcome her disapproval of her brother in order to stick by family. They weren't even married. Annabel was down as his common-law wife. "So tell us how he is, apart from his conversion to the faith."

"The poor lamb's bleating like the black sheep he is. He's

163

lost weight so something good may come of it. He's cross because he wanted a job in the library. Instead they make him spend all day in a workshop painting garden gnomes. He says it's a punishment for when he was an undergraduate and collected two hundred of them from the gardens of Finchley and sent them to the Swiss Embassy, cash on delivery. With a petition asking for political asylum. He says your crimes always catch up on you."

"Perhaps he's learning something," said Pax, searching for a moral.

"That's funny, he was never an undergraduate. He must have meant when he was articled for a year to a chartered accountant friend of Daddy's. But the story about the gnomes is true. There was a terrible row."

Pax saw a frown appear on Annabel's smooth brow. What had Nick told her about his student career? A Double First? A Blue? She resisted the urge to ask about his murky past and continued telling them about his murkier present.

"When he's not painting gnomes he helps with the weeding in the garden or goes to bridge lessons or plays snooker. They all have to do something."

"It's like a holiday camp," said Thea.

"You're wrong. It's a subtle form of mental torture," said Pax. "They find out all the things you hate doing at home and make you do them in prison. When I go to prison they'll make me play bridge and weed the garden and clean the warders' cars and watch the Royal Wedding over and over again on video. What a deterrent. Let me mope in a whitewashed cell any day."

"What do you mean, when you go to prison?" asked Annabel.

"I have decided to embezzle a large amount from the bank. I ought to warn you all that there is a great chance of my getting caught and spending the rest of my rapidly fading prime painting gnomes with Nick."

"Why are you going to rob the bank?" asked Annabel with more seriousness than he thought his remarks deserved.

"Because I desperately need the money. I shall have to flee to

164

a nice warm country like Brazil and anyone who likes can come with me."

"Spain is nicer and there's no extradition treaty," said Annabel in a matter-of-fact voice.

"That would be nice for Mummy and Daddy. They'd see more of the children," said Thea, putting a damper on the whole project.

Annabel ostentatiously swirled the shrunken ice cubes in the bottom of her empty glass. Thea asked Pax to get the meat out of the oven while she went out into the Square to find the children. When she had gone, Annabel put her hand on Pax's arm.

"Nick would very much like to see you. Can you come with me to visit him next week? Visiting is on Wednesday."

He led the way into the kitchen walking crabwise so that she wouldn't take her hand away.

"There's something on his mind he won't tell me about. I do wish you'd come. I could pick you up at the office in my car and we could drive down into the country together. Then we could have tea or something."

Or something. He felt a tightening in the knees and the crotch and the throat. "I'd like that very much. Poor Nick," he heard himself say.

He took her glass and knelt down on the floor in front of the freezer compartment. He rummaged among the frozen peas for the second ice tray. As usual it was frozen to the shelf at the back. She stood close to him, her knees and thighs touching his shoulder. They were warm and firm and soft through the thin cotton of her red dress and his shirt.

"What's that green stuff in your hair? It looks like spinach."

She began to pick at his tousled coiffure with her long, painted fingernails, pricking his scalp and gently tugging at his hair, grooming him like a monkey after fleas. He pretended that the icy tray was stuck fast so that he wouldn't have to stand up. Her bare legs were smooth and tanned, unmarked by spidery veins and hairy stubble. Her toenails were painted orange.

Forgetting his wife coming up the stairs, his children in the

165

hall, his brother-in-law languishing in jail, he abandoned the icy tray and the frozen peas and turned to bury his face in her lap. At the same time he slid his hands from the back of her knees up under her dress towards her bottom.

He was rewarded by a sharp intake of breath, a kind of reverse scream, a violent tug on his hair that brought tears to his eyes and the cry of Thea as Annabel did a standing jump backwards and landed with her high-heeled sandals on Thea's feet.

Annabel attended to Thea as she lay on the sofa with cold compresses on her ankles while Pax dished up lunch in the kitchen. He was angry with himself for making an advance at such a stupid moment. He was angry with Annabel for reacting so violently. He was angry with Thea for coming back into the kitchen. Above all he was angry that he had so completely misjudged Annabel's feelings for him. Instead of falling about his neck with strangled cries of passion she had jumped as if a mouse had run up her skirt.

In the circumstances it was just as well that Thea had not walked into the kitchen to do the mint sauce and found a tangled knot of limbs and panting bodies on the floor, half of them belonging to her husband, but it was still a disappointment.

Professional Virgins. That's what they used to call girls who kissed you on the ear when they met you and stroked your scalp and brushed their bodies against yours and made big eyes and when you thought it was time to cut the cackle and get down to business slipped out of reach of your clutching hands and slavering lips and told you to pull yourself together.

Or was she making fun of him? Did she find it amusing to flirt with this poor failure of a man, stuck in a little suburban house with an unhappy wife and a dead-end job and a leaking hulk in Saint Katherine's Dock? Did she like to see him squirm and wallow in his own inadequacy? She and Nick probably giggled about him during visiting. Poor old Pax.

He had to explain to her. He had to explain that he didn't want to have a glamorous job and a lovely family and a big house and a yacht and a mistress. He didn't want that sort of

166

success, even if there was the remotest chance of his achieving it. In fact he wanted to escape from all that, escape from a world where all that sort of thing was prized. "Tosh," she would say, "you want those things like everyone else but you want them on the cheap. Champagne for beer money."

Annabel came into the kitchen for more cold water for Thea's bandages. He avoided her eyes. The truth was that she didn't find him attractive.

"Listen, Annabel," he whispered, "I'm sorry about what happened just now. I got carried away. I didn't want to offend you. Will you forget all about it?"

"Certainly not. But the next time you put your hands up my skirt could you make sure they haven't been dabbling in the ice box first? It was like being groped by Frosty the Snowman."

Lewis the boat-builder telephoned Pax at the bank to say that the *Swan* was ready for the water. High tide was at eight the next morning which would be a good time to float her off the slipway and take her back up to Saint Katherine's Dock. One of his lads would ride up with him if he liked to help him get in and out of the lock.

Pax did like. He hoped that the lad would know how to start the engine, work the tiller, get through the lock and tie up alongside. Lewis had towed the *Swan* down to his slipway opposite Greenwich while his legs were still in plaster. Now Pax was going to take command for the first time and skipper her the four miles from Greenwich to the Tower. He hadn't the slightest idea what to do.

He ordered a minicab for six o'clock. He dressed in thick sweaters and jeans of a nautical blue and blundered around in the wardrobe for a blue wool hat that he wore when it snowed until Thea asked sleepily if there was a fire. He made sure he had his cheque book in his pocket.

He felt too sick to eat any breakfast. He opened the front door so that the cab driver would not wake the children by ringing the bell and sat in the hall cradling a cup of coffee. Was this how all captains felt when they took their first command?

The *Swan* was high out of the water, sitting on a metal cradle that ran up and down the concrete slipway. At the top end of the slip was an electric winch that hauled the laden cradle out of the water. She sat there like the yacht on his bedroom mantelpiece when he was a boy. It seemed a pity to put her in the water where the lovely curved lines of her hull would be lost from view.

Lewis pointed out where he had replaced the planks but as the hull was now covered in a thick coat of antifouling paint there was not much evidence of his work. Pax gave him his cheque – as much as he had given Harry – and they shook hands.

His crew was Jason. Lewis assured him that Jason was a dab hand at tying ropes round bollards.

Lewis held the ladder for them both while they climbed aboard. Pax moulded his face into an expression of seamanlike confidence and tried to suppress the what-the-hell-do-I-do-now sensations in his stomach. He squinted into the fuel tank but saw only the reflection of his own eye. He poked a screw-driver in and it came out dripping. Now what?

He connected up the batteries. He took the long oak tiller bar out of the cabin and slid it over the top of the rudder. He pushed the gear handle through its slot in the locker wall. He took out of his supermarket bag a can of Easi-Start, guaranteed to start any diesel engine with just one squirt into the air intake. Oh My God. Which is the air intake?

Lewis opened the wire gates into the river that kept out the flotsam. He went back to the winch and released the brake. The cradle with its precious burden moved down the slip into the yellow scum and bobbing rubbish of the Thames. He shouted to Pax to wait until he was clear of the crap before he started the engine. The problem with that precaution is that they would be cast adrift before they knew if the engine was going to start at all.

The cradle was fully submerged and still rolling down the slip when the *Swan* came alive. She floated up from the cradle, rocking in the wash of the tide. She tugged at the mooring ropes impatiently. She was like the Sleeping Beauty waking from a hundred year sleep. Lewis shouted at Jason who bestirred himself to fumble with the lashings that held the boat to the cradle on either side. He gave a push and she drifted clear, out through the scum to the middle of the river. The tide was still rising and she was carried upstream by the current, wallowing broadside.

Fighting down his rising panic Pax opened the engine locker and sprayed Easi-Start indiscriminately over the top of the engine, praying that a whiff of the vapour would find the air intake. It found his own air intake. Coughing and retching he dropped the lid of the engine locker with a bang and turned the starter key.

This was the moment for the worst to happen, for the premonitions of his accident-prone imagination to come true. It was the moment for the Easi-Start vapour to explode, for the engine not to start at all, for the wake of a passing tanker to pitch Jason overboard, for the rudder to fall off, for the discovery that Lewis had left the seacocks open. None of these things happened. Instead the unexpected came to pass. The engine started sweetly on the first turn of the key, the *Swan* nosed around at the touch of the tiller, and without further incident they began the voyage from Greenwich to Saint Katherine's.

It would be an exaggeration to say that Pax relaxed but his immediate panic was replaced by a less obtrusive anxiety. She rolled more than he expected, having no keel to steady her. He clung tightly to the boom when they passed through the wash of passing craft and he wondered what it would be like in real waves. She was lower in the water than had been apparent in the dock and the cockpit would surely be swamped in a heavy sea. The engine was loud and smoky and its sound varied disconcertingly, sometimes racing as the propeller came close to the surface of the water and then settling down again.

If he sat down in the cockpit he could not see where he was going. All he got was a view of the cabin door. He stood up on the back seat of the cockpit just in front of the X-shaped cradle that supported the end of the boom. He stooped to hold the tiller until he noticed that she had a natural tendency to turn to the left like a car with unbalanced wheels. This meant that he

169

could let the tiller push up against his legs to hold her steady on course. This left his hands free to hold the boom.

The sun came out as they passed Greenwich. It picked out the white marble of the Naval College. The elegant windows looked out at him and he held himself erect, tempted to call his lolling crew to attention. Next to the College the *Cutty Sark*, home and dry from the Australia run, reared its tall and slender masts. In her working days as a clipper she had often made the journey that the *Swan* was making now up to the Pool of London. On the hill above the College was the Royal Observatory which had set the time of many a ship's chronometer before it set out across the world. The Observatory drew the world's meridian and Pax sailed his little ship across longitude zero from the Eastern Hemisphere to the West with the pride of crossing the Equator.

Puffing out his chest he turned his back on Greenwich and forged through the glistening gunmetal water in the direction of Tower Bridge. He could see the bridge on the horizon about a mile and a half away but the Thames takes a long loop south and another long loop north which made the journey about four miles. The scenery became depressing. Between Greenwich and the City of London is barren, deserted dockland. The dilapidated warehouses, empty yards, gaunt cranes waiting for cargos that rarely come soon lose their attraction unless you are a property developer or want to make a film about what to do after a nuclear attack.

There were no other craft on this part of the river. He was grateful for an empty stretch of water to practise turning the tiller. The only danger was from large chunks of driftwood, some of them massive beams as long as the *Swan*, lurking like mines for the unwary skipper to ram.

He had remembered the night before that he had no chart of the Thames. The coastguard safety leaflet says that you should always have a chart however short the journey. He brought the *A to Z Street Atlas* instead and hid it in his trouser pocket until he was out of sight of land. Whoever heard of an old sea-dog steering by the Pole Star and the *A to Z*? He took it out and read out loud the names of the landmarks.

170

Gallion's Reach and Bugsby's Reach. They were now in Limehouse Reach, heading past Deadman Dock to Greenland Dock. Russia Dock and Albion Dock and Lavender Dock. They passed Cuckold's Point and he wondered if Thea was up yet, getting the children breakfast. They motored past Shadwell and the River Police Station, its sweet little blue launches tethered like pedalos in a park. Pax thought of Nick undrowned in Southend and now painting gnomes in the Kent countryside.

He told himself that he was happy. He pointed out to himself the reflections on the rippling water, the sound of the lapping bows and the bubbling wake. He was master of his own vessel sailing watertight from Greenwich to the Pool of London where for centuries tea and coffee, ivory and spices had finished their wind-blown voyage half way across the world. The *Swan* beneath his feet was alive again at last, ready to turn seaward and take him to distant ports and foreign shores. The sun was in his eyes and the breeze was in his face. The oak tiller nudged his leg and in return he stroked the smooth varnish of the boom.

He sniffed the air. Above the smell of engine fumes and raw diesel and the murky river there was another scent, growing stronger as they reached the Tower. He thought that his imagination was playing tricks on him. He could smell spices in the air. He told himself to pull himself together. It was dangerous to mingle dreams and reality. You only smell spices in the air as the clove islands of Zanzibar heave in sight over the horizon or as you run the tail end of the monsoon from Cochin to Colombo. But the smell grew stronger and more evocative and mingled with the boat smells of the *Swan*.

"Cor, what a stink," said Jason. It was his first contribution to their historic passage. At least it indicated that Pax wasn't going mad. "It's the Pepper and Spice Mill at Wapping." He relapsed into his stupor on the foredeck.

Yes. He told himself he was happy. He told himself that he wanted to be nowhere else. He wanted to do nothing else. He could spend the rest of his life right here on the *Swan*. Out of the rat-race, free of the cares of career and house and responsibilities. If you don't like where you are, up anchor and away. This was the life. Free as a bird.

True, there were one or two little features of nautical life that he hadn't thought of before. For example, what do you *do* on a boat while you're sailing along? You had to keep your eyes open for driftwood and other dangers. You had to make sure you were on course. You couldn't read a book or sketch the scenery. It was all very relaxing but surely there was more to it? Although he was out in the fresh air it didn't seem very good exercise. He was already feeling stiff and restless. You couldn't get out for a walk and stretch your legs. He was trapped in a space half the size of his living room at home.

Of course he was happy. He told himself so. But he could not suppress the insidious thought, the creeping suspicion that he was beginning to get a little bored. And what would it be like when there was nothing but the open sea to look at? Of course you had to trim the sails and work out your position and take sightings of the sun but you couldn't be doing that all the time. In the old days you sat round singing sea shanties and putting ships in bottles but even that would pall after a few days.

Before these gnawing doubts had time to take root they were outside the lock gates to Saint Katherine's Dock. Tower Bridge loomed over them. The giant Union Jack on the Tower of London rippled and cracked bravely in the breeze. The Tower Hotel looked down on the *Swan* from countless dark windows. How many of them concealed a tourist looking down to see what kind of job he would make of getting the *Swan* into the lock? He dropped one hand from the boom and forced his body into a nonchalant pose while the *Swan* steered herself in a wide circle until the lock-keeper noticed them and opened the gates.

Now he had to stand on the floor of the cockpit where he could reach the gear lever that stuck out of the cockpit wall. He found that he could control it with his left foot without bending down – a forward punt or a backward heel. He practised the manoeuvre a few times to get the hang of it. He hoped it would impress the brightly-coloured tourists who, even at this early hour, were beginning to line the sides of the lock.

172

It was like a new pilot's first solo landing. His heart knocking and his knees trembling and his stomach tied in a knot he inched the *Swan* through the narrow lock gates. He pushed the tiller over and backheeled the gear lever so she drifted sideways to the mooring bollards. She came sweetly to rest with barely a squeak from the white rubber fenders hanging over the side. Jason scrabbled out to throw the bow rope and the stern rope over the bollards.

"Don't tie them, Jason. If you do we'll be left dangling like a lifeboat when the water goes down. Very embarrassing."

Jason glowered at him. But Pax's instructions had been for the benefit of the spectators. He watched them out of the corner of his eye and tried to tune in to their flattering comments. He felt very proud of himself.

As soon as the water was down and the gates open he gave a clipped, seamanlike order for Jason to release the mooring ropes. Casually he kicked the gear lever, eased the throttle forwards and with a jaunty wave to the lock-master in his control box coaxed the *Swan* into the crowded marina. He had nearly done it. He was nearly there.

The *Swan*'s berth was on the other side of the dock through a maze of narrow channels between the other boats. Everything went right. He swung the tiller at the right time, kicked her into neutral, into forward, into reverse. He impressed himself with his timing and skill. This was a piece of cake.

They came to the channel where the *Swan*'s berth was. It was at the end, on the right. The channel was narrow and he had to make a sharp right-angled turn to fetch up alongside a forty foot catamaran. Facing him at the end of the channel not ten yards from where he would have to turn was a long, expensive sloop. Its white paint and new varnish sparkled like a newly-minted coin and its sails were crisp and fresh like a newly-printed twenty-pound note. On board, a tanned, fit-looking man in his forties stopped fiddling with a sail cover and stood up to watch the pretty little *Swan* heading straight at him. Pax gave him a jaunty wave and kicked the gear lever straight out of its socket onto the floor of the cockpit.

It was a memorable moment, as memorable as the timeless

instant just before the car you are driving hits a tree or the belay you are hanging from comes away in your hand or the Royal Doulton dish of Christmas turkey hits the dining room floor. The choice seemed stark. The *Swan* was accelerating down a narrow channel at ramming speed with no means of slowing down or turning round. The only uncertainty in the situation was whether he would choose to drive his bowsprit through the side of the catamaran on the right or the motor cruiser on the left or the sloop straight ahead. In that moment of clarity before disaster he noticed that she was called *Lucille*. Her skipper gazed with growing incredulity as the inevitable drew upon him.

Pax stood aside from the proceedings and with dispassionate interest watched himself struggle to extricate himself from the inevitable. He saw himself scrabble on the floor for the gear lever and try to shove the wrong end through the slot in the locker. He watched himself turn the lever round and stab at the slot with murderous despair. He watched the *Lucille* loom closer and her skipper jump out of the way of certain impalement. He turned his attention back to himself as the gear lever found its home and he slammed it into reverse. At the same time he saw himself lunge desperately at the throttle lever and push it full down. The engine roared and smoked and threw up a bubbling wake. He saw himself lose his balance and fall with his full weight onto the tiller.

The skipper of the *Lucille*, the owner of the catamaran peering anxiously through his porthole, the cowering Jason, the gaggle of passers-by on the dockside and above all Pax himself watched with varying degrees of astonishment and admiration as the bows of the *Swan* took a sharp right-angled turn scarcely a foot away from the side of the *Lucille*. The bubbling stern swung round and the *Swan* came to a dead halt in its mooring bay six inches from the side of the pontoon.

Pax kicked the gear into neutral and pulled back the throttle while Jason scampered to throw the mooring ropes round the stanchions as if trying to capture this remarkable feat for posterity before it escaped. Pax cut the fuel and sat back in the cockpit. His knees were trembling and sweat poured into his eyes and he thought he was going to faint. He pretended to tie his shoelace so he could put his head between his knees.

"Hey that was pretty close. Thought you were going to ram me. Pretty nifty though."

He was an Australian. Fearing his voice would come out in a nervous squeak Pax answered with a shrug, as if he did that kind of thing every day.

The owner of the catamaran came out onto the pontoon and walked round to where Pax was disconnecting the battery. Pax ignored him until he spoke, fearing a torrent of abuse. He was an American. "Gee, that was the sharpest piece of boat-handling I've seen in a long time. With all the Sunday Sailors you see around these days it's a pleasure to see a man who knows how to handle his boat."

"Thanks. It was nothing really. British seamanship you know."

Brimming with false modesty Pax went down into the cabin to change into his suit. It was half past ten. Time to go to the office. He had to remember to talk out of the side of his mouth. His excuse for being late was a dummy appointment with the dentist.

Still, even a day at the office couldn't spoil the achievements of the morning. He had embarked. The Voyage had begun.

❋ Chapter Fifteen ❋

Annabel arranged to pick Pax up from the bank at lunchtime. His diary recorded the Quarterly Luncheon of the Society of Overseas Bank Auditors, a non-existent function held by a non-existent organisation. It was not the first time that Pax had found his non-existent membership useful. It was followed by the monthly meeting of the Bankers' Association Operations Research Unit to hear a paper on the Operational Aspects of the European Currency Unit at the Barclays Bank Lombard Street Office. This was completely bona fide but his absence would not be noted. Indeed, his presence would have been noteworthy. In order to protect his alibi he asked Annabel to park the bright yellow Jaguar three blocks away and wait for him there.

It was a typical June day. The sky was a uniform shade of dark grey and Annabel had put the car heater on maximum. She was wearing a cream coloured wool dress that moulded itself to her thighs as she drove and rode up well above the knees. She wore white tights that made her legs look deathly pale, like legs of lamb in the butcher's, still wrapped in muslin. Although they looked unappetising he had difficulty in keeping his eyes off them, remembering the feel of her bottom ten days before.

Annabel was being brisk and businesslike. She wore little make-up with only a touch of green eye-shadow to emphasise her pallor. Her blonde hair was swept back behind her head. On the seat next to her was a smart executive briefcase in brown leather which she threw in the back as he got in. He tried to kiss her on the cheek but she gave him her hand to shake. He assumed that she was steeling herself for the weekly prison visit.

176

He was nervous about it himself. The etiquette books have no guidance for such occasions. What were they going to talk about? It was worse than hospital. At least there you could talk about the op and the person in the next bed who died in the night. In prisons, Annabel warned him, you're not supposed to talk about the trial or what the others are in for. He did not want to make Nick jealous by talking about life outside, although he was anxious to boast about his epic voyage from Greenwich to the Tower. He still basked in the glow of his memorable docking technique from which he was gradually expunging the accidental elements.

"What on earth can we talk about?" he asked as they idled in a traffic jam at the start of the Dover Road.

"This and that," said Annabel helpfully.

"Why did he ask to see me? You said he had something on his mind. I'm sure he doesn't want to hear about the quiet satisfaction of my law-abiding life."

"No idea. He didn't tell me anything."

The prospect of visiting Nick was distracting Pax from the main point of the outing which was to spend the afternoon in the country with Annabel. He had imagined several scenarios from strolling through fields of waving corn to paddling hand in hand along the beach to gazing into each other's eyes over pink gingham in a little village Tea Shoppe. Each scenario ended similarly in moans of unfettered passion, the missing element of which was where exactly this consummation was to take place.

Whenever he and Thea had tried to add a pastoral dimension to the early days of their romance they had been thwarted by razor-sharp stubble or stinging insects or inquisitive creatures of one sort or another. Like picnics, passion *al fresco* was infinitely more uncomfortable than the indoor variety. Unlike picnics it didn't seem to taste better outside. There were too many distractions. He took advantage of a suspected police speed-trap to look over his shoulder and size up the dimensions of the back seat of the Jaguar.

"What are you thinking about?" asked Annabel.

"You," said Pax, breathing deep and taking his courage in both hands.

"What about me?" she said, softly, taking her eyes off the road and looking at him with a mixture of coolness and mischief.

"What a good driver you are. Are we nearly there?" he said, breathing out with a sigh and letting courage dribble away through his fingers.

It was probably for the best. The fast lane of a motorway was no place for a declaration of adulterous passion, not if you wanted it to lead anywhere except a pile-up on the central reservation. He waited until they were parked in a lay-by on the road leading up to the prison, whiling away the twenty minutes before visiting time.

Again he breathed deeply and took his courage in his hands. He sidled to the edge of his seat and put his arm round her shoulders. He stroked her hair. Her businesslike facade began to crumble. She put her head on his shoulder and shivered. With his left hand he restarted the engine and turned the heater on to maximum. Still stroking her head he dabbled the fingers of his left hand in the warm air from the defrosting vents on top of the dashboard.

"Is it hard for you?" he asked tenderly.

"It's easier with someone like you to lean on," she said and snuggled as close to him as the gear lever allowed. It was time for action as well as eloquence.

"Oh Annabel," he said, putting his left hand on her knee and sliding it boldly up under her dress. She intercepted his hand with both of hers and pushed it firmly away.

"But I've been warming it. Honestly."

"It's not that. I just couldn't. Not before we go in and see him."

She lifted her head from his shoulder and kissed him on the cheek, leaving him in hope that after they came out she might feel differently.

Pax had expected a visiting room out of a James Cagney film — a barred room divided down the middle with a wire mesh

178

screen and eagle-eyed guards ready to smash their truncheons down on smuggled notes and cigarettes. Instead they were taken to the dining room. It was a new extension to the building and looked like a modern factory canteen. There were bright-blue carpet tiles on the floor, bright-yellow curtains on the windows and bright-red Formica on the tables. The walls were mercifully white but covered with British Airways travel posters.

"A riot of colour," whispered Pax.

"Those posters are worse. They're like skiing posters in an amputee ward."

Pax thought she must have got the remark from Nick. Wit was not one of Annabel's strong points. Pax thought of adding "or like Durex ads in a monastery". That wasn't very witty either and he wanted to keep their relationship on a more romantic plane until he got her into the back seat of the Jaguar.

"They've got a captive audience," he said lamely. The joke fell deservedly flat.

They were told to sit down at one of the bright-red tables. Annabel chose one in the corner by the window, at the opposite end of the room to the self-service counter. A man in a sports shirt and cricket flannels was serving tea and biscuits and cigarettes behind the counter. Half a dozen tables were already occupied, three people at each huddled over brown plastic trays of tea cups.

Pax tried to distinguish between the inmates and the visitors. He looked for tell-tale signs from the James Cagney films. The cigarette cupped in the hand, the wary eye out for the brutal warder, the head hanging low in shame. It seemed that only the visitors behaved his way, overawed by their surroundings. The prisoners in their ordinary clothes looked quite relaxed. Only the warders were obvious. They wore blue trousers and blue shirts and some wore blue ties and jackets as well. One of them sat by the door idly leafing through a motoring magazine.

Nick came in and looked around for them. He was wearing an open-necked white shirt and grey trousers. He had lost weight and his hair was cut short. The hair that Pax had pulled out to save him from drowning had been replanted but in a less systematic pattern than before. He saw them and waved and put on a springy step as he walked across the canteen towards them.

He hugged Annabel and kissed her full on the mouth. Pax looked out of the window at a cricket game on the playing field and wondered how he was going to make small talk with a man he had every intention of cuckolding in his own car as soon as he had left his company.

"Hi, Pax old boy, how good of you to come. Listen. You're not supposed to give me money or anything but you can go up to the counter and buy us tea and biscuits. Do you mind?"

"Of course not." He steeled himself to look his brother-in-law in the eye. He was glad of the excuse to leave them together until he had recovered his composure.

"I'd like tea. Annabel will have coffee. And then whatever you want. Then if you could get two hundred cigarettes in assorted brands of ten, fifteen Mars Bars and twenty of those packets of Bluebird chocolate biscuits. That should do it."

"My God, how have you lost weight?"

"We don't eat them, Pax. They get cleared away on the tray and thrown into a special rubbish bag. Then we share them round tonight. If the warder asks you, you say you're a chocolate addict and a chain-smoker. But he won't. Don't worry."

"If it's against the rules, why take the risk?"

"Rehabilitation. Training for life outside again. Practising what you can get away with. Come on, Pax. You've got five hundred experts in here on what you can and can't get away with."

Pax queued at the counter with a heavy heart. He would have been less depressed to find him chained to the wall of a damp cell than incarcerated in the false liberality of this garish place. Nick with his dreams of glamour, sophistication and wealth, the big deal, the beautiful mistress, the fast life, was now reduced to trafficking in Mars Bars while his girlfriend dabbled in adultery with his brother-in-law. It was all so squalid.

He placed his order with the inmate behind the counter who

180

filled it without batting an eyelid. It cost nearly twenty pounds. That reduced his cash resources to three pounds and fifty pence. He had not counted on the expense of prison visiting. He wasn't going to give Annabel much of a good time in the country on that budget. A gin and tonic each at the most.

He put the loaded tray down carefully on the table. The other two were silent and expectant as if they had been exchanging quiet confidences while he was away. They made an elaborate play with the milk and sugar while they tried to think of something to say.

"How are the gnomes?" asked Pax, forcing his lips into a cheerful smile.

"I have a theory about gnomes. I've backed it up with research in the library. We have a debating society and I even spoke for ten minutes on the subject."

Pax felt a twinge of compassion. It sounded like school. He imagined the Governor's report to the parole board when Nick's application came up: ". . . useful member of house . . . tries hard at cricket . . . did well in debating cuppers . . ."

"From ancient times people have put fertility symbols in their gardens. The Romans had a god called Priapus. They stuck his statue in the flowerbed. He was supposed to get the birds and the bees going. Well, I think the garden gnome is a direct descendant. Look at them. They all leer at you like dirty old men. And you know what the most popular model is? I should know. I have to paint more of them than any other. It's the gnome holding the fishing rod in his crotch. I needn't tell you what the fishing rod is supposed to represent."

Pax and Annabel laughed politely. Nick looked serious. Pax wondered why he had steered the conversation in this direction. Had Annabel said something to him? Had he given himself away? He began to feel uncomfortable. Adultery needed more nerve than he had anticipated.

"It's the ones with the fishing rods I can't stand. They prey on your mind. Whatever I say, Pax, don't look surprised. Just carry on smiling and nodding. This is a normal conversation."

"Of course, Nick."

Obviously the experience of prison had made him slightly

potty. It was best to humour him. He could always call the warder over if Nick became dangerous.

"The next most popular ones are those that sit on toadstools. I want you to do something for me, Pax. Have you got gnomes in the garden? You are the only person I can trust."

"No I haven't. Of course I will." Pax nodded.

"I always do yellow waistcoats on the toadstool sitters. I've just let Annabel into the secret. She needs you as much as I do. But the fishermen have red coats. Don't you think that's sweet?"

"Yes. No. I mean no. Go on. Ha ha."

Pax found the subterfuge confusing. It was obviously a common trick among the prisoners to disguise a serious conversation in tittle-tattle and Nick was expert at it. Pax had always been hopeless at codes and backslang and rhubarbing on stage in the school play and now he was glad he had his back to the warder. Annabel nodded and smiled as if they were discussing last night's television.

"I got the hook on a fishing rod caught in my finger the other day. Don't be surprised at this, Pax. I want you to go on your boat down the Thames and pick something up for me. How is the *Swan*? Annabel tells me you're quite an expert now."

"Not bad. The bottom's been repaired so she's watertight. It's the rest of the gold coins you were bringing in isn't it? It's lovely on the river."

"You've been lucky with the weather. But I got a good game of cricket the other day. You're dead right. I had time to tie the bag to a buoy before I ran myself aground. I made thirty-five runs and I caught two people out. I forgot about the other damn bag in the heat of the moment and that's why I'm sitting here now. Are you teaching little Thomas to play? Tell him from Uncle Nick to keep a straight bat."

"I'm trying to. He's better at it now than I am. Never was much of a sportsman. Not a hope, Nick, you can forget it. I'm not getting mixed up in that sort of business. Not for a lousy ten thousand. Or a hundred thousand. My advice is to give it up to the police and get yourself out of here. Do you play tennis as well?"

"I did a gnome with a tennis racket the other day. This is my only hope, Pax. Mine and Annabel's. I would have waited until I got out and did it myself. But I read that they're surveying for a nuclear power station down there. I'm scared they'll move the buoy. Also the Frogs are due out of prison on parole before me. They might put two and two together and get there first. We do frogs as well and sweet little robins and windmills with sails that go round and round."

"Count me out. I hate gnomes and frogs and windmills."

"It's not peanuts we're talking about, old boy. It's over a million. Your cut would be over a quarter of a million. The best one is a windmill that drives a handle with a gnome on the end. It looks as though he's turning it himself. I don't do those. I do the traditional plaster ones."

"Can I have a Mars Bar?" Pax ripped open the packet with shaking hands and stuffed chocolate in his mouth. His words were muffled in the gooey fudge. "Say that again."

"You heard right. I do the plaster ones. There's over a quarter of a million in it for you, Pax Brown. Just for a trip down the river. I'm not greedy."

"A quarter of a million?" slurped Pax, mopping the dribbling chocolate from his chin. He wished he smoked cigarettes.

"A quarter of a million. That's a lot of gnomes. But they're very popular."

"Perhaps one with a fishing rod, then. But I couldn't handle a boat on my own, not all the way down river."

"Annabel will come with you, won't you darling? I've been promising her a trip on the river. Haven't I, old girl?"

Pax grabbed for another Mars Bar although the first was already making him feel sick. The other two began an animated discussion about the wallpaper in their dining room at home. They had seen the inmate from behind the bar coming over with a wet cloth in one hand and a black plastic bag in the other. He swept the cigarettes and sweets into the bag and looked aggrieved at the two Mars Bar wrappings. Pax tried to smile at him but his teeth were stuck with caramel. The man took away the tray and wiped the top of the table.

A million tied to a buoy in the Thames Estuary. A quarter

of a million for him. Twenty-four hours on the *Swan* with Annabel thrown in for good measure. The second Mars Bar was making him feel even more sick.

"Where can I get one of your gnomes? I'll think about it," he said in a faint, distant voice.

"Any garden centre. I'll tell you the make. I knew you would. But you have to realise that it's urgent. The French are let out next month."

"A garden centre? Will they have the ones with the yellow waistcoats? How do I find the buoy?"

"You should find a good selection anywhere. We turn enough of them out. The chequered buoy that marks the opening of Havengore Creek. It's on Maplin Sands. You'll find it on the map. How are Thea and the children? Annabel tells me she was round at your place the other Sunday. I really appreciate your looking after her, you know."

"What do I do with it when I've got it?"

"Stand it on a level surface and plant nasturtiums round it."

"Pax, darling, you look a bit pale."

Pax felt more than pale. He felt thoroughly insubstantial. The combination of the prison canteen environment, his daydreams about Annabel, meeting Nick, the obsession with gnomes and now the story of a fortune in gold coins dangling in the Thames Estuary had suffused his life with an unreality that no amount of pinching or pulling himself together or Mars Bars or long drinks of water could dispel.

While Nick and Annabel made small talk he tried to make sense of what he had just heard. The first possibility was that the story was entirely true. Nick had had time to dump the smuggled coins and they were still there like ripe fruit or seasonal oysters, ready for the gathering. But why not wait until he got out of prison and he could collect them himself? Either because he was afraid his former accomplices would get there first or because he knew he would be followed as soon as he walked out of the prison gates.

The second possibility was that the story was a figment of the imagination. But whose? Had Nick's ambition for wealth and power turned into delusion? Twelve hours a day locked in a tiny cell and dreaming what life could be like outside could lead to all kinds of confusion between reality and daydream.

He might also be trying to keep Annabel's respect and admiration. He had been caught but it wasn't for the pittance that had been found on the boat. It was for big money. The kindest thing would be to play along and humour him. He could come back in a couple of weeks and say the loot had disappeared.

The last possibility was the most worrying. Perhaps the story was a figment of his own imagination. Had he really heard what he had heard? The conversation had been about gnomes and the interpolations had been provided by his own fevered mind. He was doing his best to be unfaithful to Thea for the first time. He was bored to death with his job. He was lumbered with a leaky boat that had already swallowed his life savings and plunged him into debt. He desperately wanted to throw off his present life. The only escape seemed to be a large amount of money falling into his lap. Add to these ingredients the stress of the prison visit and Hey Presto! A fiction that solved all his problems at once.

The two people who could settle his doubts were sitting opposite him. They were having a heated argument over the colour they should paint the hall of her flat. The tables around them had filled up. The whole room had ears.

"You're sure about the, you know, the things. I'll go and get them if you like. You're sure I'll be able to find them."

"Absolutely old boy. Any garden centre. One with a fishing rod. Everything in the garden will come up roses."

"Did you hear what I heard?" asked Pax.

They were sitting in the car park facing the prison, a rambling Victorian pile. He kept his eyes on it as if he expected it to disappear like Aladdin's palace along with the hoard of gold coins as soon as he turned his back. Annabel too was staring into the middle distance. Her voice was as distant as her gaze. "About the money? Yes, I heard."

"Do you think it's really there?"

"Why not? Do you doubt Nick's word?"

"Of course not. Why should he tell a deliberate lie? I just think he may have been mistaken. Prison does strange things to people."

"We have to trust him, don't we? He trusts you and me."

This augured badly for a bit of hanky-panky in the back seat, although he wasn't sure he was completely up to it. He felt sick and bloated from Mars Bars and glasses of water. A headache was coming on.

"He certainly is trusting us. It's not the sort of secret I would share with anyone unless I was desperate. A million pounds would bend the conscience of a lot of people. How does he know I'm not going to take the first plane to Brazil?"

She turned round to him, her eyes wide. "Oh don't say that. Poor Nick. You couldn't."

"Or I could hand it over to the police on the promise that Nick would be released early and any other charges would be dropped. I might even get a reward."

"You couldn't do that either." She rummaged in her handbag for a handkerchief.

He was not so sure that Nick's trust in him was very flattering. Nick needed someone to go down the river for him. One option was to find a person of the highest standards of decency and integrity and courage. Pax could not see in himself any evidence of these qualities. Another option was to find a person so lacking in enterprise, ambition, courage, sexual drive and attractiveness that he could be safely sent down the river with his beautiful mistress to pick up the loot and bring it back like a devoted spaniel. Pax feared that in Nick's opinion he fell into the second category.

He could live with Nick's opinion. What was harder to come to terms with was that he was probably right.

"Let's go, Annabel. I can't stand this place."

They drove back towards London along country roads, avoiding the motorway, whiling away the time until the pubs opened. Pax tilted his seat back to ease the pressure on his complaining abdomen. He surreptitiously unbuttoned the top of his trousers, a move he had been anticipating at the beginning of the afternoon for different reasons. He tried looking at

Annabel's knees, imagining her in the back seat with her skirt around her waist, remembering the feel of her soft, firm flesh, but it was no good. The mood had gone. Supine in his seat he looked up at the grey sky though the windscreen like a switched-off television.

Annabel had said nothing since they had left the prison. She drove fast, her eyes fixed on the road. Suddenly she braked for no apparent reason and pulled off the road into the entrance to a field. She stopped the engine and looked at him inquisitively. "Well? Are we going to do it?"

He released his seatbelt and struggled into an upright position. He knew he should lean over, despite the gear lever, and take her in his arms. But his indigestion had worked its way down and he was pretty certain that if he shifted his buttocks on the seat he would fart. That would not be a good start to foreplay.

"Let's go for a walk first. It looks so pretty round here."

There were elder bushes on either side of the car and a field of long grass in front. The wind was chill and the sky that deep shade of English grey that promised nothing so dramatic as rain but only the continuing prospect of more greyness for days to come. The grass underfoot was neither wet nor dry, just limp and damp. The earth was soft without being muddy. There was no view. A couple of dead elms stood in the field. There were no birds or bees to be heard above the thrumming of a distant tractor.

Pax stood downwind and bent over to fiddle with his shoe-laces. Then he buttoned up his trousers. Feeling easier in body if not in mind he joined Annabel at the five-bar gate and put his arm round her.

"Shall we get back in the car?" he said.

"I thought we'd got out for a walk."

She was wearing high heels so they had to walk along the road. They strolled aimlessly for a few minutes between the high hedges and overgrown ditches until they came to another field of grass and dead elms. They turned round to go back to the car. She had her arms folded, hugging herself for warmth. He picked up a stick to slash away at the grass by the side of the road. It wasn't how he had pictured their afternoon in the country.

He followed her round to the driver's door, spun her round by the shoulders and gave her his best shot at a smouldering gaze. He pulled her to him and kissed her. Her lips were soft but unresponsive and although she let his tongue in between her teeth she gave him no encouragement. She kept her arms folded so it was like embracing a shapeless parcel.

"Let's get in the back seat."

"Not now, Pax. Not after we've just seen Nick. You heard how much he trusts us. It wouldn't be fair on the same afternoon. Let's wait until we're on the boat. It will be very beautiful then, I promise."

She pecked him on the end of the nose, swivelled out of his embrace and got in the car. He hammered on the window and she wound it down.

"But you said when we stopped. You said, 'Are we going to do it?' What have I said? What have I done?"

"I didn't mean that. I meant are we going to take your boat down to the chequered buoy at Havengore Creek and get Nick's money. We are, aren't we? Together?"

She wound the window up and started the engine. Pax went round to the other side feeling more relieved than frustrated. He had done what was expected of him and now he could go back to feeling sick and worried in peace.

❋ Chapter Sixteen ❋

Pax stretched lazily on the crumpled bed and wondered where he was. There was no movement. They must be becalmed. The late afternoon sun streamed through the porthole in a brilliant shaft. It was already low in the sky. In an hour or so it would suddenly disappear as if it had been switched off. Nightfall was sudden in the tropics.

He was alone in the cabin. She must have gone outside while he was still asleep. He could not hear her moving around. She was probably sunbathing on the bleached teak of the foredeck. He smiled to himself at the thought of her lithe body, tanned evenly all over.

It was stuffy in the cabin although the hatches and the main door were open. Through the skylight he could see the white mainsail hanging limp from the boom. Above the gunwhale strake and below the dangling sail ropes the eastern sky was beginning to turn from blue to a translucent and darkening purple. He thought of Nick looking at a tiny patch of grey sky out of the high judas window in his cramped, whitewashed cell.

He sat up on the bed with his feet on the floor. He took a sharp knife from the hog and a fresh lime from the raffia bag that dangled from one of the breast hooks. They had bought the limes and a few mangoes and a pineapple on the quayside that morning before setting off. The squeezer was already on the table. He squeezed the lime into a glass and fetched ice and cold soda from the small refrigerator in the galley.

He resisted the temptation to sip it straight away and carried it up the steps into the cockpit, swirling the tinkling ice in the glass.

"What a lovely sound. And what a lovely body," she said.

189

He stretched again, standing on tiptoe, straightening his arms like the Leonardo man with a circle drawn round him. He saw her look at his tanned, muscular body with frank admiration and smiled at her.

He stepped up onto the foredeck. The strips of new black stuff between the freshly payed planks felt slightly warmer than the wood to the soles of his feet. His senses had become alert and finely tuned in a way he had never experienced on land.

He handed the glass down to her. She sat up in the shade of the limp foresail with her back against the mast. He kissed her behind the ear. She was naked. He could smell the perfume and salt and sweet woman's fragrance. He nibbled the top of her breasts so he could taste it too. She pushed his head away and he felt her hard nails and soft fingertips in his scalp.

Her blonde hair was streaked by the sun and sea. The golden colour of her tan brought out the fine purple line that marked the edge of her soft, pink lips and emphasised the whiteness of her even teeth. Without make-up her large blue eyes looked rounder, giving her a vulnerable, startled look like a young deer.

He sat down beside her, their bodies touching from the shoulders down to her long, slender flank. She took a mouthful of lime juice but did not swallow it. She kept it in her mouth which she pressed to his. He forced his tongue through her lips and sucked at the cool, tart liquid. She began to swallow too. A tiny drop of juice fell on her thigh and she left it there, glistening in the sun. She took another mouthful from the glass but instead of waiting for her mouth he eased himself down so he was lying flat on the deck beside her. He licked the drop from her thigh. He carried on licking, widening the circle of his tongue until with a moan she too lay back on the deck with her legs apart.

They finished the rest of the glass later.

He lay on the deck, propped up on his elbow. He watched her rise gracefully to her feet. Their bodies were glistening. It was as if he could feel every tiny drop of perspiration, his and hers,

190

on his tingling nerve-ends. She stood on the side of the deck with her toes on the deck edge-rubber. She was silhouetted against the sun, now large and low in the evening sky. She looked over her shoulder to him and smiled.

He stood beside her on the deck. The sea was a glassy calm. It was suddenly disturbed by a pair of dolphins breaking the water beneath the bow. Wheeling and gliding they played around the boat, arcing over the water and gambolling in each other's wake. As suddenly as they had appeared they were gone, another couple luxuriating in each other and the solitude of the sea.

They dived off the deck together. The water was wonderfully cool. They tried to gambol like dolphins but this was not their element. They held hands and trod water and kissed and floated on their backs. Her long wet tresses floated around her head like a Medusa.

"You are my mermaid," he said, closing his eyes and letting himself drift, weightless.

For the first time since they had set sail that morning he felt a breeze on his cheek. He savoured it. It was blowing off the land way over the horizon. It carried the perfume of cinnabar and cloves and dusky camelias. The moon would soon be rising and they could sail through the gentle night, watching the phosphorescence in their wake until they drifted off to sleep in each other's arms.

"Pax," she whispered, "the boat."

He opened his eyes. The sea was no longer like a mirror. It was ruffled by the breeze skittering over the water. The same breeze was also tugging at the white sails of the *Swan*. The foresail flapped lazily and her bows were turning in the direction they had been sailing before they were becalmed. She was fifty yards from where they floated.

Pax eased into a fast crawl, knifing through the water. The breeze picked up and the sails began to fill. He swam faster but he could hear the bubbling sounds from the bow and the creak of the mast as the *Swan* got under way.

It was not only the freshening breeze that chilled. An icy fear began to grow inside his chest. He looked over his shoulder.

She was swimming valiantly, trying to keep up. Ahead the *Swan* was heeling slightly, gathering speed. He put his head down and swam for all he was worth.

The sun had gone and the rising moon was half over the horizon when he gave up. The *Swan* was out of sight and the wind was strong. She would sail empty, a *Marie Celeste*, on the course her tiller was lashed to, until she ran aground. People would find her and wonder what had happened to the crew. Or she would remain undiscovered on a deserted reef until she broke up and sank into the coral waters.

Exhausted, he swam slowly back in the direction he had come. He wanted to hold her hand, comfort her, let her comfort him. At least they would lie once more in each other's embrace before they were claimed by the infinite darkness of the sea.

There was no sign of her. "Annabel!" he called, his voice cracking with thirst and salt. "Annabel!"

She had disappeared like a mermaid. He was naked and alone. "Oh bugger," he said, and thought of home.

Pax came into the bedroom naked and dripping. It was meant to be a silent protest about the fact that there were no towels in the bathroom or the airing cupboard or draped over the banisters on the landing. But he trod on a small piece of transparent Lego outside the bedroom door and came hopping in with a howl, leaving a giant Man Friday wet footprint on the brown carpet before falling on the bed, jostling Thea who was sitting cross-legged in her nightdress clipping her toenails. The resulting exchange of words was rushed and confused.

"Bloody Lego should be in the playroom."

"You've made the sheets all wet."

"This house is like a pigsty."

"Why couldn't you call from the bathroom."

"The children ought to be made to tidy up or they'll grow up like you."

"You rot the carpet by walking on it like that."

"Cutting your nails in bed is a filthy habit."

"You were hogging the bathroom. I can't help it if you're selfish."

"I'm selfish? Because I don't want to wallow all night in toenail clippings?"

"I pick each one up and put it in the rubbish."

"Which particular rubbish? This bedroom is full of rubbish."

"Most of it's yours. Don't blame me for your own shortcomings."

"My shortcomings? I'm out all day. It's like coming home to a rag and bone man."

There was a short interlude while Pax, deliberately hobbling, went into Thomas's room where he would find a bath towel on the floor. Thea made an elaborate play of changing the sheets and inspecting her toes in the hope of finding a cut from the nail-clippers that could be blamed on him.

Now was the time to make peace, before the row escalated to legitimate grievances. As he rubbed himself down on the landing Pax struggled with the temptation to go in, give her a hug and laugh off the business with the Lego, but in the end he overcame it. It had been several weeks since their last argument about the boat and the explosive atmosphere had been building up again. Even then, the manner in which he had bought the boat and the spending of the deposit meant for Romona Terrace was too large and overwhelming an issue to be the focus of a flaming row. They had discussed the issue calmly and rationally and come to a *modus vivendi* on the subject, which is to say that they stored up all the emotional grievances for a later date.

The next stage of escalation concerned the house and the children.

"How can you want a bigger house when you can't even manage this one?"

"This isn't a house, it's a shoe box stood on end."

"It's practical and easy, even for a total slut."

"With a man-about-the-house like you? Give me a slob any day."

"The kids like it."

"Why are they always round at other people's houses then?"

"Because they can't stand the mess at home."

193

"Nobody lives in these houses with children. You're too selfish to care."

"Selfish? You're so immersed in your petit-bourgeois life you're involuted."

"Don't use words you don't understand."

They continued this overview of their current domestic situation while he put his pyjamas on and brushed his hair and she finished making the bed. He went back to the bathroom to brush his teeth and ostentatiously hang the towel up on its proper rail while she rummaged in a pile of newspapers and magazines on the floor under the dressing table for the latest estate agent's house list to make a point of reading it in bed. It was now time for the old chestnuts to be brought out, nuggets of grievance from previous rows dating back to before they were married and which had stood the test of time.

"What about all those things you said about my mother . . ."

"It wasn't my fault the application wasn't posted . . ."

"Don't twist what I said. We were expecting Sarah not Thomas . . ."

"You've got a perverted memory . . ."

"That built up a wall between us which we'll never knock down . . ."

After these relics of previous arguments had been carefully taken out and given an airing in order to place the present row in its historical context, it was time for the immortal themes of money and sex to put in their appearance. They were both convinced that other people were enjoying more of those commodities than they were.

"Go on, tell me how much we spent on housekeeping last month, go on . . ."

"Do you have any idea what the rates are . . .?"

"I wouldn't trust you with Monopoly money . . ."

"You want me to scrimp at home while you fritter it away on boats . . ."

"Whatever I bring home, I don't think I'm getting good value for it . . ."

"Value for money? What is this house, a cash and carry . . .?"

194

"I earn a bloody good salary I'll have you know . . ."

"You've been in the same job for ten years . . . Sugar Daddy's home! Take his money and run!"

"Listen, I can make a lot of money. Just don't expect to see me very often."

"Anyone would think I sit round painting my nails and buying new dresses . . ."

"You want me in the Big Time, like your brother Nick . . ."

"I could buy it cheaper on the street . . ."

"My God, by the time I come upstairs you're fast asleep . . ."

"Every time I even mention sex you start to yawn. See, you're doing it now . . ."

"No I won't do those things, they're disgusting . . ."

"When we were first married we had nothing else to do . . ."

"Talk to me for five minutes first, that's all I ask . . ."

"Sometimes I think there'd be more life in a plastic doll . . ."

"I'd like to take the initiative sometimes . . . You take it so seriously. Why don't you put notches on the bed . . ."

At the end of this phase of the proceedings they were lying on their sides, back to back, with their arms folded, each waiting for the other to roll over and put out a conciliatory hand and each convinced that they had made the first approach last time.

"What's the time," he asked as coldly as he could.

"Half past twelve."

"I have to be up early in the morning to go to the office. Good night."

He waited for the touch of her hand but it didn't come. Stuff it then. Instead, she said she was going down to make herself a cup of tea.

"Tea? At this time of night? I'm going to sleep."

"Oh," she said, feigning surprise, "before we've finished talking?"

"There's no point in carrying on now. It will all seem different in the morning."

She rolled out of bed, put on her dressing gown and went downstairs. He defiantly put out the light and closed his eyes. He relaxed his limbs, took a few deep breaths, let his jaw sag

195

and tried to think of something peaceful. He was still wide awake when Thea came back up and defiantly switched the light on but he pretended to be asleep. It achieved the desired effect.

"How could you go to sleep at a time like this," she hissed and shook his shoulder. He grunted and asked if it was time to get up. Had she not just changed the bedding he would have received the hot cup of tea full in the face.

Their row now entered its final and most wounding phase, the exposure of personal inadequacies. Up to now the accusations and counter-accusations had been about incidents and behaviour. Now they turned the spotlight on character deficiencies, known to the experts as Home Truths. Pax knew that there was no point in simply enumerating what he thought were her personal failings since she was indifferent to most and even proud of some. What he had to find were her anxieties about herself. Likewise she would only score a bullseye on him if she touched on something he was deeply concerned about. For example, he didn't mind being unambitious and idle but he did mind being a daydreamer who did not have the courage to put his dreams into practice.

"You are totally incapable of genuine sympathy . . ."

"I've never known anyone so indecisive . . ."

"Why are you so aggressive all the time . . ."

"Because you're so defensive . . ."

"Give me one example in the last three months . . . see, you can't . . ."

This was no longer back to back, staring at the wall, or lying on your back staring at the ceiling and being careful not to touch the other person, this was eyeball to eyeball stuff. And Thea was the first to strike a hit.

"You sit and fantasise and wait for somebody else to make it all come true . . ."

The world suddenly became a very lonely place for them both. It had stopped being a distraction, a catharsis, almost an entertainment.

"I don't think we can go on living together if our relationship is built on nothing more than convenience . . ."

"Let's admit it. We are different people now . . ."

"What are you doing?"

"I'm getting dressed. We might as well admit it now. I can't stay here . . ."

Last time it had been Thea who had got dressed, driven the car around for twenty minutes and come back to find him pretending to be asleep. Living in a small house they could not go through the intermediate stage of sleeping in separate bedrooms. It was his turn to make a token flight to freedom but he was handicapped by not knowing where the car keys were.

"Why should you leave me here? I'm going if anyone's going," she said, springing out of bed and looking for her underwear in the various piles in the bedroom.

It was like a pyjama race at an infant school sports. The faster they tried to pull their clothes on in order to get to the front door first the more they became tangled up. Thea won by not bothering with socks. Pax chased her down the stairs and called after her as she disappeared into the garage not to expect him to be still there when she came back.

He sat on the bed for a few minutes, wondering what to do. Having made the threat not to be there when she came back, pretending to be asleep would be a climbdown instead of a demonstration of callous indifference and putting the chain on the door would be merely malicious. He sipped the tea Thea had brought up but it was cold. This of course was his opportunity for a real break, a test of whether he genuinely meant what he had told Thea this evening. With a feeling that he was taking a new and perhaps irrevocable step he pulled a suitcase from under the bed and began packing. But would Annabel come and fetch him? He rested his hand on the telephone before realising that there was an intermediate stage between abandoning his own home and moving in to someone else's. He tiptoed into Thomas's room and took the sleeping bag down from the top of his wardrobe.

He was outside the square, hidden in the shadow of a hedge, when he saw Thea drive back and park in the drive. He watched and waited while she let herself in the front door. He saw the lights in the rest of the house go on and off and her silhouette in the bedroom window as she looked out for signs of movement. Then the bedroom light went out and he could picture her lying in the dark with her eyes open, waiting for him to come sheepishly back with his suitcase.

He tried to reconstruct the row. He could not remember how it had started or what they thought they were arguing about. At the time it seemed as though they were leaving no stone unturned but in fact they had avoided all the real issues. They had simply vented their frustrations and anxieties in an emotional froth.

They hadn't talked about his attraction for Annabel. It wasn't love but what was it? They hadn't talked about Nick and his fortune dangling from a buoy in the Thames. Did he really want that money and what would he do with it if he got it? They had not talked about the *Swan*. What did it really mean to him? They hadn't talked about each other. They had simply used each other as punch-balls.

And what was Thea worried about? What were the real issues for her? He had no idea. Perhaps now was the time to go back to the house and ask her. Thea, what is important to you? What do you want of me? Of yourself?

No, dammit. For once he was going to do what he said he was going to do. If he asked her those questions she wouldn't give a straight answer. She would think he was getting at her. And anyway, he wouldn't give her the satisfaction of opening the door to him.

He turned his back on the house and walked in the direction of the Post Office where he could phone for a taxi, the suitcase banging against his knee.

His first night on the *Swan* was not what he had imagined. She creaked like a galleon. Even in the flat calm of the marina she swayed and rolled and complained. He lay awake trying to identify the different squeaks and groans and then waited for them like the next drip of a leaky tap.

There were faint scuffling sounds. Rats? On the few occasions when he dozed off he woke with a start, sure that something had run over his face. Staring at the ceiling he listed

198

all the logical arguments against rats and mice but was not so convincing on the subject of cockroaches. He wished Thea had never told him he slept with his mouth open.

He blamed his wakefulness on the stuffy atmosphere and the smell of rot and mildew. He wrestled with the catches on the brass portholes. He managed to open one but the chill breeze made him shiver. He hung his underpants over it to break the force of the draught and huddled in his sleeping bag trying to drum up a sense of satisfaction that he was spending his first night afloat.

The bunk was not long enough for him to stretch out. At five o'clock in the morning stretching was the most desirable thing in the world. The whole cabin was pressing in on him. He couldn't get out of his mind the Edgar Allen Poe story of the man who thought he had been buried alive in a coffin until he realised he was in a ship's bunk. How would he get out if they sprang a leak in the night?

He listened for drips and gurgles. He prayed that the boatbuilder had done a good job under that smooth layer of antifouling paint. He didn't have a torch so he couldn't look for tell-tale drips or tiny bubbling springs under the floorboards in the bilges. He contented himself with feeling such planks in the side of the hull as he could reach with the back of his hand. They felt damp.

This discovery led him to examine the bedding he was lying on. He had not thought to examine the cushion under his sleeping bag. It was made of foam rubber encased in rubberised cotton. He put his hand inside and squeezed the foam. Water trickled through his fingers. No wonder he felt stiff and cold. He was bound to catch a chill.

He hoped that Thea was lying awake too, wondering where he had gone and if he would ever come back. It served her right. It would teach her a lesson. She would take him seriously in future. But these thoughts became less of a consolation. They began to ring hollow. He even felt twinges of remorse which he hastened to suppress. It was a petty way to behave, unworthy of mature human beings. But how could he go back now?

199

He gave up the struggle for sleep at first light. He sat on the edge of the bunk and cradled his head in his arms resting on the table. This was going to take some getting used to. And he hadn't even left the marina yet. What would it be like at sea, leaning over at an angle and the waves beating at the portholes? At last, exhausted by the night's emotions and discomforts he dozed off into a short and fitful sleep.

He woke up at eight o'clock, stiff, shivering and with a headache. He shuffled to the cabin door and scrambled into the cockpit. It was drizzling but he welcomed the freshness on his face. Anything was better than the cramped, damp and stuffy cabin. He couldn't straighten his legs, he had a crick in the neck and one shoulder remained obstinately higher than the other. He clutched the boom and tried to force his body out of its Richard the Third posture.

Clutching for crumbs of comfort he noticed how pretty and brave the boats would have looked in the early morning sun if it had not been raining. He congratulated himself on being able to get out of bed to such an idyllic scene. He would only decide whether he had rheumatic fever after a hot shower and a couple of aspirin. Painfully he scrambled back into the cabin for his towel and spongebag.

A shower in the Yacht Club did something for stiffness and cramp but nothing for the feeling of fatigue and nausea. He had grown soft, he told himself sternly. Last night was nothing for a fit man in the prime of life. He had to take himself in hand, toughen up, prepare himself in mind and body for the voyages he had dreamed about. They were now within his grasp. He had made his break with suburban domesticity.

But wait, he said to himself in reply. I have not grown soft. I always was soft. I have always needed eight hours' sound sleep in a warm bed or I feel rotten for the rest of the day. I have only been camping once in my life and I caught pneumonia. I have never been in the Army or the Scouts or the Cubs. I have begun the Canadian Air Force exercises more times than I've done press-ups. I usually stop within a week because I've strained myself or caught cold doing them in front of an open window or got bored with them. I am not cut out for this and never have been.

He sloped sadly back to the *Swan*, hoping there were no tourists around to see him in yesterday's office shirt, old painting trousers and black brogues without socks. He struggled into his office shirt and suit in the cramped space of the cabin. By shifting the table he could almost stand upright under the centre hatch. It was impossible to dry himself properly. His clothes felt clammy. There was no mirror for him to tie his tie and comb his hair. He had forgotten to bring an umbrella or a raincoat. Shivering and unkempt he walked as fast as his aching legs would permit to the coffee bar next to the office to force down breakfast.

I have scored a moral victory, he told himself over his third cup of tea. I have made the break. I have taken the first step. I have cast off into the tide. Nothing can stop me now unless I have to spend the next two weeks in bed.

Thea was asleep. She lay on her back in the middle of the giant four-poster, her arms spread wide for her absent lover, her hair cascading in wild abandon over the satin pillows. The embroidered sheets, perfumed with lavender, were around her waist, tossed and rumpled in her restless dreams. Her lace nightdress was parted to the waist and a shy pale breast was half-exposed to the impudent rays of the sun's first light.

She stirred and whispered his name and woke with a start. Her hand flew to her mouth and she stifled a timid cry. He stood by the side of the bed. His face was brown and lined and weathered by the elements. His hair had turned a golden blonde in the sun and salt of the sea. His eyes were lapis lazuli from beyond the ocean, ultramarine. His body was strong and sinewed. His sailor's coat was torn and stained with salt and blood. One sleeve was empty. She took fright when she saw it and then she saw the sling across his chest and the good strong hand inside it.

In his other hand he carried a large leather bag. He lifted it with an effort and threw it on the bed. Deftly he undid the catch and lifted the bag by its bottom. Out onto the satin sheets poured ducats and crowns, sovereigns and pieces of eight, a river of gold, shining in the early morning sun.

She gasped and gazed at the riches in disbelief. She looked up at him with eyes moist with love and admiration. He leaned over and seized her in his strong arm, forcing the breath out of her willing body. He pressed his mouth to hers, forcing her soft lips apart. The room whirled around her and she closed her eyes. All resistance melted and was replaced by an overwhelming longing.

With one masterful rip she was naked. She sprawled on the satin and gold and he pleasured her hard, with his boots on.

He spent the morning fighting off the temptation to have a lie down in the sick room. This was a small, airless cubicle carved out of the stationery stores to comply with the regulations about working conditions. In theory it was meant for anyone who felt unwell. There was an unspoken convention that it was for pregnant women and those who fell down unconscious on the job. Hangovers and sleepless nights on boats and other symptoms of an immoderate life did not count.

At lunchtime he phoned Thea.

"I went to the *Swan* last night."

"I guessed you had. I expected you would sooner or later."

"Did the children miss me?"

"No. They thought you were still in bed."

"That's good."

"How did you sleep?"

"Marvellous. Like a log. Must be the sea air. What about you?"

"Marvellous. I had a very good night. Have you got a cold?"

"No. It must be the bad line. Never felt better."

"You sound hoarse. Are you coming back for your clothes?"

"Some time."

"The children will miss you at the weekend."

"I'll see you on Saturday morning then. If that's all right."

"Fine with me. I'll explain to the children."

"Listen, Thea, there's something we have to talk about."

"I thought we'd done all the talking last night."

"It's to do with Nick. And the *Swan*."

"That's nothing to do with me."

202

"Don't walk away like that. It's important."

"You were the one who walked away. Last night. Remember?"

"All right, if you won't listen I'll find someone who will."

"Try a psychiatrist."

"Goodbye."

"Goodbye."

He put the phone down and noticed that the door of his office was open. Doreen was sitting at her typewriter, concentrating on her work with the intensity of an ardent eavesdropper. She stood up from her desk and came into his office.

"Can I get you a cup of tea? And one of my pick-me-ups?"

He looked at Doreen properly for the first time. Usually he tried to avert his gaze. When he did look, his attention was absorbed by the clothes she wore. Today she was wearing a voluminous rugby shirt with black and yellow horizontal stripes and a navy-blue split skirt, either half of which would have made an ample garment for any of the girls in the typing pool. She would have made an All Black think twice. All that was missing was a scrum cap.

Now he looked past even this outfit to her sad brown eyes. They looked at him with a moist, melting lustre.

"No thanks, Doreen. And could you close the door? I have to make a few confidential phone calls."

"But you look a bit under the weather. No more bad news from home is there?"

He forced himself to look at her face again. She was smiling at him, her bright-red painted lips parted to show the lipstick stains on her front teeth. Her eyes seemed to be getting bigger.

"What do you mean, no more bad news?"

"Nothing. I just thought there had been a bit of a problem with your wife's brother. I wouldn't like to think of you being upset, Mr Brown."

"Doreen, I am very busy. I have a diary full of engagements. I have some important telephone calls to make. I do not feel ill. I am fine. I do not feel like a cup of tea. Please close the door of my office when you go out. And I would be very grateful if you would not listen in to my private conversations."

203

He expected her to march out in a huff. But she stood her ground. Her brown eyes were still luminous with passion but her lips had lost their smile.

"Please do not speak to me like that, Mr Brown. I am not a tea-towel to be trampled under your feet."

Pax struggled with the metaphor. She must run her kitchen like Thea did. "I apologise. I'm a bit tired. You're right. But I have a lot of work to do."

"Since when? You've never worked hard. The only time I've ever known you busy all day was when you were looking for that stuff on Collectors' Coins Limited which your brother-in-law was tied up in."

Panic. He felt submerged in a butt of icy water. He forced the words through a reluctant voice box. "What are you talking about? What do you know about that?"

"Don't worry, Mr Brown. There was only one memo and I destroyed it while you were off sick. And now look at the thanks I get. We're a partnership, Mr Brown. Didn't you ever realise?"

There was nothing he could think of to say. Doreen continued, her lips quivering now and her brown eyes moister than ever.

"Your diary's always full, isn't it. You're always rushing off to lunches and meetings all afternoon. You're ever so busy, Mr Brown. Then why doesn't anyone ever come here? Why doesn't anyone ever telephone you or write to you? How do you make all these arrangements? Telepathy?"

"Doreen that's silly. I'm often on the phone. It's just that I call them."

"I've heard you. You have these busy and important conversations with the Speaking Clock and the Weather Forecast and the Recipe of the Day. Mr Brown, when I first heard you, I thought you were insane. And then I realised what you were up to."

"That's ridiculous. You don't know what you're saying."

"And if I spent as much time on the toilet as you do, I'd go for a check-up."

Pax stood up behind his desk to confront her. He forced

himself to look at her face. "That is all none of your business. How I run my job and fulfil my responsibilities is no concern of yours. You are paid to type and answer the telephone. I have a brilliant career ahead of me, Doreen. What if I were fully occupied at this job? How would I cope when I got promoted to higher things? I have to keep something of myself in reserve. If you don't like it, you can work for someone else. I'll ring up Personnel this afternoon."

Her eyes were filling with tears. Her bottom lip was quivering. "That's all the thanks I get. I've protected you, Mr Brown. I've seen you sleeping behind the files and told people you were busy. I tell Mr Pinkish and everyone else how hard you work. When they call from America I tell them you're in conference when you're reading on the toilet. I know what those little pencil crosses mean in your diary. If it wasn't for me you'd have been out on your ear years ago. We're a team, Mr Brown, whether you like it or not."

She pulled a tiny handkerchief, embroidered with rosebuds, out of the sleeve of her rugby shirt and dabbed her eyes. He came round from the other side of the desk and put his arm round her shoulders. She felt surprisingly soft and feminine.

"Doreen. What can I say?"

"Nothing, Mr Brown. Too much has been said already."

She took a deep breath, gave a big sigh and walked out of his office, closing the door quietly behind her. Perhaps everyone is in someone else's daydream.

He sat down at his desk and dialled Annabel's number.

❖ Chapter Seventeen ❖

Walking arm in arm with Annabel along the dockside towards his yacht on a fine summer evening Pax wondered why he was not happy. Two months ago this would have been an idle fantasy, an outlet for his frustrations and anxieties about his marriage and his home and his job. Now, against all expectations, it had all come true. He had made a break with his former existence and was about to sail off into the sunset with a beautiful woman and a million pounds in unmarked gold coins.

"I think we should leave tomorrow. Let's see what time they open the lock," said Annabel, squeezing his arm.

"But tomorrow is Saturday."

"So what?"

"Saturday is, well, Saturday. I have to go home for some clean clothes. And see the children."

"Who cares whether it's Christmas Day. It's our day. Tomorrow we start a new life, just you and me."

"I."

"What?"

"You and I. Never mind. I just don't think Saturday is a good day for that sort of thing. Banks aren't open. Monday strikes me as a better day. I mean, you have the rest of the week left."

"Are you getting cold feet?"

"Me? What a silly idea. I just haven't made up my mind yet. I was going to think it over tonight. And then you telephoned me at the office. I didn't say I was going, did I? I just told you that I'd moved onto the boat."

"But there's nothing to think about. We just sail down the river, you and me together, and see if there's anything tied to

206

that silly old buoy. Then we can decide what to do. And we'll have had a lovely little trip on your boat. I haven't forgotten my promise, you know."

She steered them through the tourists and office workers to the lock-master's office. It had stopped raining and the sun had come out. He tried to bask in the reflected glory of the attention given to Annabel. She was wearing a pink silk blouse open to the waist and a short white skirt slit up the thigh. He did her justice by pulling in his stomach, forcing his stiff legs into a stride and moulding his face into a debonair mask, but his heart was not in it.

The lock opened at ten o'clock in the morning. That was two hours before high tide.

Pax shook his head regretfully as he put their drinks down on the table in the Yacht Club bar. It was the same table that he and Nick had used when they had lunch and he was introduced to the hairless Carlo. "Ten o'clock is too late. We couldn't get down there by nightfall. We'd be better waiting a few days. Then we can get an earlier start."

"Have you looked at a chart to see how far it is?" she asked sweetly.

She leaned over to ferret through her shoulder bag. He could see her plump, firm breasts. She had small, pink, girlish nipples. Thea's were large and brown because she had suckled his children.

She put a map on the table folded into a blue cover. "Stanford's Coloured Charts for Coastal Navigators No. 5, The Thames Estuary," it proclaimed around a picture of a ship's wheel. She started to unfold it and Pax looked uneasily round the bar.

"Relax. If we can't look at a chart in here, where can we look at one?"

She was right. Nothing was more natural than to study a chart of the Thames in the Yacht Club bar but he was still uneasy. He felt like Long John Silver opening up a map of Treasure Island.

He had never seen a chart before. His first reaction was that it did not look as pretty as a land map. The land was plain white with very few details such as one or two essential place names. The shallow water was pale blue and the deep water dark blue. The land was bordered by sandy-coloured bits and there were also sandy-coloured islands. On the water there were a few red lines and little red and yellow blobs.

Any sparse elegance the chart may have aspired to was disfigured by an acne of tiny little numbers on the smooth blue water. They were whole numbers with a few fractions close to the shore. Pax pointed to them knowingly and explained they indicated depth. Exactly what depth he could not say. Scouring the small print at the side of the chart he discovered that "soundings are given in fathoms at Chart Datum."

"What's a fathom?" asked Annabel.

"Full fathom five thy father lies," was his only answer and the sum total of his knowledge about fathoms. They were either a yard or two yards or the same as a rod, pole or perch.

There were a lot of words as well as numbers. It was apparent that the literary qualities of the Thames Estuary far outweighed the pictorial. The ring and romance of the names caused him to whisper them into her ear like a love spell or a ritual chant.

"Kentish Knock and Middle Sunk Sandbanks. Fisherman's Gat and the Wallet or the Warp. Columbine Spit by Old Ham Gat and Spaniard Middle Sand runs into the Cant. Barrow Deep to Shipwash and Medusa Channel. Beware Blacktail Spit and Clite Hole Bank and trust Scar's Elbow Bell."

"That's all very well. But where's Havengore Creek?"

They pored over the chart. Pax half hoped that it wouldn't be there, that it was a name Nick had read in a book. He spotted Southend where they thought he was drowned.

"There it is," she cried, stabbing her finger in the middle of a sandy-coloured patch. "Havengore Creek."

The sandy-coloured patch was Maplin Sands, the largest sandbank on the chart. From the sandbank several parallel little creeks ran inland and joined up to make the river Roach, a tributary of the Thames. Annabel rested the tip of her finely-polished, red-painted fingernail on a little black blob in the middle of Maplin Sands labelled "Cheq. B."

"X marks the spot. Thank God it's near the shore. I was afraid it was going to be out in the dark blue bits somewhere. Oh Pax, isn't this exciting?"

He had a feeling you were safer out at sea than close to the shore but decided not to mention it. He had a much cleverer idea. He went to the bar and asked Malcolm, the steward, if he had a road map of the east coast. He came back with the *Reader's Digest Book of the Seaside*.

"Look. I've got a much better idea. There's this small road which runs from Southend right across this heathland to the end of Havengore Creek. We'll buy a little rubber dinghy and paddle out to the buoy. Or we could hire a pedalo in Southend. A lot less trouble than taking the *Swan* down there. We can drive to Southend in an hour."

"A little rubber dinghy? A pedalo? Do you realise how much a million pounds' worth of gold weighs?"

"I hadn't thought of that."

"And did you know that the bit of heathland between Southend and Havengore is a military firing range? You can't get within ten miles of that buoy by land."

"I just thought there might be an easier way."

"Well there isn't. We've got it all worked out. We need a big boat that won't attract attention. We don't want to hire one because no-one would let us have one without a crew. And they might ask questions."

We've got it all worked out. Annabel and Nick? They must have had a very full conversation in the canteen while he was getting cigarettes and Mars Bars.

"Come on, Pax. This is the best way. We go gently down the Thames to Southend, round the corner to Havengore buoy and pick up Nick's money as it gets dark. Look at the map. You don't even have to go out of sight of the shore. And if the coastguard sees us or one of those army people on the range, what could be more innocent than an old fishing boat tying up on the buoy for a few minutes to sort out the engine? Then we can either come back up the Thames in the dark or we can find somewhere nice and quiet and romantic to spend the night before we come back on Sunday. No-one will even notice us."

"I'm still not sure. I have to think about it. I promised to see the children tomorrow."

"Oh darling, please. I'm so excited. For me?" She put her left hand on his shoulder and leaned over. Her silk blouse fell open again. She opened her eyes wide and parted her moist lips. This time when they kissed she gave all her mouth to him, her tongue quivering and darting. She thought she could make him change his mind by using her body. She was playing on his masculine pride, his virility, his lust. She thought she could make him forget his inhibitions, his caution, his common sense, his loyalty to his wife and his family and his children with the promise of a few moments of sensual pleasure with her luscious body.

She was right.

"I want you," he heard himself whisper as he nuzzled her ear.

The rest of the world receded somewhere beyond the boundary of his senses. All that he could see and hear and feel and touch and taste was concentrated on her warm and soft and giving body. He would do anything, say anything, believe anything in order to love and hold and lie with her. The *Swan*, the bank, his home, his children, nothing else mattered any more. As he drank at her lips and pressed himself to her breasts even Thea was forgotten.

But not for long. Drawing breath he looked over Annabel's shoulder for a moment and saw Thea looking in at them through the window.

At first he thought she was a figment of his guilty conscience. He smiled wanly back at her expression of disbelief and hurt and anger. She turned on her heel and walked briskly back along the dockside in the direction of the car park. Without a word to Annabel he stood up, knocking the glasses over, and forced his way through the crowded bar and out onto the dockside in pursuit. He caught up with her fifty yards from the car. He could see Thomas and Sarah in the back seat, faces pressed to the window. They waved at him.

"Thea. I can explain. You've got it all wrong." He took her

210

arm to make her stand still but she shook it off violently.

In better, happier days they had sat hand in hand on the sofa and made fun of the soap operas and B movies. Sometimes they turned the sound off and improvised their own dialogue, strings of terrible clichés interspersed with nonsense and vulgarity. How they would have jeered and clapped at the stream of time-honoured quotations he now poured into her ears.

"You're making a terrible mistake . . . That's the first time I've even touched her . . . She's lonely and upset. I was just trying to help . . . I wouldn't do anything to hurt you or the children . . . There's nothing between us. I promise . . . If you love me you must believe me . . . Just give me a chance to explain . . ."

She got in the car and almost slammed the door on his fingers. She wiped her cheeks with the heel of her hand. She opened the window a crack and spoke for the first time. "Go back to your boat and your mistress and we'll talk when you've come to your senses."

The bewildered faces of his children stared back at him through the back window as she drove off in a cloud of exhaust and a scurry of gravel. He gave a feeble wave.

Annabel was waiting for him by the chain fence, looking down at the *Swan*. She was looking as demure as one can in a slit skirt and open-fronted blouse.

"I suppose you'll be getting your things from the boat and going home. You're not to worry. I'll find some other way of getting to Havengore. I'm sorry I caused you so much trouble."

He felt calm and in control for the first time. He knew exactly what he was going to do. His mind had cleared. He was free of doubt and indecision. His words were measured and authoritative.

"I want you to go home right now. Pack some sensible clothes and a lilo and some blankets, unless you've got a sleeping bag. Tomorrow morning I want you to buy two big four-gallon petrol cans and fill them with diesel fuel. I shall expect you here no later than a quarter to ten. I'll look after the rest. The chandlers are still open."

She looked at him as if she had noticed something about him for the first time. She stood on tiptoe to kiss him but he turned his head away. There would be time enough for that later.

He was woken by a clap of thunder and the tattoo of raindrops on the cabin roof. The berth rolled beneath him. He clutched at the shelf by his head to stop himself falling out. The *Swan* was heaving in the swell, straining at her ropes. Abandon ship. Where had he stowed the lifejackets he had bought that evening? He sat up, cracked his head on the ceiling and lay down again.

The torch. He had to have the water-resistant torch. He groped on the shelf until the world outside the portholes turned to day in a brilliant flash of lightning. Water was streaming down the portholes. Inside and out. There was water on the floor.

Dear God. I don't want to drown.

He suppressed the fear that the water was coming up through the floor. He found the torch and flashed it up to the cabin roof. It was dripping from the seams and the portholes. There was no immediate danger unless they were swamped by a tidal wave. He had better check if she was dragging at her moorings. Resisting the temptation to dive back into his berth and put his head under the bedclothes he struggled into his new orange anorak and new waterproof hat. Feeling like Christopher Robin off to rescue Pooh he forced open the cabin doors and scrambled outside.

The cockpit was awash. The din was tremendous. The rain beat savagely on the boats and on the water, ropes clattered against the mast, thunder boomed and rolled. Bracing himself against a violent squall of wind and rain he wondered whether he should have invested in a safety harness. The wind whipped off his hat and he clawed at the choking tapes on his Adam's apple, bringing a lump to his throat. Water trickled down the back of his neck and lashed into his eyes. A brilliant flash of lightning threw everything into negative, searing the upright line of the mast into his retina. He wished he had listened to the weather forecast.

If it was like this in Saint Katherine's Dock, what the hell would it be like on Maplin Sands?

Thea got out of bed at three o'clock in the morning to make another cup of tea. She shifted from one foot to the other on the cold kitchen floor while she waited for the kettle to boil. Her mug was upstairs by the bed so she rummaged in the sink for another to rinse under the tap. As there was no-one else to make tea for there was no need for the teapot. God knew where the lid was in this mess anyway. Slowly and deliberately she poured milk into the mug, added a tea bag and poured on the boiling water. She poked the tea bag down with the handle of the butter knife and stirred it.

She got a chair out of the dining room and stood on it to reach the Paracetamol from the top of the cooker hood where the children could not reach it. As she turned and pressed it the ratcheting noise of the safety cap echoed in the silent house. Mustn't wake the children. She took two out and looked at the rest in the jar. There was no point. They would only make her sick.

She went back upstairs and put the tablets on the bedside table next to the phone to wait until the tea was cool enough to drink. She lay on the bed in her dressing gown and buried her face in the darkness of the pillow. She would look a sight in the morning. Perhaps if she had a bath it would help her get to sleep.

She sat up and reached for the mug. It left a brown ring on the cover of the *Reader's Digest Book of Home Improvements* that Pax had been reading. He wouldn't be needing it on the boat. Boats didn't need loft conversions and kitchen extensions. She picked up the tablets and looked at them in the palm of her hand.

She threw them on the bed and put the mug back on its brown ring. She began to rummage on the floor for her clothes as if she had suddenly remembered an urgent appointment. She dressed quickly and started to look for her handbag. She found it on top of the washing machine in the garage. She put on her old quilted raincoat and went out into the Square. A fine dew

213

was falling, making sickly haloes round the street lamps. She unlocked the car and left the back door open.

She ran back up to the children's room. Never disturb a sleeping child. But this was an emergency. She scooped Thomas up in his duvet and carried him downstairs to the car. He opened his eyes, asked if they were going on holiday and fell back to sleep again. She went back for Sarah who did not wake at all. She stood on the front step, trying to think if she had forgotten anything. She had. She fetched the *A to Z* from the record rack in the living room and a scrap of paper from beside the telephone with an address scribbled on it.

She rehearsed her speech as she drove through the glistening, deserted streets. It wasn't for herself that she was doing this. It was for the children and for him. She would be happy to creep away into the night for ever if she knew that they would be happy. She knew they did not really want her. She knew that she was a drag on them all. She knew she was a terrible wife and mother and home-maker. She could make it on her own with just her memories. But it was more than just their own lives. The children would be devastated. And the rest of his life would be ridden with guilt. She would beg. She would plead. She would implore. The only thing she could not decide was whether to take the children out of the car and hold them at her side, bleary-eyed and pathetic in their duvets, while she made her speech.

After several wrong turnings and stops to check the *A to Z* she drew up outside the address on the piece of paper. It had taken nearly an hour. It was half past four in the morning. The street was deserted. All the lights were out in the house. She felt sick in the pit of her stomach. She sat there, wondering whether to turn round and drive back home again. She had been a fool to come. And what about the children? They were fast asleep. If she dragged them out into the drizzle they would catch their death of cold.

As in a dream she opened the car door and went up to the front door of the house. She found the bell to Flat B and pressed it. She couldn't hear anything. Perhaps it didn't work. She had better go home. She gritted her teeth and pressed it again. She was about to turn away and go back to the car when the light in the hall went on. She could hear someone padding in bare feet. She wanted to run away and hide but they would see the car anyway.

The door was opened by a large, fat man in a towelling bathrobe. He was totally hairless with not even an eyebrow or a nostril hair to mar his smooth, buttery skin. He had the wide-eyed, newborn look of a slightly jaundiced baby. Thea's knees felt suddenly weak.

"What the hell do you want?" asked the man, his baby face puckered into a scowl. His voice was deep and North American.

"I was looking for Annabel," she said as loud as she could.

"At this time of night you ought to be in bed or asleep. Come back in the morning."

"It's urgent. Life and Death," she squeaked.

He looked her up and down. He balled his fists as if he was about to hit her. Now her knees were actually shaking. He grunted and turned away from her but left the door open. He padded off down the hall, clenching and unclenching his hands. While she waited she rehearsed her speech again. She looked back at the car. The children were still asleep.

Annabel appeared wearing a red silk kimono and pink ear-muffs. Thea felt scruffy and unwashed in her old quilted mac. The hairless man stood behind Annabel, glowering. Her bright-blue eyes, puffed with sleep, widened with surprise.

"Thea! What is it?" she said like someone who already knows.

Thea could feel her heart pouding in her head, her stomach pounding in her chest. Her legs were beginning to shake. It was time for the speech.

"If you ever go near my husband again, I'll slit your fucking ears."

Annabel's hands flew to her ear-muffs. She clutched the hairless man's arm and looked up at him to defend her. He stared at Thea, looking right through her, and then a crocodile smile flickered over his baby face.

215

"That's my kind of talk. Don't worry. She'll do as she's told." He closed the door.

She drove slowly home. She felt very tired. Somewhere deep inside there was a tiny glow of achievement. She felt she had passed a milestone. She had done something she had never done before. For the first time in her life she had used THAT word.

Pax woke up cold and stiff. He rolled out of his berth gingerly to avoid going into a rheumatic spasm. There was a lot to do today. He would start with a cup of tea, brewed on the new camping gas stove he had bought at the chandler's the night before. He set it up in the galley and looked for the matches. They were bobbing around the food cupboard with the sodden box of tea bags and the burst bag of sugar. He took a few matches out of the box and put them under his left armpit to dry. The box itself he put under his right armpit. But it was no good. The striking paper was too far gone. He would have to wait until the shops opened. He disentangled the sticky matchheads from his underarm hair and began to repack and dry out his stores.

The rain had stopped. It was cold and grey. He flicked the pools of water from the cockpit seats with his hands and brought out the stores from inside the cabin. He tried not to think that they had cost him his credit limit on both his credit cards. It was an investment, wasn't it?

Lifejackets. Lifebuoy with winking light that automatically goes on in the water. It was winking now after spending the night submerged under Pax's berth. There were no instructions about turning it off so he covered it with his orange anorak. He had no wish to be plucked to safety before he had even got out of the dock. Twenty yards of Terylene rope, just in case. Distress Flares (Keep In A Dry Place). Aluminium paddle for steering in case the tiller breaks or paddling in case the engine breaks. Inflatable life-raft. Spare anchor with three fathoms of chain. (Not enough to reach Thy Father) and thirty feet of warp. Water desalination tablets. Portable bilge-pump.

This was a selection from the Coastguard's Hints to Boat-

216

owners. Ignorant, he had chosen them pretty much at random. He was on safer ground with the other stores, remembering the bits and pieces that always came in handy on a caravan holiday. Candles. Tin opener. Saucepan. Cockroach powder. Aspirin. Two mugs. Two plates. Two sets of cutlery. Two champagne glasses. Sticking plaster. Safety pins. Spanner. Toilet paper. Bucket.

He threw into a black plastic bag the waterlogged food. Tea, matches, the little sugar that had not dissolved, biscuits, bread, a Victoria sponge. He toyed with the idea of trying to match the labels with the tins they had come off but there was no time. You can recognise a corned-beef tin and they would have to take pot luck on the baked beans, alphabet spaghetti and Irish stew. Unscathed were the milk, butter, brandy, sausages, soap and Champagne.

Champagne with Annabel. One hand toying with her luscious body, the other with a fortune in gold. Somehow this vision didn't belong with the world he lived in, at least up to now. Fussing with his tins, whiling away the time before she arrived, he repeated to himself that he was really changing his life. Gone were the vacillation, the idleness, the compromise. Before he was swallowed up by death he would have tasted the carefree life of action and adventure. And it was starting right now.

At nine o'clock he went to the shop for a box of matches, a pound of sugar, a packet of chocolate digestives and little plastic bags to put them in. He shut himself into the cabin and got the stove going in the galley. He warmed his hands over the saucepan while he waited for it to boil. He started to shiver but could not diagnose whether it was a chill or apprehension. Annabel would be here in a minute and then there would be no going back.

He imagined her in here with him when it was all over. Tousled blonde hair, a pink jump-suit open to the waist, long slender fingers running through his scalp. His hand shook as he poured the boiling water over the tea bag in his mug. A shudder ran down his spine as he heard a woman's tapping footsteps on the pontoon by the side of the *Swan*. He felt the boat rock as

217

she stepped into the cockpit. He took a deep breath and opened the cabin door.

It was Thea. She wore her old quilted raincoat. In one hand she carried a purple nylon duffle bag, in the other her green wellies. Although it was only half past nine she had brushed her hair and put on make-up. She could not cover up the red rims round her eyes. They looked at each other as they would have looked at themselves in a mirror.

"Are you having a jumble sale?" she asked.

"There was a storm last night. A Joseph Conrad job. She sort of sank from the top down. There's biscuits in syrup and pre-wetted toilet paper." He avoided her gaze by fiddling with the tea bag.

"Is that tea?"

He sidled back into the main part of the cabin so she could get down the steps. She backed down them, clutching the rail, as if she feared imminent capsize. She groped her way to the port berth and sat down. He handed her the mug.

"That's yours, isn't it?" she asked.

"You have it. I'm going to phone Annabel or head her off in the car park."

"You needn't bother. I've seen her. She's not coming. She was very understanding."

He poured hot water into the second mug and added tea bag, milk and sugar. He still avoided her eyes.

"Nice little home you've got for yourself in here. Very cosy."

"When did you see her?"

"Four o'clock this morning. Her boyfriend opened the door. He wasn't very pleased. I was a bit abrupt because I didn't want to leave the children on their own for very long."

"You mean you drove across London at four o'clock in the morning? On your own? And you left the children?"

"I put them in the back of the car. They went to sleep. I set out at one but I got lost."

"And there was someone else there? Really?"

She nodded and looked at the floor. He put his elbows on his knees and let his head sag. He suddenly felt very tired and stiff and empty. "I'll just shove all the gear inside and then we'll go home. That's what you want."

Thea stood up and looked down at him. "The hell we will. Georgina's looking after the children. I've come to sail down the river with you.

"Leave off, Thea. You don't have to do that. It's just a waste of time. Let's go home."

She reached out and forced his chin up so he had to look at her. Her mouth was set and her pupils had narrowed into pinpoints. "So all this business about boats and the sea and a new life and getting away from the petit bourgeois life was all talk, was it? All you wanted was a bit on the side. And when you can't have that, the rest doesn't matter. Let me tell you, I may not have her tits but I can pull on a rope as well as she can."

Did she want him to hug her? Argue? Plead for forgiveness? Take her seriously? She probably didn't know, any more than he knew what he wanted. He didn't know how he ought to feel, which he had always thought worse than not feeling anything.

"Oh shit," he said, "where did you park the car? I'll have to go and get some more diesel."

By five to ten the cockpit was more or less clear although the cabin looked as though the Customs and Excise had been having a practice. Thea was busy in the cabin, muttering about the damp bedding. Pax connected the battery, squirted Easi-start liberally into the engine compartment and hesitantly turned the key, half hoping it would not start. With a cloud of blue smoke and an asthmatic cough the engine chugged into life. This time he manipulated the gear lever with exquisite care. Leaving her in neutral he cast off fore and aft. With the tiller hard over and little nudges from the engine in reverse gear the *Swan* backed gently out from her berth and turned to face the lock. He steered her nervously down the narrow passage between the other boats.

He started to whistle but it did nothing for his growing feelings of foreboding.

❊ Chapter Eighteen ❊

The storm of the previous night had blown itself out, leaving a grey, sullen day to match his mood. The river was like old soup. Indescribable filth lurked in its depths while croutons of more buoyant rubbish bobbed on the surface with streaks and whorls of creamy foam. He sniffed the air for the smell of seasoning from the Pepper and Spice Factory but the wind was blowing in the wrong direction. He stood on the back seat of the cockpit holding the boom with two hands while the tiller nuzzled his leg. He kept a sharp lookout for driftwood that could hole the bows and rope that could choke the propeller like bindweed.

As they passed the River Police station at Wapping, Thea came out of the cabin. She had found the Arran sweater she had knitted him while she had been pregnant with Thomas. His first impulse was to ask her crossly to take it off. She probably wanted to look adorable in it with the sleeves rolled up and the hem almost to her knees, like a woman in a man's shirt. But her face was pale and she was shivering. He decided that she had not put it on for effect.

"Are you all right?"

"It's very stuffy in there. I'll be O.K. in a minute."

It sounded more of a hope than a promise. She huddled in the corner of the cockpit facing him with her back to the cabin. He pulled himself straight and sucked in his stomach and set his jaw resolutely to the horizon but she closed her eyes and he let it all flop down again.

"Pax, can I ask a question?"

"Anything you like."

"What are we doing here?"

Pax looked down at the scenery. Cranes and chimneys. Piles

of coal, scrap, gravel. Slag. Timber. Oil tanks. Containers.

"Is that a philosophical question?"

"I'm in no mood for that sort of thing. You know what I mean. Where are we going? What were you going to do before? With, you know."

"I tried to tell you on the phone from the office. I said we had to talk. You wouldn't listen. You told me to talk to a psychiatrist."

"I am sorry. I am truly sorry for not listening to you after you had run away from home to spend the night on the boat and phoned me from the office at lunchtime. Now if it's not too much trouble could you please tell me where we are going and what you intended to do."

"Your brother Nick was guilty of smuggling gold coins into this country to evade French exchange control and British value added tax. Only a fraction of the booty was discovered. The rest, so he says, is tied to a navigation buoy off Maplin Sands just round the corner from Southend at the mouth of the Thames Estuary. There could be a million pounds' worth. Nick asked me to take Annabel and the boat and see if it was still there. That's where we're going now."

His bald statement had its intended effect. She was speechless.

He immersed himself in the "Port of London Authority Handbook of Tide Tables, Particulars of Docks Etc." a slim blue hardback of a hundred pages, which he had bought at the chandler's the evening before. This was a more authoritative source of information about the Thames than the *A to Z*. He was not at all embarrassed to pull it out of his orange anorak.

Half the book was taken up with tide tables. For every day of the year they listed high water and low water at seven places on the river from London Bridge to Walton-on-the-Naze at the mouth of the estuary. One of the places was Shivering Sands, a name that sounded so fictional that he looked it up on Annabel's chart.

The book had a lot of information that was interesting but not immediately useful. There were instructions for gaining access to the Tilbury Grain Terminal and a list of Authorised

221

Explosive Anchorage Areas. It also contained a lot that was completely incomprehensible to him and that he hoped was irrelevant to their present mission.

There were some nuggets that were very useful. The distance from Tower Bridge to Southend Pier was forty-three land miles. Round the corner to Havengore Creek was six or seven miles. They had fifty miles to do.

The speed of the *Swan* was six knots, say seven miles an hour. For the next hour they were going against the tide that was still rushing upstream at about four miles an hour. So their actual speed was about three miles an hour. For the hour after that there would be slack water which meant they would go at seven miles an hour. When the tide turned they would speed up to eleven miles an hour. That would last for four hours before the tide turned again. What time would they get there?

It was like an eleven-plus arithmetic problem. He wished he had paid more attention to taps filling up baths and trains speeding towards each other. It had taken him twenty-five years to discover why he was supposed to learn that junk. By his reckoning, in which he had no great confidence, they would be past Southend at six o'clock. That should give them two hours to find the buoy, see if there was anything tied to it, and turn for home.

They motored slowly past Greenwich. Pax remembered his last trip with Jason and smiled at his excitement and anxiety. He was beginning to feel a bit more confident. It was really pretty easy. The engine seemed to be going smoothly although he still could not get used to the variations in pitch and tone as the propeller came near the surface or the exhaust dipped deeper under water. Every ten minutes or so he opened the engine locker and felt the top of the engine with the back of his hand like a mother with a feverish child.

They picked up speed as the tide went slack. There were few other craft on the river. A barge train passed them going upstream, tossing them in its wake and making Thea clutch the seat. The tiller swung abruptly to one side and cracked his shin on its return. He ignored the pain and forced his lips into a sailor's whistle in case she looked at him. The bright yellow

222

Woolwich ferry passed in front of them and this time he shouted a warning about the wash.

"I'm hungry. Shall we have something to eat?" he asked, to break the silence.

"Would you mind getting it yourself? I don't feel like food."

"You're not feeling seasick are you?" he snapped, more a command than a query.

"You can't feel seasick in a flat calm," she snapped back, more a question than a reply.

He showed her how to stand on the seat with the tiller against her legs. She preferred to stand on the cockpit floor with the tiller in her hand, craning round the side of the cabin to see where she was going. She held it hesitantly, letting it jostle her arm as the wavelets hit the rudder. He told her to stay close to the right bank and shout if she saw anything in the way. He went down into the cabin to make himself a sandwich.

She had cleared up the galley, spread waterproofs on the berths and laid out the sleeping bags. Her duffle bag was on the floor, blocking the way into the forecabin. On the narrow shelf next to one berth she had put her handbag and a photograph of the children in a silver frame. Sticking out from under the pillow was a lacy nightdress she only wore at Christmas and on their wedding anniversary. It looked very domestic. He thought of the old couple who had lived on the boat under a willow tree. He felt a prickling in his nose.

He made a cheese and tomato sandwich and took it outside. He ate it sitting on the cabin roof with his back to Thea. After Woolwich the river widened out. If this had been a pleasure trip he would have made an effort to see beauty and interest in the scenery. As they were on a different kind of errand he saw how flat and dull it was. Under the grey sky there was not even the despairing charm of ugliness. He no longer resisted the suspicion that had crept upon him on his first passage from the boatyard to the Tower. Just pottering along looking at the scenery was boring. There was nothing to do. The only thing that made this voyage interesting was the goal at the end. And when he had the bag of money in his hand and made it up with

Thea, what would be left? Only the boring scenery.

He took the tiller back from Thea. She slumped in the corner of the cockpit facing him. All the determination that had brought her here seemed to have drained away. She sat with her knees tucked under her chin and his sweater pulled down over her ankles, like a morose dwarf with enormous tits.

To pass the time he decided to rig up one of the sails. He had not taken them out or looked at them since he had bought the boat. They were all heaped up in the cabin underneath the foredeck. It would also give Thea something to do to take her mind off herself. He would have to cajole her gently into activity.

"Come on, Thea, snap out of it. Take the tiller please."

He scrambled up onto the foredeck, lifted off the hatch and put it to one side. A smell of rot and damp and mildew rose from the depths as if he had opened an old tomb. He lay on the deck, reached inside, and pulled up the first piece of canvas that came to hand. It felt soft and slimy. It was decorated with dark green gorgonzola patches. He dragged out a couple of square yards onto the deck until he found an edge sewn round a rope. Every yard or so along this edge were horseshoe shaped rings of metal. The base of the horseshoe was a bolt that could be unscrewed.

A steel cable ran from the top of the mast to a bronze ring bolted to the front of the deck. A Terylene rope was also attached to the metal ring with the same sort of shackle that was on the sail. The rope ran to the top of the mast, through a pulley and down the other side of the mast where it was wound round a wooden cleat. This was obviously for hauling the sail up.

He laboriously unscrewed the sail shackles and fixed them round the steel cable. He attached the end of the Terylene rope to the end of the sail. The theory was that when he untied the other end of the rope from the wooden cleat and pulled on it the sail would rise gracefully to the top of the mast. It would look like a picture of Y is for Yacht.

"Oh God. What's that terrible smell?" Thea gagged. Her face was deathly pale. Her nose had grown pointed and fleshless. She abandoned the tiller and sat down on the cockpit seat, retching into her hand.

The sail stuck half way up the cable. It flapped menacingly in the breeze. Originally white it was now various shades of nauseating green and yellow. The stench of putrefaction was overpowering as it unfolded. Black, slimy things dropped from its creases. It seemed alive and evil.

The *Swan* wallowed head to wind without a hand on the tiller. The breeze blew the smell straight down into the cockpit.

"For God's sake, hold on to the tiller," he shouted.

"To hell with the tiller. I'm holding on to my stomach."

He had to take the sail down anyway. He had shackled it on upside down. Taking deep breaths to windward through his mouth he hauled it down, trying to ignore the slime on his hands. He resisted the temptation to bundle the sail straight back through the hatch but painstakingly refitted the shackles to the cable the right way round. It might come in handy if the engine broke down, although they would probably not be the ideal circumstances in which to learn to sail. He shoved as much as he could into the forecabin and stuffed the rest tightly under the bowsprit.

He made his way back to the cockpit and took the tiller, pointing her seaward again with the ebbing tide.

"I hope you haven't got a bug. Or what about food poisoning? You didn't eat shellfish last night did you? Tinned salmon? Fried scampi? Prawns in garlic?"

"Shut up about food. I need to go to the loo."

"Just let me check it out first. I didn't have time this morning because of repacking everything. We call it the head, you know."

"We can call it the belly-button for all I care. Quick. I need to go now."

The first drawback was that the head was in the forecabin, which, as they had just discovered, was full of nicely ripening sails. He gingerly opened the door from the main cabin and took a deep breath. His worst fears were confirmed. It smelt like the kind of chemical closet that induces a fortnight's constipation on a caravan holiday. And he hadn't even opened the concertina door to the loo yet.

It was a small compartment, three feet from floor to ceiling and wide enough for a moderately-built man if he hunched his shoulders. It was not possible to go in frontways and turn round. You had to back in with your drawers already down.

The lavatory pan was half full of black sludge. A handle was supposed to pump sea water in from outside to flush it. He tried carefully a couple of times with no result, then more vigorously. It snapped off in his hand, the metal eaten through by rust. "Won't be a minute," he said to Thea as he dangled a bucket over the side. Her face displayed discomfort and despair. But the water only diluted the sludge and sloshed over the edge of the pan. He fiddled with various knobs and taps that might be seacocks to let the water out. Since seacocks also let the water in he hesitated to force them.

He broke the news as gently as he could. She took it badly. She grumbled bitterly as she retreated into the privacy of the main cabin with the bucket. He took the opportunity to pee over the side.

Somehow it wasn't what he had imagined.

The lights of the beach-side night club were hidden by the fronded palm trees but they could still hear the music from the band, pulsating with exotic rhythm. She kicked her shoes off on the soft white sand and they stood watching the lazy curl of the surf made brilliant by the silver moon. Then he took her in his arms and they danced to the sound of the sea and the music. She rested her blonde head on his shoulder. He could feel the warmth of her cheek through his white tuxedo.

The life he had left behind all seemed like a dream in the tropical moonlight. He touched her earring, a half-sovereign from the hoard they had collected many months before from the buoy in Havengore Creek. That was real. Gold was real. Her delicate ear and the rest of her perfect body were real.

Thinking he was caressing her ear out of affection, she nuzzled closer to him. The scent of her body rose to mingle with the perfume of orchids and musk that lingered on the night air. He let his hands wander through the folds of her long

226

silk evening dress. He stroked her back and kissed the side of her neck. She sighed and her moist lips sought his.

"Let's go back to the boat," he whispered.

"No, Pax, right here. I want you now."

She gently slipped from his embrace and lay on the sand, her arms outstretched. Her eyes were wide and shining in the moonlight and pleading for him. He slipped off the tuxedo and with a sensual smile slowly undid the buttons of his money belt. He tossed it onto the sand by her side.

It was a relief to get rid of the weight.

"I say. Did you hear about that man Brown? Seems he kept gold coins in a money belt round his waist. He got back to his yacht the other night – you know, the *Swan*, over in the lagoon – after some shindig or other at the beach club. He fancied a swim, dived in without thinking and sank to the bottom like a stone. That fancy piece of his, what's her name, is offering a reward for the body. Half shares. But it's too damned deep."

"What a way to go. There'll have to be an autopsy if they find him."

Thea lay in a foetal position on the floor of the cockpit, her eyes fixed on the dial that showed the engine temperature. He was standing on the seat, holding on to the boom, the tiller nudging his leg. He had offered her a blanket but she preferred to be cold. She would be all right in a minute. She felt better when she couldn't see the water.

"Pax. Do you wish she was here instead of me?"

"Do you want an honest answer?"

"Yes."

"I don't know."

She heaved herself into the lotus position, still on the cockpit floor, clenching her teeth. She took deep, regular breaths, the Lamaze method for avoiding puking over the side.

"You were kissing her."

"Yes, I was kissing her."

"Did you ever do anything else?"

"No."

She opened her eyes, gulped in air and tried concentrating on the end of Southend pier, the nearest static object. She tried to speak without moving her mouth so the words came out like a ventriloquist's, without b's and m's.

"What are we going to do if the money's there?"

"I don't know. Let's find it first."

"What were you going to do before I barged in?"

As the estuary widened they sensed the beginnings of a deep sea swell. His knuckles whitened on the tiller. The propeller raced as it came near the surface of the water.

"Go away somewhere. Buy a boat. Give it all up. Somewhere warm and exotic. Enjoy life."

"With her."

"With anyone who'd come. With you, if you like. We needn't get a boat. We can stay inland. In the mountains. You don't get altitude sickness do you?"

"What would we do there? You and me and the kids? What would be so different from what we do now?"

"Of course it would be different. We'd all be liberated, relaxed. We'd go fishing together and make a tree house and tell stories. We'd be together. Enjoy each other. You and me. I don't know. It would be different."

"And that's what you were going to do with her. Find yourselves a tropical love-nest. You and Annabel. And the money. And the boat."

She made a rasping, gurgling sound that turned into a retching cough. She held on to the gunwhale with one hand and her stomach with the other. She took more deep breaths. If they had been on dry land and she hadn't been about to throw up over the side he would have thought she was trying to stop laughing.

"So what would *you* do if the money was there?" he challenged.

"Get on dry land and never set foot on a boat again."

She was not in the right frame of mind to talk about the dawning of a new life. Her complexion was greenish and waxy and she looked shrunk in on herself. She looked up at him, put her hand over her mouth and retched again.

No. She couldn't be laughing.

*

Opposite Southend pier the engine began to stutter. Pax grabbed for the throttle and eased it back but it had no effect. He kicked the gear lever into neutral. The engine recovered for a few seconds and faltered again.

"What's the matter?" asked Thea, standing up.

"Get the lifejackets. Just in case."

He put on his calmest voice. Not that it mattered much what kind of voice he used for such a request. The content of the message eclipsed the style in which it was delivered. "I say, you chaps, don't get excited but I think we may have to abandon ship" has the same effect as "every man for himself," or whatever they teach you at naval school.

Acute fear overcoming chronic nausea, she bolted into the cabin.

In some ways it was a relief not to have the noise of the engine drumming in his ears and vibrating under his feet. He could hear the sounds from the shore quite easily over the water. At the water's edge children shouted and screamed. Further along the shore a funfair mingled disco with steam-organ music. From the seaward side a steamer's siren bleated a message of doom. Seagulls mewed as they circled overhead and wavelets lapped against the drifting hull.

Thea struggled through the cabin door in an inflated life-jacket, carrying her duffle bag.

"Listen to the sounds of the sea," said Pax, trying to calm them both.

"To hell with the sounds of the sea. Get the engine going."

He opened the engine locker and picked up a spanner. It was more symbolic than useful. He had no idea what to do. He felt the temperature with the back of his hand. Hot but not boiling. He jiggled the hoses and copper tubes and electric wires that festooned the main body of the engine. He found a dipstick and examined it like a nurse with a thermometer. He tested the tension on the rubber belt. He gave the cylinder block a few ringing taps with the spanner. Finally he composed his face to express disappointment.

"Let's call the whole thing off. There are some fishermen

229

over there. If we wave to them they'll give us a tow. We should never have come."

"Are you sure we haven't just run out of petrol?"

With a refill from one of the cans the engine started first time.

The Voyage continued.

Maplin Sands is an enormous sandbank ten miles long on a straight stretch of shore between two headlands. Half way between them is Havengore Creek. The shore is flat and marshy and criss-crossed with ditches and rivulets and creeks. At high tide the water laps against the reed beds. At low tide it uncovers the sands, nearly four miles wide. The chequered buoy marks the edge of the sands and the beginning of the deep water channel that goes into Havengore Creek. It is between two flashing buoys five hundred yards apart.

It took him twenty minutes to work that out from the chart. He sat with the tiller under his armpit trying to keep the bows against the oncoming waves, poring over the chart in the failing light. The little numbers scattered over the blue danced before his eyes. Gusts of wind fluttered the page and drops of spray confused his vision. Thea was lying rigid on a berth inside the cabin staring at the ceiling above her head and shivering.

All he had to do was follow the line of the edge of the sands between the flashing buoys and he would come to the chequered one. That was easier said than done. The sands were already half covered by the rising tide. His inexperienced eye could not detect the colour of shallow water. The wind was blowing them onshore and although it was not very strong he underestimated its ability to blow off course a shallow draught boat without a keel.

He thought of putting down the leeboards but was afraid of getting them stuck in the sand. It was not yet dark enough for the flashing buoys to be flashing but grey enough so that he repeatedly lost sight of them. The first time they ran aground with an insidious crunching sound his stomach dropped to his knees. He had the presence of mind to throw the engine into

230

reverse before they were pushed broadside onto the sandbank and with the help of the rising tide they floated off. Thea struggled through the cabin door in her lifejacket, clutching her handbag.

"What was that?" she squeaked.

"Nothing. Just ran aground, that's all. We can get out and walk if we have to." He neglected to add that the tide could run faster than they could across the two miles of sand to the distant-looking shore. They ran aground three more times before he got the hang of it.

The waves were getting bigger. The sun was setting behind a massive bank of dark clouds in the west and the sky in the east was already black. There was a pale haze on the horizon and over the shore. Pax's general sense of anxiety and foreboding was being replaced by well founded fear. It was totally irresponsible for the parents of two young children to be cavorting out to sea in the dark, one of them seasick and the other incompetent.

At eight o'clock he thought he saw the chequered buoy. He shouted at the top of his voice. Thea staggered into the cockpit clutching her green wellingtons to her chest.

"Where is it? I can't see anything. Pax, I can't see anything at all. It's pitch dark."

"It's back there. I'll circle round. I'll have to be careful not to ram it."

First he took a good look round to make sure they were not being spied on. But they were outside the main shipping lane, there were no fishing boats or yachts and now the shore was hidden by a thin, white mist. Unless anyone was specifically looking for them they were alone. He turned in a large circle and went back to where he thought he had seen the buoy. He was sure he had gone too far and circled again.

"What are you trying to do? We've been going round and round for ten minutes?"

"*You* do it if you're so clever. Otherwise shut up."

The shore disappeared. There was still some light in the west but the rest of the sky was dark and filled with scudding black clouds. The swell was cresting into white-topped waves.

"Couldn't we look for it in the morning?" she asked, plaintively.

One dash of spray in his face was enough to convince him. They would make a run for the shore, find a sheltered place to anchor, and come back at first light in the morning. With a pounding heart and fingers crossed he set a course north-west which in theory would bring them to the beach across Maplin Sands.

It was the worst part of the voyage. The mist closed in and they lost sight of the flashing buoys. Foghorns began to bray but it was impossible to tell if they were about to be run down by a tanker or if it was miles away. In the distance they heard bells. They were cutting across the direction of the sea swell but there was no means of telling which way they were being pulled by the current. The tide was on the turn but he had no idea what effect that had on the rips over Maplin Sands. The compass card swung wildly between north and west. He begged it to stand still for just one second. Thea fought down her nausea and, clinging to the cabin side, peered through the murk for hazards.

He had imagined the shore looming through the mist so often that when it really appeared he ignored it. He felt the bow scrunch against the sand and swung the tiller hard over. The *Swan* heeled over. There was an ominous swishing, tearing sound as she ran aground and miraculously floated free. Thea turned on him wide-eyed.

"What have you done now?" she shouted.

"Got us to the shore," he said, as nonchalantly as he could.

They nosed their way down the shore until they came to the mouth of an inlet. He throttled back and puttered cautiously down it. There was just enough light to see a short wooden jetty before they rammed it. A board on a post announced that it was "Ministry of Defence Property. No Photography. No Trespassing." He cut the engine and went onto the foredeck to tie up to the post.

He used a super-granny. This is for use by people who cannot remember if a reef is right-over-left-and-left-over-right or left-over-right-twice. He did left-over-right-twice followed

232

by right-over-left-twice and another one each for luck. The result looked like macramé and would take a devil of a time to untie but it was the best he could do until he learned bowlines-on-the-bight and round-turns-and-two-half-hitches.

He went back to the cabin. He stood under the low ceiling trying to decide whether he looked more dashing with his knees bent or his shoulders hunched. Thea was sitting on her berth, her eyes fixed on the dark porthole opposite her. Her hair was lank and lustreless, her face pale and lined.

"We did it," he crowed.

"Did what?"

"Got here. Without drowning."

"We've got to get back. Also without drowning."

He dropped his dashing pose of the romantic seafarer. He felt tired and stiff and hungry. He had taken them down the Thames into the open sea, almost found the chequered buoy and navigated back to a safe mooring in the thick fog. Just now he had been proud of his achievement but his elation had already melted away. Would it have been different with Annabel, the woman of his dreams? Wouldn't he have felt strong and masterful, taken her in his arms, lowered her gently backwards on the berth and taken his prize?

Right now all he wanted was a fried corned-beef sandwich and a hot cup of tea and to crawl into his sleeping bag for the rest of the night in preparation for tomorrow. He ferreted in the galley drawer for the candles and stuck one on the corner of the sink. He set up the camping gas stove and attacked the corned beef tin with the opener.

"We'll soon have a hot meal and a cup of tea. That will cheer us up."

She didn't answer. He looked round and in the flickering candlelight he could see tears streaming down her cheeks. She made no effort to stop them. They dripped onto his Arran sweater.

"Let her snivel," he said to himself, turning back to the corned beef. "She wanted to come and now she's here. I didn't ask her. Annabel wouldn't have sat there feeling sorry for herself. Thea's not cut out for this sort of thing. Our lives have grown apart. It's time to make the break. This is probably the last night we'll spend together . . ."

He prised the meat out into the frying pan and went over to her. He sat down next to her and put his arm round her. Habits die hard. "What's the matter?"

"You wish *she* was here, don't you?" she sniffed. "You think that *she* wouldn't sit here feeling sorry for herself. You think I'm not cut out for this sort of thing. Our lives have grown apart. You're hoping this is the last night we'll spend together." Her shoulders began to shake.

"Thea, sweetheart, what on earth gave you that idea? How could you think that? You were so brave out there. Lots of people get seasick. Nelson. My mother."

He kissed her on the cheek. It was wet and salty. He hugged her shoulders, held her hands on her lap. She turned her face so he pecked round her eyes and ears and finally kissed her on the lips, warm and wet and slobbery. It wasn't Annabel, it wasn't new but it was familiar and warm. He put his hands inside her sweater and tried to ease her down on the berth.

"I have to go to the loo."

"You can go outside. You can get onto the jetty from the foredeck. There's no-one around. Take your wellies though, it might be marshy."

"If it's not bobbing up and down it will be heaven."

She mopped her face on her sleeve and forced a smile. He helped her scramble over the foredeck onto the jetty. She clumped over the planks, holding a roll of toilet paper, and picked her way into a clump of long sea grass between two sand dunes. She squatted out of sight and he went back to the cabin to light the stove. Tea first, then the corned beef.

The tide was running out fast. In an hour or so the creek would probably run dry and the *Swan* would nestle into the sand on her flat bottom. They would stop bobbing up and down. They would eat their supper and crawl into their separate sleeping bags. And then he would get out of bed and crawl into hers. For old times' sake.

She screamed his name. He put out the stove and scrambled

into the cockpit. She was waving and shouting at him from the end of the jetty, a dark shadow in the white mist. The land on either side of him was moving. He realised with horror that the *Swan* was sailing backwards down the inlet towards the sea. What had happened to the super-granny? He ran onto the foredeck to retrieve the rope and found that the knot was still firmly in place but the post had broken off from the jetty. The *Swan* was dragging the board with it like a sea anchor. He left the rope trailing and went back to the cockpit.

"Don't worry. I'll start the engine. Don't go away," he shouted.

She had left the jetty and was running along the bank after him, waving the toilet paper. She stumbled in and out of puddles and had lost one of her boots in the mud. She called his name as she floundered through the grass and the reeds.

He checked to see that the battery was connected and confidently turned the starter key. The engine stuttered into life. He pushed the gear lever forwards. The *Swan* stopped moving backwards and began to make way towards the shore. His self congratulation was rudely shattered by a protesting whine under his feet. The cockpit shuddered, the engine raced and faltered and only recovered when he threw it into neutral. Instinctively he looked over the stern to see that the mooring rope, still tethered to the Ministry's post, had wrapped itself round the propeller.

"Don't panic. I'll drop anchor," he shouted.

The *Swan* began to drift backwards again on the tide. She had nearly cleared the inlet and waves were buffeting the hull. He went onto the foredeck and clumsily unscrewed the shackle that held the anchor fast. Forcing himself to keep calm he threw the anchor overboard. The chain ran through a hole into the forecabin. He watched it rattle out. The water was shallow and the anchor should hold well in the sand so there was nothing to worry about.

The water was deeper than he thought. The *Swan* was still running backwards and the chain was still clanking out of the forecabin. How silly of him. The anchor was probably stuck fast on the bottom but they were being dragged out by the tide.

All he had to do was hold on to the chain to stop it running out and they would stop. But how do you stop the chain running out without breaking your fingers?

He was still considering this problem and wishing he had researched it beforehand when the end of the chain came on deck. In reality it was only a second but in that wonderful moment of lucidity when time stands still before disaster strikes it seemed like an age between noticing that the end of the chain was not attached to anything and watching it disappear for ever over the bows and into the sea.

He looked for Thea but she had disappeared into the mist. Faintly above the noise of the waves against the hull and thumping of his heart he heard her call his name, like the distant mewing of a seagull. He opened his mouth to call back but shut it again. There was no point. He was alone.

The *Swan* was drifting broadside to the swell, rocking from side to side. It seemed as if she was being pushed towards the shore but in fact the tidal stream was taking her out to sea against the direction of the waves and the rising wind. On top of the sea swell were choppy wavelets spitting spray. He would have expected the wind to blow away the mist but it seemed to be getting even thicker. He could not see the shore or any lights but the sound of bells and sirens grew louder. He wondered if he was drifting into the middle of a sea lane.

The first priority was to free the rope that was tangled around the propeller. He leaned over the stern and tugged hopefully at the two free ends but it was clear he was dealing with the grandmother of super-grannies. Every one of the engine's thirty-six horsepower had been dedicated to tightening, unravelling, twisting and knotting the rope around the propeller and its shaft. He would have to cut through it.

He found the breadknife in the galley and tied it to his belt with a long piece of string. The way things were going he was bound to drop it in the water. There was a small piece of teak deck at the stern behind the cockpit. The hull sloped inwards so the propeller was under an overhang. To reach it he had to lie on the small piece of deck with most of his torso hanging vertically down. He wished there was someone to hold his legs. The tiller rail cut into his thighs and the edge of the deck into his stomach.

It was like getting string out of a lawnmower blades but on a grander scale. How do the bits that get wrapped round last end up *under* the bits that were wrapped round first? The first couple of layers were easy because he could cut across the rope and he began to feel he was doing well. Then he found he could cut only lengthways down the rope because the propeller was in the way of the knife. He hacked away with growing desperation. The water came up to his elbows, chilling his fingers so he could not feel the knife handle. A wave surged to his chest and the next one splashed over his head. He felt it sluicing down his neck inside his orange anorak.

Foghorns and sirens were getting louder. He forced out of his mind the fear of being run down by a ship. Even if he saw one coming straight at him there was nothing he could do to get out of the way. He would be invisible from the bridge and without a radar cone would be invisible on their screen. He forced his aching arms to saw away, tugging on the strands that came free with fingers that felt like clumps of frozen sausages. He tried to ignore the tingling in his legs, the shooting pains in his feet, the pain in his abdomen that felt as though he was being sawn in half, the cramps in his shoulders, the heavy throbbing in his chest. Ignoring them made them feel worse.

The bellowing roar of the tanker's siren seemed to come from all round him. Three short blasts and a long. He looked up to see the tall black mountain looming out of the mist. A brilliant searchlight dazzled him. It ignored the scrap of driftwood and the wormlike creature clinging to it. The siren boomed again. The searchlight and the bridge lights lit up the mist but all there was to see was a foul black monster and its bow wave looking like teeth. The wormlike creature dropped its knife and tried to wriggle back into the cockpit. A cramp knotted its legs and he clung helplessly to the tiller.

"Oh God," he cried, and closed his eyes.

He had often lain awake in bed wondering what his last thoughts would be when he died. The Last Things, the World

237

to Come, his wife, his children, his mother? Or would it be something like the best bacon sandwich he had ever had or the only goal he had ever scored in a football match? Waiting with his eyes closed to be smashed by the tanker's bows and minced to little pieces by its propeller all he could think of were the times he had lain awake in bed wondering what his last thoughts would be when he died.

The bows passed ten feet from the stern of the *Swan*. The bow wave tilted her up on her nose and threw her upwards, forwards and down. Green water surged over the foredeck, engulfed the cabin and broke where Pax was clinging to the tiller. The *Swan* tilted and shuddered and at last her bows came up again into the air. She was sucked back towards the tanker's hull, smacking up and down on the water, heeling and pitching. The rusted black side of the ship, the skin of a scaly Leviathan, seemed near enough to touch. The *Swan* was thrown against it and snatched back again by the waves before she smashed like an orange box.

Then came the bubbling, boiling maelstrom of the wake. He was like a crone on a ducking stool as the stern reared into the air, plunged under water and reared again. She tilted on her side. Instinctively he scrambled as far as he could away from the water and saw the bottom of the hull. She righted slowly and he scrambled back.

As suddenly as it had appeared the ship was gone. He lay on the stern, coughing up water and wanting to vomit. He realised he had beshat himself and his eyes stung with anger and self pity. He wanted to crawl into the cabin, lie down, and wait for the next ship. He fell back into the cockpit, shivering. The breadknife, still tied to his belt by the long piece of string, caught on the tiller rail.

"Sod you," he screamed into the wind.

He picked up the knife, leaned over the stern and hacked away at the rope again.

After the wake of the tanker the sea seemed calm but in fact it had considerably worsened in the past half hour. The wind was gusting more strongly and whipping up white horses on the wave-tops. They smashed against the side of the drifting

Swan, slopping up to the cabin sides, pouring into the cockpit. The self-draining holes in the floor could not cope. As soon as the level went down a foot it was flooded again.

The last piece of rope came free. Unless any had been sucked down the shaft towards the engine it was clear. But what about the battery and the engine itself? They had been doused with sea water. And the gear box could have been damaged when the engine strained against the jammed propeller. He turned the key. It started first time.

With more optimism than was justified by the circumstances he turned the bows into the wind and waves.

His optimism soon evaporated. He had escaped the tanker by a hair's breadth and the propeller was free and the engine had started. But what was he going to do now?

The waves were three or four feet high. They smashed into the *Swan*'s bluff bows and came coursing down the side of the cabin to the cockpit where he stood knee-deep in water. The mist had lifted but it had started to rain in thick, blinding squalls. Gusts of wind tried to turn the *Swan* broadside and it took all his strength to hold the tiller steady so the bows met the force of the sea. She rolled from side to side through what seemed like a hundred and eighty degrees. She pitched so the bows were buried in green water and the stern stuck up in the air, the engine racing as the propeller came out, smacking down again with a hideous jar.

He was completely lost. Rising on the crest of a wave before the sickening plunge into its trough he glimpsed flashing lights, white and red, but he could not tell how far away they were. In the distant sky he saw the beams of lighthouses reflected on the scudding black clouds but he had no idea whether they indicated danger or safety.

His eyes were stinging and his throat was parched with salt. He shivered with cold. He was faint with hunger. His body was a mass of bruises. He longed to get into the cabin to change his trousers and find the chart and put on a lifejacket. With the breadknife string and bits of shredded mooring rope he lashed the tiller to the tiller rail as best he could and made for the door.

What remained in his bowels turned to water. The cabin was flooded. As the *Swan* heeled over the water covered the portholes on one side. When she rolled it all rushed over to cover the portholes on the other side. The contents of the cabin were afloat in a sodden mass. There would be no dry trousers and no dry chart. He leaned over from the cabin steps and picked up his lifejacket as it floated by.

He had to start pumping. The water would flood the engine locker. The *Swan* would be swamped and would sink. A wave flooded the cockpit and forced its way past him into the cabin. He grabbed the lintel as the *Swan* shuddered crabwise. He slammed the door shut and huddled on the floor of the cockpit waist-deep in water while he struggled into his lifejacket.

The pump. With every wave that came inboard she lost a little buoyancy. Each time the bows went down into the waves they took longer to come up. He shuffled on his bottom to the pump locker, opened it and put in his hand to find the pump handle. It wasn't there. He groped wildly around. It must have rolled down into the bilges. He didn't have a spare.

As the wind had increased in strength it had veered round so that it was now blowing diagonally across the direction of the waves, forcing the *Swan* broadside to the seas. He picked up the breadknife that still dangled from his belt and cut through the ropes that held the lee boards up on either side of the hull. They slid down into the sea under their own weight. He wished he had thought of them sooner. They made it easier to steer into the waves and stopped her rolling as much. They may also have prevented her from capsizing when the squall hit her two minutes later.

It hit without warning. The wind tore at his clothes, forcing him against the lashed tiller. At first he thought it was a tidal wave but the water that deafened and blinded him was rain. The *Swan* was wrenched around and thrown broadside to the waves. The tiller broke free from its supergranny and threw him across the cockpit. His coccyx struck the edge of the seat and pain shot up his spine. A giant wave hit the *Swan*. She heeled over, engulfed in green, frothing water. His weight was thrown against the tiller and instinctively, despite the agonising pain in his back he pushed with all his strength. The old oak tiller bent and cracked under him. The bolts that held the rudder groaned. But with a shudder the brave *Swan* lifted her bows and turned to meet the next wave.

"Hello darling. I'm home."

He hung up his orange anorak in the hall, letting it drip salt water over the carpet. Thea came down the stairs to meet him. She flung her arms around his neck in spite of his soaking sweater. They kissed. Her lips were warm and familiar, like part of his own body.

He followed her wearily upstairs to the living room. He was dog-tired and the base of his spine hurt.

"Sit down and I'll make you a cup of tea. You look exhausted."

"I've had a busy day."

While she was making tea in the kitchen Thomas and Sarah came down in their pyjamas. They screeched "Daddy" and jumped on him. Sarah snuggled up to his chest while Thomas pummelled him. They didn't mind his wet clothes. Their small, lithe bodies were like extensions of his own. He told them the story of the Owl and the Pussycat who went to sea in a beautiful pea-green boat.

Thea brought him tea. He warmed his hands round the mug. While he drank it, she stood behind his chair and massaged his shoulders. He took the children upstairs and tucked them into their bunks and said their prayers with them. Then he took off his own clothes and got into his own bed. Thea slipped in beside him.

"Did you have any trouble getting back?" he asked, putting his arms round her.

"No. I just caught a bus. How's the boat?"

"At the bottom of the sea."

"I'm sorry."

"I'm not. I'm glad it's all over. I'll be able to collect on the insurance. I never want to set foot on a boat again. I'm not cut out to be a sailor."

She nestled her head into his chest and stroked the small of his back. He was still waiting for the warmth to come back into his body. "Were you in love with her?" she asked quietly.

"Yes. I fell in love with her. It was one of those things you can't help. I thought she was so beautiful and at the same time so defenceless. She needed me to protect her. I wanted to be with her, be inside her, go away with her. For a time I felt she had always been part of me. It was very private. I couldn't imagine her and me belonging to everyday life. It was more than an infatuation. It was a passion. I don't know how to explain it. But it's all gone now, I promise. Will you have me back?"

"Of course I will. I think she'll get over it."

"Who?"

"Annabel."

"I wasn't talking about Annabel. I was talking about the *Swan*."

"I thought you meant Annabel."

"God no. She was just an accessory to the *Swan*, like a brass clock. A touch of lust now and then but nothing ever happened. Romance and sex don't mix."

"What will you do now?"

"Stay at home. Play with the children. Make love to you. Learn to cultivate the garden. That's what really matters. It's very simple really. Life is about staying alive. Everything else is a bonus. I love you, Thea."

He was about to push inside her damp and welcoming warmth when she pointed over his shoulder.

"What are those lights?" she asked.

"Distress flares," he replied.

242

❖ Chapter Nineteen ❖

The orange flare burst in the sky and hung there. It was over to the right in the direction the wind was coming from. It was like a firework. Where were the *oohs* and *aahs?* He tried to say *ooh* but his lips were cracked with salt.

The *Swan* was low in the water, exhausted with the battle against the sea. Filling with water from the top she would soon give up the struggle and settle for peace beneath the waves. Her top planks were rotted. Her nails were rusted. Her bolts were loose. Her pintles were slack. He waited for her to split open like a ripe pod under the next crashing sea.

He was past caring. The sooner she sank the better. He was numb with cold. His body ached. His face hurt with the wind and salt. He had no idea where he was. He was in the middle of a gale at night on a lee shore without a chart or a radio or an anchor. The distress flares he had bought yesterday were lost in the bilges with the handle of the bilge pump. The engine was still valiantly throbbing but for how long? As soon as it stopped the *Swan* would turn broadside to the wind and it would all be over.

He had finished praying. He had dragged out all the rusty incantations and repeated them until they were meaningless. He had finished making rash promises of what he would do if he were saved. He would go to church on Sunday, be a loving husband and father, become the best auditor in the City, give a tenth of his income to charity, sell flags for the Lifeboat Institution, visit his mother once a week, stick to his Canadian Air Force exercises and throw himself and the gold bullion on the tender mercies of the Director of Public Prosecutions. He had said all that and mixed it up with his long-neglected prayers until he confused and forgot them again. All he could remem-

243

ber was the first line of the hymn they used to sing at school, "For those in peril on the sea", which stuck in his mind because it had been written by someone called Whiting.

The orange light in the sky went out. He was not the only one in peril on the sea. They probably had a radio as well. Help could be on the way to them already. Into his dulled mind came the faintest glimmer of hope. If only he could find the other vessel in time he might be rescued with them. It was his only chance.

He took a bearing on the spinning compass-card, shoved the tiller over and headed into the teeth of the wind. As the *Swan* laboriously wallowed round he saw on the left hand side, further away than the orange light had been, a white flare followed by two more. It was the signal from the coastguard that the distress signal had been seen. Help was on the way. He whispered to himself the prayer he had so often whispered to the alarm clock in the morning. "Just give me five minutes more."

The waves were as violent as they had been but less high. Instead of washing over the deck they struck the hull shivering hammer-blows. The *Swan* heaved and bucked but seemed in less danger than before of being taken straight to the bottom by a giant sea. The wind was less strong, although vicious gusts whipped rain and spray into his raw face. He kept his eyes on the spinning compass-card, forcing out of his mind the thought that the current and the waves and the wind could be taking him in a completely different direction. He gripped the tiller under his armpit and hoped.

He tried to blot out from his vision the black, surging waves and the indigo sky. He wished he could close his ears to the wind whistling through the rigging, the sea smashing against the hull, the creaking and groaning of the timbers and the tattoo of rain on the deck. He wanted to disown the bitter metallic taste in his mouth, to distance himself from his shivering, aching body. But the Other Pax who had stood aside and watched so many times was not there. For the first time in his life he was rooted in himself.

Another orange flare shot into the sky, hanging like a

monstrous sun. Rising on the crest of a wave he saw in its lurid light a listing steamer to the right of where he was steering. She was aground on rocks or a sandbank. This barrier was protecting the *Swan* from the full force of the open sea which is why the waves had become less violent. On the other side of the steamer the waves crashing against her hull sent sheets of spray high in the air and over the decks.

There were red and white lights on the deck and a flashing searchlight. Behind it was a group of men huddled against the superstructure. They had bright orange lifejackets. The flare in the sky went out but he could still see the searchlight and he steered towards it. Although he was still a quarter of a mile away from the stricken ship the wind and current were helping him on.

Another flare, this time white. It was from the lifeboat that rounded the sandbank on which the ship was aground. High in the water it crashed into the sea and rose again like a cork. Pax fought back his hope and panic. Oh God, let them see me. What if he arrived too late?

The lifeboat reached the calmer sea between Pax and the sandbank in the lee of the wrecked ship. Lifeboatmen in yellow suits appeared out of the wheelhouse. One of them held up a gun. He fired a line. It went straight over the heads of the sailors on the deck of the steamer. Hands clutched at it in the air and hauled at it. A lifeboatman shouted commands through a loud-hailer but Pax could not understand them. The words were whipped away by the wind. He was still two hundred yards away.

The line was made fast. The seamen pulled over the rescue tackle. Before they could reach it the ship was struck by a sea like a tidal wave. Green water poured over the listing deck. She floated free of the sandbank, tilted and swung. A loading derrick tore loose. The boom was catapulted over the deck rails and harpooned the lifeboat through the wheelhouse. One end was still attached to the derrick. The steamer heeled over, forcing the lifeboat under water. Coupled like knotted dogs they would drag each other to the bottom.

Pax saw this much with dull, despairing horror. Then a

second sea struck them all. It swamped the *Swan*. He could feel her going down beneath him. The water choked his eyes and mouth and nose. So this is it. He was about to force his arms off the tiller and strike out for the surface when the brave little boat struggled up to the air again. But the engine had stopped.

For the time being the two massive waves had spent the force of the storm. The sea was calmer and the wind dropped. He was now to windward of the two doomed vessels. Both of them were listing heavily, one towards the other, coupled by the derrick. The lifeboat was almost under water. Its helpless crew clung to the uppermost rail. The crew of the steamer were huddled under the superstructure. One of them hacked despairingly at the derrick with an axe.

When the storm came back they would all be finished.

With numb, clumsy fingers Pax took the belt off his trousers. He tied the tiller to the tiller rail as best he could. He forced his cramped body past the cabin onto the foredeck. Sobbing with the effort and the pain he shoved the hatch on the foredeck to one side. He dragged out the mouldering foresail that he had rigged up that morning. He pushed back the hatch. Clinging to the base of the mast he found the right rope and pulled with the weight of his whole body. He saw the skin tear away from his unfeeling hands and blood drip onto the deck.

Flapping and cracking and stinking in the wind the mottled green sail inched up its cable. Half way up the free corner of the triangle broke loose and flapped out over the water. The rope that was fixed to it snagged on the boom. Pax grabbed it with his bleeding hands, pulled it back and fixed it to the bottom of the mast with a super-granny. It billowed like a spinnaker but he could not haul it up any further. Two of the shackles had snagged. But it caught the wind and the bows turned in the direction of the lifeboat.

He struggled back to the cockpit and untied the tiller. Without the engine the *Swan* seemed more responsive to the sea and the rudder. Instead of fighting the elements she moved with them. She was making headway towards the two wrecked ships. Their crews watched her silently. She had become their only hope.

Ten yards from the side of the lifeboat Pax pushed the tiller hard over. The bows came into the wind and the sail flapped. The *Swan* came alongside the lifeboat, bashing the hull. Hands stretched down to clutch at her. He looked up to the grained, anxious faces of the lifeboatmen. The strength of his own voice took him by surprise. "Steady now. One at a time. And bring something for a pump handle."

"Thanks, Skipper," shouted the lifeboat coxswain as he came on board.

If this was death it wasn't so bad after all. It was warm and white and soft. He couldn't move his body but he didn't feel any pain. The light hurt his eyes but the salt stinging had gone. There was a metallic taste in his mouth and a nasty smell of disinfectant but it was preferable to the nightmare he had left. The world was dry again and it didn't move up and down.

Someone was holding his hand. It felt soft and warm against his grainy skin. He opened his eyes.

"Hello love," said Thea.

"I'm glad you got back all right."

"I found a coastguard station. They were very nice."

"Did you tell them about the money?"

"Yes. There was nothing there. I think Nick made it up. To keep Annabel on the hook."

"How are the children?"

"Fine. They're very proud of you."

"Did they find the *Swan*?"

"They think it must have sunk. I'm sorry."

"I'm not. I never want to go on a boat again as long as I live. Farmhouse holidays from now on."

"You'll get the insurance, won't you?"

"I think so. Go and buy Mavis. We're still living together aren't we?"

"Of course. Now you have to get some rest."

She kissed him lightly on the lips and left him to go back to sleep.

They had saved the newspapers for him.

247

LONE HERO IN SEA RESCUE DRAMA . . . Pax Brown, 35, single handed . . . Stricken merchant ship . . . Gale force ten . . . Worst storms in living memory . . . Turned his back on safety . . . Unwritten law of the sea . . . Outstanding seaman-ship . . . Engine failed . . . Only the foresail . . . Hearts of Oak . . . Lifeboat Coxswain, 55, forty years of service . . . The Nelson spirit . . . Brave little *Swan* . . . Every man saved . . . Commendation for helicopter crew . . . Last to abandon his boat . . . Civic reception . . . Duke of Edinburgh, Master of Trinity House . . . This Island Race . . . Duty and self-sacrifice . . . Did not think of himself . . . Wife's tears of pride . . . Thomas, 7, Sarah, 5 . . . Inspiration to all Englishmen . . .

He started to chuckle. His ribs hurt and his throat was sore and his lips were cracked but he chuckled some more. He started to laugh. Tears ran down his chapped cheeks. He held his stomach. He whooped and snorted and cackled, caught his breath and laughed again.

In the corridor outside the student nurse ran to get Sister. "Delayed shock. We'll give him a sedative."

But the *Swan* had not sunk. Left in peace at last by frightened, silly, ridiculous men, with the tiller lashed and the sail made fast, she began her solitary voyage on the wind and tides. She followed Barrow Deep past Knock John towards the Shipwash lightship, her gunwhales barely above the water, wallowing in the waves but refusing to sink. The beam of the North Fore-land lighthouse picked out her brave silhouette and passed blindly on. As dawn broke through the lightening clouds she crossed Middle Sunk Sands, sailed through Fisherman's Gat and turned back on the flood tide to South Shingles.

The gale died down to a stiff breeze. The white horses were tamed. The storm clouds scattered. Morning found her cruis-ing past the Drill Stone through the gentle swell towards the Tongue Sand Tower. The warm south wind made a belly of the sail.

A dead calm followed the storm. While Pax was filling the hospital with laughter she floated motionless. The water was a flat mirror, reflecting the clear blue sky and a few fluffy clouds. The cockpit was full of water and the foredeck was level with the sea. The sail, washed clean, hung limp. A seagull stood on the tiller.

A tremor of wind scuttled across the sea. Ripples lapped against the honey-coloured bows. With a shiver of excitement the canvas began to fill. The seagull shat, flapped its wings and flew off towards the land. The *Swan* turned slowly to the sun and set sail again towards the unattainable horizon.